faking summer

THE BAYSIDE LAKE SERIES

JESS BRYSON

EDITED BY
SARAH WATERMAN, A3W EDITORIAL

To those who are often overlooked
I see you
You are enough
Now, believe it

the playlist

1. Blue Bird (feat. Alison Krauss) – Carter Faith
2. Girl I Never Met – Corey Kent
3. Never Been Done Before – Chase Wright
4. Afterglow – Morgan Wallen
5. This Town's Yours – Canaan Cox
6. Wanna Be Saved – Austin Williams
7. Take My Word for It – Trevor Snider
8. Dancing in the Rain – Chase Matthew
9. Right Where You Left Me – Taylor Swift
10. How to Not – Tommy Acker
11. Rescue – Kane Brown
12. Lie Like Me – Andrew Jannakos
13. Guess Is as Good as Mine – Jaden Hamilton
14. She Will – Lil Wayne
15. All I Forgot – Ashley Cooke & Joe Jonas
16. Some Things I'll Never Know – Teddy Swims
17. Whiskey & Smoke – Ryan Montgomery
18. Dopamine – Hudson Westbrook
19. Take It or Leave It – Tyler Rich
20. I Don't Like You Anymore – Maddox Batson
21. Let 'Em Talk – Ty Myers
22. It Won't Be Long – George Birge
23. Indigo – Sam Barber
24. Stargazing – Myles Smith
25. Number One Girl – ROSÉ
26. Lose Control – Teddy Swims
27. If I Know You – Jagger Whitaker
28. Beautiful Things – Benson Boone
29. Bad Decisions – Dylan Schneider
30. Stay a Little Longer – Myles Erlick
31. Constellations – Jade LeMac
32. Rhinestone Ring – Abbey Cone
33. Door's Unlocked – Noah Hicks
34. Coming Home To – Austin Williams
35. One Day Left – Chris Bandi
36. Better Boy – Nate Smith

a note from the author

Dear Reader,

If you're here after reading Rival Summer—welcome back. We're heading back into that same wild, unforgettable summer—but this time, you'll see it unfold through two new perspectives.

Different eyes, different hearts, and a whole new side of the story.
Whether it's your first time visiting or a return trip, I hope this story sweeps you away. May this summer be the best one yet.

Content Warning:
This book contains depictions of:
• Alcohol consumption
• Physical assault
• Sexual assault

With Love,
jess

prologue

CAROLINE

My mother meticulously arranged her fancy plates, each adorned with a delicate ivy pattern along the edges. These plates only surfaced from the depths of her china cabinet for occasions worth noting—and tonight was all about Charlotte, my older sister, who had just scaled another mountain on her path to becoming a doctor. She'd scored a 520 on her MCAT.

I watched silently as Mother placed the last gleaming fork beside the napkin which was folded into a perfect triangle. The clink of silverware served as a reminder of all the achievements that always played on repeat around here—Charlotte, the perfect child, and my brother Cooper, the baseball prodigy who had recently accepted a coaching position at a nearby college. He went pro for a few years, then blew out his knee, but luckily loves coaching. With every clink, I hear their accolades echo off the walls of our home and deep into my consciousness.

Hardly anyone noticed me as I took my seat at the dinner table. Typical Caroline, blending into the background. It was as though I was just another empty seat at the table.

Mom was gleaming with pride as she clasped her hands

together. "Today is such a special day," she announced, her voice swelling with emotion. "Charlotte is making her dreams come true, and we're all here to support her impressive accomplishments."

The words left no room for interpretation—this was Charlotte's moment, and by extension, Cooper's too. Their successes were always celebrated, always making my parents proud. I was the only one who didn't make them proud, or so it seemed. But still, I was happy for Charlotte and Cooper. They were my siblings, after all, and I knew someday my success would come. At least I hoped so.

Charlotte leaned back in her chair with a soft smile. "Thank you," she said, her voice brimming with gratitude. "I couldn't have done it without my family." Laughter and praise was passed around the table along with the food, along with stories of her unwavering determination and the success of Cooper's team this season.

My mother turned to me, her gaze piercing, as if she'd only just remembered I was there. "So Caroline," she began, her tone deceptively casual, "anything exciting happening with you? Still 'just' teaching dance and cheerleading?" The way she said "just" made it sound like it wasn't even a real job.

I straightened my spine, meeting her gaze with an assertive tilt of my chin. "As a matter of fact, yes, I'm still teaching," I replied, my voice steady despite her judging eyes. "I'm also still President of the Blue Devils' committee, just like you and Charlotte were." I let the words hang in the air for a moment before continuing. "But you probably forgot all about that."

Cooper's hand collided with mine in a solid fist bump. "You go, girl," he said, his eyes crinkling with genuine pride. Unlike the others, Cooper's faith in me had always been unwavering, never judgmental.

"Oh, that's right," my mother said, her eyes scanning me, as if looking for something I had missed. "But tell me, Caroline, will you be dating this summer? Your aunts are always asking me when you're going to settle down." She paused, a delicate arch in her brow. "All of your cousins are married or engaged, on the right path. Your sister is engaged. Your brother is married. The grandparents on your father's side are starting to wonder if there's something strange going on with you."

My parents met when they were sixteen, and their parents even earlier than that. They didn't understand the dating world today. I could almost hear the whispers at family gatherings, feel the weight of their stares.

"Caroline doesn't date," my sister let out an obnoxious laugh.

I reached for my wine glass, fingers curling around the stem as I convinced myself to take a sip and not fling it at my sister. "And how would you know?" I asked.

"Because, darling Caroline," she began, her head tilted, lips pursed, "you have never brought anyone home. Not to any family event, nothing."

"Maybe I just like to keep things private," I said, shrugging. "And you'd all scare off anyone I brought home anyway, with your interrogation and high standards."

My gaze drifted beyond the confines of our dining room, wishing I was anywhere but here. I had plenty of time to date, to figure out if marriage is even something I wanted. But if I did bring someone home? Yeah... my family would scare them off in record time. The judgment. The unrealistic financial expectations. The whole "A real man should be able to support you" nonsense—when all I want is to support myself. It's exhausting. And honestly? I wouldn't blame anyone for never wanting to come back.

My mother and sister exchanged knowing glances. "We just want it to be someone successful and from a good family. You'll never be able to afford the lifestyle you want on your own," my mother chided. "You just graduated college, you're about to turn twenty-two, and your father and I are not going to support you forever," she added, punctuating the sentence with a delicate sip of her wine.

I swallowed, refusing to let her get to me just before Charlotte chimed in. "Caroline, we know you're not dating anyone. But maybe if you smiled every once in a while someone would want to." She shook her head slightly. "You don't exactly scream approachable. No idea how you were a cheerleader all through high school and college."

Not missing a beat, Cooper leaned forward, elbows on the table, and shot me a conspiratorial wink. "Nah, I think she's perfect how she is." His words were a small relief amongst the skepticism hanging on the other side of the table.

The subtle dismissals faded away as Dad finally spoke up, casual and unaffected. He looked up from the glowing screen of his phone, which often seemed surgically attached to his palm, and announced with oblivious cheeriness, "Well, I'm ready for dessert—anyone else?" His eyes, usually so keen and observant when it came to his work, missed the tension that had settled around the table like an unwelcome guest.

I felt my shoulders drop, the weight of insignificance settling in. I pushed my chair back, the sound barely registering over the clinking of cutlery and the murmur of conversations. My words, attempting to carve out some space for myself, fell flat, not even gaining a glance in my direction. "I think I'm over dessert. I'm going to bed early."

Mom was already rising to fetch the dessert she'd made, her hands reaching for the apple pie—Charlotte's favorite, while Cooper and my dad talked about baseball.

The energy in the room never wavered, even as I turned and slipped away. As I made my way upstairs, the sounds of their joy was another reminder that, per usual, my absence didn't make a difference.

one

CAROLINE, **age 11**

My pink glitter headphones rested around my neck, one ear free to keep me tethered to reality as I skipped to school with my best friends. Life was an open book with a happy ending, its pages untouched by the smudges of disillusionment. My hair, a blonde tangled mess secured in a high ponytail that swayed with each movement.

"Look," Sam breathed out, in awe. Her finger extended toward our classmates clustered at the front of our soon-to-be new kingdom: sixth grade.

A group of boys near us were particularly animated, their voices rising above the rest. A circle had formed around one bench, where one of the boys had his arm outstretched, revealing a gnarly scar that had impressed all the others.

"Those boys are cute," Sam mused, scanning them slowly as she tried to decipher which one stood out the most to her. The boys continued to react to the wound as if it were a spectacle from another planet, each grimace and gasp more dramatic than the last. I watched, half-amused, half-curious, until it happened—my eyes locked onto one of them, refusing to let go.

Stacey leaned in close, her voice a conspiratorial whisper, "That one is Reese. He looks like a Disney prince, I bet he could have any girl he wanted." He pushed back his dark hair. "Whoever it is, I'll put gum in her hair," Stacey declared with a hair flip.

"Also," she continued, "my mom said his dad has more money than the president."

"Does the president have a lot of money?" Sam asked, tilting her head, brows knit in genuine curiosity.

"I think so," Stacey replied, shrugging one shoulder.

None of us knew quite how much money the president had, but we shook off the confusion and our attention snapped back to the boys congregated around the bench. Their laughter was untamed and seemed to ripple through the courtyard.

"He is kind of dreamy," Sam admitted, her gaze fixed on Reese. He lounged effortlessly, his easy smile so disarming it felt criminal in the worst kind of way. "It's those green eyes and those dimples," she added, her tone almost wistful. "He has that going for him, plus his daddy's money. I'm sure he gets whatever he wants."

He didn't have to say a word. There was no grand gesture or cheesy line. There was just something about him—something irresistible and powerful—that made my heart flutter with excitement for the very first time. And that's exactly when I realized I was having that butterfly feeling I had heard and wondered about.

Stacey, her lips curled in a playful sneer, flicked a dismissive hand toward the boys. "Well, I'll take any of them in that circle," she joked. "Except maybe the one with the scar."

Third period became my sanctuary, the one hour of the day I looked forward to. Reese sat two rows in front of me—even the back of his head was dreamy. I willed him to feel my gaze, compelling him to turn around and notice me.

Each morning, I curated my appearance with him in mind, spraying myself with perfume I had stolen from my sister. Anything to unlock an elusive glance from him, to finally get on his radar. I watched the way he pushed back his hair—an act so mundane but that inexplicably fascinated me. All of his movements were effortlessly cool. He was somehow given the gift of skipping any adolescent awkwardness. Even the simple act of sliding off his backpack as he settled into his seat was more interesting than anything I had heard in our Social Studies class all year.

But then, reality intruded in the form of Evan Rockwell and a crumpled piece of paper striking my face—completely unwelcome in the midst of my daydreams. The sting from the paper ball's impact lingered on my cheek as I turned towards Evan. "What was that for?"

Evan leaned back in his chair, a smug look creasing his features. "I see you over there, drooling over Reese," he said, loud enough for nearby desks to hear. My face flushed a deeper shade. "He likes you too, you know."

I glanced at Reese, who remained oblivious, caught up in the conversation he was having. Still, that did nothing to steady my racing heart. "He does?" The question slipped out, and along with it a vulnerability I hadn't meant to expose.

Evan's grin widened. "Yeah, he told me himself." He was part of the crowd Reese was always in, so his credibility was hard to dismiss.

An unsettling thrill skittered down my spine as Evan leaned in closer. "He wants you to go to the dance with him," he said, and my tiny heart pounded harder. "But he's shy, so I told him I'd ask you."

Shy? Reese Carrington? The notion seemed laughable, that for some reason he had sent Evan—one of his minions—to ask me, so it must be true. I sat there, palms damp against the cool surface of my desk. It felt as though a spotlight had been switched on above my head, illuminating me in its harsh, unforgiving glow. An urge to leap up and scream wrestled with the disbelief cementing me to my chair. The sixth grade heart throb, liked *me*?

I froze, lost in a tumultuous sea of emotion while the fantasy of Reese and I going to the dance played out in my head. I nodded, feeling as though I had somehow stepped into a moment every girl dreams about. "Yes," I whispered. "I'll go with him."

Evan's smile grew. "Cool. He's wearing dark blue, so make sure you match him," he instructed. "He'll meet you by the punch station."

The final bell couldn't ring soon enough. My legs jittered beneath the desk. I was a tangle of nerves and excitement. When we were finally released, it was a rush of sound and motion, everyone spilling into the halls where echoes of locker slams and laughter mingled.

"Spill it!" Sam demanded, seeing the excitement written all over my face.

"Reese Carrington asked me to the dance!"

Sam squealed, grabbing both my hands as we bounced on the balls of our feet, our high ponytails swinging in unison. "Oh my gosh, this is huge!"

The week that followed was a blur of whispered secrets and giddy anticipation. Sleepovers became strategy sessions, each night spent sprawled across my floral comforter, discussing everything Reese. We were huddled together, air thick with the scent of bubblegum lip gloss as we dissected every encounter, every glance he'd *almost* shot my way.

"Imagine slow dancing with him," Stacey mused one evening, "your hands on his shoulders, his on your waist, being that close to him. I bet he smells like a hotel lobby."

Sam chimed in, "And when a slow song comes on, it'll be like... like magic. The way it is in the movies."

"Stop! You're making me nervous," I laughed, though my stomach dropped at the thought. I straightened up abruptly, and the sudden movement made my friends freeze, their wide-eyed gazes following me. I strode across the room, flung open the door and yelled down the hallway, "Cooper!"

A moment later, I turned on a slow song on my computer, transforming my room into an intimate stage set for a dance lesson I'd never forget. Cooper appeared in my doorway, his expression mildly irritated.

"What?" he demanded, leaning against the frame with crossed arms.

"Will you..." My voice faltered under his gaze. I swallowed the lump in my throat, motivated by the urgency of the task at hand, "teach me how to slow dance?"

From my bed, my friends' giggles and cheers erupted, filled with mischief and encouragement.

Cooper let out a long, drawn-out sigh, the kind that meant his patience was being tried. "Are you serious?" he asked, skeptically.

"You have to help her," Sam piped up. "She's going to dance with the cutest boy in sixth grade!" She was almost begging. It was the same hope I felt, to not make a fool of myself in front of Reese.

"Does Mom know you're going to this dance?" Cooper asked, curiously. But I knew he was giving in.

"Y-yes, she does," I stammered, feeling the weight of his protective gaze. "Can you help me now?"

"Fine," Cooper finally relented, his voice full of an older brother's unspoken contract to guard his sister's heart.

"Stand here," he directed, positioning me with hands that had lost their childhood clumsiness and were now replaced with teenage grace. I watched, entranced by the transformation from annoyance to instructor as he took my right hand in his left and placed my other hand on his shoulder.

"Relax, Caroline," he said, a smile playing at the corners of his mouth. "Just follow my lead." And so we began, swaying to the rhythm of Ed Sheeran.

I stumbled once, twice, laughter bubbling out. Sam and Stacey were still perched on my bed in their curlers and pajamas. They watched with wide eyes, their giggles soft and sweet.

"This is actually kinda fun. Maybe I'll ask Mom to sign me up for dance class," I said with a laugh. "See? You're getting it," Cooper encouraged. For a fleeting second, I saw not just my brother but the young man he was becoming—the one who unknowingly turned heads as he passed by others.

The song ended, and Cooper released me, a mock bow accompanying his retreat. "There. Don't step on the guy's feet too much," he teased, ruffling my hair before he walked out, closing the door behind him. I collapsed onto the bed, the springs creaking under the sudden weight.

"Your brother is really cute," Sam whispered, her eyes gleaming with mischief. "Do you think he'd take me to the dance?"

With a gasp of disgust, I grabbed the nearest pillow and launched it at her, igniting a burst of feathers and laughter. We tumbled into each other, a tangled mess of limbs and giggles until sleep wrapped around us, pulling us gently into our dreams.

At school on the day of the dance, I found myself trapped in the worst kind of war zone—dodging rubber missiles while the stench of sweaty gym socks and old floor polish clung to the air. Crouched in the back, I braced for impact, questioning why this torture was considered physical education. "My mom let me get the short blue dress," I murmured, glancing at Sam and Stacy, who were also just hoping to make it out alive.

"Thank goodness," Sam grunted, hiding behind Stacey. "She was determined to make you wear Charlotte's old one."

Time froze as a ball rocketed toward me, a blur of an incoming disaster. It was then that Reese came out of nowhere, intercepting the ball, catching it just inches from my face.

"Looks like you owe me for that save," Reese teased, and my body froze. His voice had that effortless flirt to it, almost as if he was reassuring me that he was just as excited as I was about the dance. To anyone else, it was just a casual snag, barely a moment at all. But to me? It was everything. My brain short-circuited, my heart did some kind of palpitation, and I was pretty sure I was about five seconds away from melting into a puddle of swoony mess. My lips parted, but I lost my ability to speak. I could only manage a smile before he wound up and hurled the ball back at the other team.

"Girl, he just saved your life," Sam whispered in awe.

Stacey, ever the hopeless romantic, clasped her hands over her heart. "For the first time in my life, I think I'm seeing real love before my eyes," she breathed out, her sentiment coming from every rom-com we ever watched together.

Laughter rippled between us as we skipped our way back to the locker rooms. Our laughter and excitement never stopped—it rode with us, all the way home and as we got ready for the dance.

When the dance had finally arrived, my mom pulled up to the curb, then turned to me.

"You know," she began, letting a smile break free, "I met your father at a school dance."

I unbuckled my seatbelt. "I know, Mom."

"I heard there might be a cute boy you're going with tonight," she added.

"Really, you're being so embarrassing," I muttered, turning away to hide the blush on my face.

"Have fun, sweetheart," she said, as I pushed the door open. "I'll have cookies at home waiting for you to tell me all about it."

"Thanks," I shouted, stepping out into the night, and closing the car door behind me.

The gymnasium was lit up with starlights, transforming our middle school dance into pre-teen enchantment. Sam, Stacey, and I arrived in a whirlwind of satin and tulle, the scent of hairspray and sweet perfume trailing behind us like pixie dust. Our dresses, meticulously chosen to flatter and sparkle, rustled as we moved. Mine was the color of midnight to match Reese's dark blue attire.

"Remember to breathe," Stacey whispered, her fingers gently rearranging a stray curl that framed my face.

"This is your night, girl," Sam added, beaming at me with a confidence I desperately tried to mirror. "Live it up for all of us." Their hands on my shoulders felt like the passing of a baton as they walked me to the punch station, their pep talk infusing me with borrowed bravery.

"Go get him," Stacey said with an infectious grin. They smoothed the fabric of my dress one last time before leaving me standing alone, my heart hammering with nervous anticipation.

My palms were clammy, fingertips grazing the cool surface of the punch bowl as if it would help me somehow. I took a shallow breath, willing my lungs to expand fully, to steady the tremors that threatened to betray my composure.

Then, he entered.

The overhead starlights seemed to conspire in his favor, spotlighting him. His hair fell just right—as if each strand had been set into place by angels. In that moment, he was the embodiment of every daydream I had indulged in since third period. My reality was colliding with fantasy, and the butterflies ambushed me again. Not just in my stomach but in my heart and in every inch of my body.

But then, she appeared.

Emma King, with her expensive dress and smile that outshined the strobe lights. She glided in after him, and my pulse hitched. Reese paused and turned to her, offering his arm. She happily accepted, looping her own arm around his.

He was exactly how I dreamed he'd be, he looked as cute as I thought he'd look—only I wasn't the one on his arm. The air around me turned icy, as if the warmth of the dance had left when they entered. My friends' gazes found me, their pity-filled eyes glassy, mirroring the sheen of the gymnasium floor. I felt exposed standing there at the punch table, clutching the edge like it was the last shred of dignity I had left.

Evan sauntered in then, surrounded by Reese's loyal followers, their easy laughter filling the room. Each chuckle, each pointed finger, jabbed at me—a relentless, rhythmic, excruciating pain.

Evan pulled Emma away from Reese, then whispered something in her ear. Her laughter was soul crushing as she approached me. But then she turned, her fingers picking up a full cup.

"Whoops," she cooed as she turned back to me, her voice dripping with feigned innocence. She let go of the cup, and I just watched —helpless or simply unwilling to step away.

The punch cascaded down my front, a waterfall of intentional malice, drenching the fabric of my dress. A gasp rippled through the crowd, yet all I could hear was her venomous chuckle.

"Heard you were trying to steal my date," she laughed bitterly. "He'd never go for someone like you."

In those moments, you make a choice between fight or flight, and my flight was instinctual, a desperate scramble away from the ridicule. The cool night air outside slapped my tear-streaked face, sobering but not cleansing the humiliation that stained my cheeks. I collapsed onto a bench, its wooden slats unforgiving against my crumpled form.

Sam's shoulder became my sanctuary, her embrace a shield against the pain and embarrassment. The sobs that wracked my body were like violent waves, and with each tear, I drowned a little more in disillusionment. The taste of my tears on my lips was a bitter testament to the cruelty that had unfolded. I begged my mom to let me crash at Sam's that night—I couldn't go home, couldn't face her, couldn't bring myself to say what had happened.

I would never forget—the sting of betrayal, the weight of eyes filled with scorn, the sharp night air as I gasped for breaths between sobs. A cruel joke had been played on me and I was shoved under a spotlight for everyone to see. Reese had become my nemesis, the embodiment of everything wrong in this world. Crushes were no longer filled with excitement and hope, they were traps, waiting to capture the innocent, and steal their joy.

That night, beneath a sky that offered neither comfort nor stars, I learned the hardest lesson of all: the world could be cold, and hearts colder still.

two

REESE, **age 16**

"Reese," Dad barked through the bluetooth in my truck, shattering the peace of my morning drive, his tone as sharp as the control he had over my life, "you need to go straight to the batting cages after practice. That first hit you had in the game last night? Weak." I didn't need to see him to know the look of disappointment on his face, like always.

"Your coaches focus too much on your arm and not enough on batting," he continued. I gripped the steering wheel tighter, my nails biting into the leather.

"Great advice, Dad," I muttered, unable to resist a sarcastic remark when I got the chance.

"See you later tonight, smart ass," he replied, ending the call.

As I pulled up to school, I narrowed my eyes, realizing my spot was taken. It was Caroline. She'd had the audacity to park in my space, of all places. She drove an old red sports car that looked like it was held together by hope, duct tape, and a couple of well-placed zip ties.

She leaned against it casually, surrounded by a few of the other cheerleaders who seemed to have become her shadows this year.

"What the fuck," I hissed under my breath as I rolled down my window. My fingers drummed an impatient rhythm on the dashboard, and I tilted my head slightly and called out, "That's my spot, can you move?"

She glanced over with those ocean-deep eyes that never seemed to settle on one color. Today's shade was more grayish than normal. She barely made the effort to look my way, even in my oversized truck. "For you? No."

A chuckle escaped me—not out of amusement but disbelief. "Are you serious?"

Caroline's laugh was soft but full of sarcasm. "Do I look like I'm joking?" She crossed her arms over her chest. "Why are you the only one with an assigned parking spot, anyway?"

"Maybe because my dad donated the new fieldhouse," I retorted, the words leaving a sour taste on my tongue. I hated talking about his money or donations because he only ever did it when there was something in it for him. It was all just another thing he'd never let me forget. But it had its perks. Like getting my own spot close to the school entrance.

"That's convenient," she said with a lift of her brow, tone dripping with insinuation. "Why don't you check back tomorrow? Looks like it's taken today." And just like that, she turned her back to me, long blonde hair swaying with the motion, dismissing me entirely. Caroline knew how to provoke me, to press buttons I didn't know existed. I just didn't know why she did it.

"There are no other spots. I'd have to park a mile away!"

She didn't turn back to look at me, she just laughed. "Sounds like you'll finally get to see what it's like to be in our shoes," she called out.

"Why are you being such a dick?" The words tumbled out before I could catch them, but they didn't faze her. She simply held up a hand, palm outstretched as if to silence me. I shook my head, incredulous.

I turned the wheel, the growl of my truck's engine roaring as I peeled away. Just as I got to the end of the lot, Evan emerged from between two cars. Evan and I were cool but only because he was on the baseball team and we ran in the same circle of friends. He was someone you could count on to be at all the parties, but never someone you could actually trust.

"Where you going?" he asked, an eyebrow raised in confusion.

"Caroline's on one today," I said, not bothering to shade the truth. "She took my spot, so I'm gonna be late to class."

He nodded slowly, as if weighing the gravity of my predicament. "Why don't you have her towed? You know if you get a tardy, Coach will have us all running laps in practice."

"Nah, all good," I said, forcing a nonchalant shrug. "I'll find a place to park." Caroline had the upper hand at the moment, but today was far from over. I was highly aggravated, but I liked something about the way she fired back at me—the way she gets worked up. Towing her car may have been what Evan would do but it wasn't my preferred method of retaliation. I'd find another way to get under her skin.

"Alright," he conceded, with a hint of respect. "Better man than I am." And with that, I left him standing there.

After what felt like a walk from the next town over, I ran into Caroline again in the hallway—the cheerleaders had the luxury of hosting and prepping for today's pep rally, which means they were excused from class.

"I'm sure the whole team's going to love the extra laps we'll be running today because I'm late," I said, sidestepping Caroline with a pointed look. "Big thanks for that."

She turned to me, a pleased smile on her lips as she cocked her head. "Anytime," she quipped. "You all could use the extra laps, anyway." She eyed my stomach like I wasn't ripped underneath my shirt.

"Has anyone ever told you how unpleasant you are?" I asked. My patience was wearing thin.

"Hmm. Let's see, I've been called ice queen, a witch, bossy, don't even get me started on my so-called target addiction... okay, maybe I'll claim that one."

"Cheerleading doesn't seem like the right sport for you." I paused, rubbing a hand across my jaw. "Maybe you should take up fencing... especially with that sharp-ass tongue of yours."

She stopped dead in her tracks, the rubber soles of her shoes squeaking against the polished floor. Spinning on her heel, she faced me, those striking blue eyes flickering from ice to stormy as they met mine.

"Coming from you?" she shot back. "People here don't actually like you, you know." She jabbed a pom-pom at my chest. "They just suck up to you because your dad has money."

Her words hit harder than I wanted to admit, but I wasn't about to let her see that, so I let out a low chuckle. "I don't think you've been paying attention. I'm adored around here," I said, pushing off the lockers and taking a step toward her. "I'm basically a legend. They'll probably name a wing after me once I graduate."

"Who adores you?" she asked, tilting her head in a motion that sent her blonde hair shimmering down her shoulder. "The pathetic freshmen girls who follow you around? That doesn't count, Carrington."

My grin widened, as I closed the distance between us by half a step. "Aw, you have been paying attention... that's cute. How long you been watching me, Caroline?"

"I haven't," she hissed through clenched teeth, and I caught the faintest quiver of anger in her voice. "You're the absolute worst, and I couldn't care less about anything that has to do with you."

Bingo. That was the spot, the nerve I'd been aiming for. There's an art to poking just enough to rile someone up without pushing them over the edge. And Caroline? Well, she was literally hanging on the edge.

"Am I?" I said, letting the words roll off my tongue slowly, savoring the taste of victory. "Because you started this. Were you just trying to get my attention? Is that what you wanted?"

"I'd rather plummet to my death from the top of a pyramid," Caroline spat out, putting a hand on her hip.

"Right. And it seems like every day now I keep finding someone's lunch leftovers in the bed of my truck. Someone who really likes peanut butter and jelly. Got any idea who that might be?"

Caroline didn't move. She was the embodiment of the raging spitfire I knew her to be. "Maybe someone got confused," she replied, her sarcastic tone making the corners of my mouth twitch involuntarily. "Thought your truck was a dumpster, perhaps? You should probably get that checked out."

"Gotta say, Caroline, maybe you should spend less time worried about me and my truck, and more time worrying about your cheer routines. They're almost as shaky as your self-control around me."

She crossed her arms, the subtle shift in her stance revealing nothing but confident defiance. "At least I know how to stick a landing," she shot back. "Can't say the same for your curveball."

"Damn. You're chaos." I grinned, enjoying this more than I should. "Good one."

"How about this? You stay away from me, and I'll do the same," she said, dropping her arms.

I inched closer, the hallway suddenly feeling like the narrow confines of the mound with everything riding on my next pitch. A half smile played on my face, as I let one corner dip just enough to flash her a dimple.

"I'll stay away, Chaos," I murmured, "if you stay out of my parking spot."

She straightened up, her grip tightening on the straps of her pom-poms. "Never having to speak to you again might be worth the extra walk," she retorted. "I'll take it into consideration, but no promises because making you miserable is also quite satisfying."

And with that, Caroline spun around and walked away. I leaned against the lockers and watched the space Caroline had just vacated, as if her fiery spirit had left an imprint. She was the only girl in high school who seemed to draw a line in the sand with me, the only one who didn't try to erase it, who didn't scramble to stand at my side.

I couldn't understand why she hated me, but there was something about her resistance that intrigued me. Most girls fell at my feet, eager for any attention I might give them. But not her. Never Caroline.

three

CAROLINE, **5 years later**

The pinch was as familiar as it was painful, Yaya's grip so tight it was like she thought someone might steal me from her. "Asteri mou," Yaya cooed, pink lipstick smeared on her teeth. "I can't believe you're twenty-two, you are beautiful." Yaya was still stunning in her old age. Her jewelry was always on point, but her lipstick never stayed in the lines. She had been married to my grandfather for forty years before he passed away, and then she left Greece to live close to us. "But when I was your age, I was married with four kids already. Do you still like men? Because I don't care about your preference as long as you're married."

"Yaya, I—" My voice came out muffled and strained as her fingers held firm. "Yes, Yaya, I like men," I managed to blurt out, the words barely escaping the confines of her affectionate torture. "I just haven't found the right one yet."

I knew the concern in her voice all too well. "Do you need me to set you up? What about that nice man who sells insurance?" Her eyebrows arched in anticipation, as if the mere suggestion could script my future. "He has a great wealthy family."

"Yaya, no," I began, the protest rising from my chest, but before I could finish, her hand shifted. She turned me sharply to the side, and with a pinch to my ass said, "You have such a tight bun, I don't see what the problem is."

Heat surged through my body, my face red with embarrassment. The parking lot suddenly felt like a fishbowl, and I couldn't shake the feeling that someone had just caught Yaya getting a snag of my behind. Mortified didn't even begin to describe it.

"Caroline, we need to get in line now or we're never going to get a table." My sister Charlotte interrupted. Grateful for the diversion, I composed myself and followed her lead.

The line for the restaurant filled the waiting area. I fell into step beside my sister, the burn of Yaya's pinch lingering, an unwelcome reminder of the unfair expectations that my entire family had on my love life.

I trailed my sister to the hostess stand, the scent of garlic and oregano overwhelming us. The hostess—her attention shackled to a tablet—barely glanced up as she delivered the verdict: an hour wait.

"An hour?" The words slipped from my lips, shooting my sister a sidelong glare—who'd assured me all was arranged for my birthday dinner. "I thought you had it handled."

"They don't take reservations!" she hissed, rolling her eyes.

"We'll just wait," I murmured, accepting our fate.

Once dinner was over with, I could get to the real fun. I knew my friends had planned something epic tonight for my birthday—plans a world apart from cheek pinches and insurance salesmen.

My family and I stood in line. My parents chatted while my sister and her fiance exchanged stolen glances, their hands subtly entwined. My brother was on his phone, exuding detached interest. His wife, who also happened to be a gorgeous model, stood behind him.

We had been waiting to be seated for nearly fifteen minutes when the heavy wooden door swung open, and in walked Reese Carrington along with his family. The moment Reese strutted inside the restaurant, all heads turned his way. He was in a black dress shirt that hugged his athletic frame, his dark hair tousled and falling in messy perfection. I caught sight of the cuff adjustment—a subtle but deliberate motion that drew attention to his newly ink-stained skin beneath. It was just a glimpse, but it was enough to reveal the edge of a tattoo, which I'm sure was some act of rebellion.

He approached the hostess stand, all eyes still on the bad boy who played life like a game only he knew the rules to. The hostess herself seemed momentarily disoriented. It was almost comical the way her jaw fell open, like Harry Styles had just walked in.

And there I was, rolling my eyes at this disgusting spectacle.

The hostess, the one who had barely acknowledged us, now paid no attention to her tablet. Her demeanor shifted instantaneously from polite indifference to eager accommodation.

"Right this way, Mr. Carrington. We have your favorite table ready," she said, abandoning her post to lead them through the maze of tables.

Reese's little sister scurried after the hostess. His stepmother, a striking woman with an air of polished grace, and his father who was on the phone and wearing an expensive looking suit, also made their way to the table.

Reese and my brother locked in a handshake and patted each other on the back, tied together through the baseball world.

As Reese passed me, he caught my eye and flashed a roguish wink. I clenched my jaw, keeping my voice low.

"Entitled ass," I whispered, my gaze tracking Reese's confident stride. "How? They don't do reservations."

My brother raised an eyebrow at me but said nothing, the corner of his mouth twitching in amusement at my barely contained irritation. The faint echo of Reese's laughter mingled with clinking of glasses, as they were seated swiftly. They didn't bother another glance back at those still waiting.

"Ben Carrington just won a huge case," my mother's voice drifted from where she stood next to my dad. "I bet they're celebrating tonight. Heard he got his client eight million."

"Money and good looks, those are the kind of men we need to be having dinner with," Yaya added.

We all knew about the Carrington family. My fingers curled into my palm, nails pressing into my skin. I forced a neutral expression in an attempt to hide the snarl fighting to surface. He was the one person who aggravated me to no end. Images stormed behind my eyes—flashbacks of every time Reese's perfect life had collided with mine. With his annoyingly perfect looks, his unreal green eyes, and that arrogant tilt to his chin, as if he'd won life's lottery and knew it. He always got to walk through life on a red carpet—because of wealth and connections. No need to work hard and prove yourself when you're Reese Carrington.

An hour had trickled by in a slow, syrupy crawl before we were finally ushered to our table.

"Finally," my sister exhaled, as she smoothed out her dress. Her eyes sparkled with the reflection of the candlelight when she leaned toward the waitress, conspiratorial. "We're here for my sister's birthday. She's been dreaming about your manicotti for weeks—it's her favorite. Well, that and peanut butter and jelly."

The waitress—in a black apron sporting more stains than I could count—flashed a sympathetic smile, her pen poised above her notepad. "I'm so sorry, hunny," she began, her words oozing regret, "that table over there ordered the very last one." She gestured across the room at Reese's table.

His infamous green eyes were locked onto his plate, where manicotti remnants lay half eaten. A heavy sigh escaped me as I buried my face in the warmth of my palms. "I'll just take the lasagna," I murmured, my voice muffled by my hands.

"You got it, hunny." Her notepad scratched softly against the table as she scribbled the order down.

I stood abruptly, pushing back from the table with a scrape that felt too loud, too sudden. "I'm going to the bar to get a drink," I announced, and no one acknowledged me.

I found myself tracing circles on the counter top as I waited for my drink.

"Looking for the kids' menu? You won't find it at the bar," came a deep, smug voice from beside me.

I turned, already bracing for the inevitable. Reese leaned against the counter, green eyes flickering with mischief as they met mine.

"Funny," I quipped, rolling my eyes, "I was actually looking for the trash—oh, and there you are."

"If I remember correctly, you've always had trouble recognizing trash cans," he said, obviously referring to my discarded school lunches.

"That's not true at all—I'm looking right at one."

His laugh, a rumble of amusement that somehow seemed both genuine and rehearsed, filled the space between us. "Is there ever a day you don't run your mouth?" he teased, a cocky smile playing on his lips. He leaned in closer, his warm breath barely grazing my ear as he added, "If you need something to do with it, I can help you out with that."

"Well," I began, "I would be stuffing my face with manicotti for my birthday, but you ruined that—like you do everything."

He cocked a brow, his grin pure mischief. "Birthday, huh? Let me guess... twenty-two?"

"Early eighties, actually," I shot back, my sarcasm so thick you could spread it on bread.

Reese's smirk deepened, his voice a slow, teasing drawl. "That so? Gotta say, you wear eighty *real* well."

"I know," I said, reaching past him, brushing the cool surface of the bar top with my fingertips before I picked up my drink. "And if you'll excuse me, I have to get back to my second favorite meal." The words slipped out, a bitter reminder of the manicotti-shaped hole in my birthday celebration.

"Happy birthday, Chaos," he said, casually sipping his drink, as I turned and walked away.

After dinner, our mostly empty plates were scattered across the table. Once the waitress picked up our empty plates, my mother was quick to let her know, "We will take the bill now, when you're ready."

"Oh, hunny," she interrupted. Her hand fluttered up, waving off the concern before it could fully form. "It's already been taken care of."

The air around me seemed to still, the ambient noise of clinking glasses and murmured conversations fading to a distant hum. My mom searched the waitress's face, trying to understand. "Taken care of?"

"Yes," she confirmed with a nod.

"For the whole family?" Dad asked, overhearing the conversation.

"Indeed," the waitress replied. "The Carringtons have taken care of everything. And," she added with a smile, "they've also spoken with the chef—a pan of manicotti made from scratch has been arranged for your family to take home. It'll be packaged up shortly."

Yaya leaned across the table. "I knew it," she whispered. "That lawyer is into me. He's my type of man, too. Rich, thoughtful, and looks just like a Greek god—and I would know." She gave a knowing smile.

As my family continued to chat, their voices mingled with the soft notes of a piano somewhere in the background, but all I could do was stare dumbfounded at the now-empty table Reese and his family had occupied. Why in the hell would Reese Carrington pay for my birthday meal? And why would he convince the chef to make manicotti from scratch?

I nodded at the waitress, a silent acknowledgment that I heard her, though understanding eluded me. Reese had never been one for random acts of kindness—not without a motive, a play for power. We'd spent the past how many years hating each other? What game was he playing?

$four$

REESE

The pom-pom hit my face with a smack, blinding me momentarily. Cheerleading could very well be the damn death of me. I blinked rapidly to adjust my vision, as I tossed my practice bag on the floor.

"You almost took my eye out, Lo!" I scolded my little sister, Lola. She ignored me, lost in her own world of chants and cartwheels. She had been practicing in the living room all day. She'd started before I left for practice, and when I got home she was still leaping and kicking with complete disregard for the innocent bystanders passing through the house.

"You've been at it for hours," I added dryly, sidestepping a discarded cheer shoe as I made my way to the kitchen.

She glanced at me mid-headstand. "Yeah, I'm panicking," she said, out of breath. "I have tryouts for Elite cheer in a few weeks. The only reason I didn't go with mom and dad to the beach house this summer. I have to focus, and bootcamp is coming up next week."

I nodded, peeking back at her legs flying through the air again. "Well, I can't stand the music. I'm gonna go meet the boys for a drink. Text me if you need anything."

She didn't even glance back at me to respond. The door closed behind me with a gentle click, sealing away the endless loop of cheer music.

The neon sign of Gin & Jerry's Pub buzzed as I pushed open the door and stepped into its familiar darkness. My eyes adjusted, scanning for any sign of the boys, but of course—late as usual. I slid onto a barstool, catching the nod from RJ, a bartender I knew well. Middle-aged, with a long dark beard and a no-nonsense vibe, he barely paused before reaching for a frosted glass.

"Evening, Reese," he grunted, sliding my usual order across the bar.

"Hey, RJ." I returned a nod. The cold bottle touched my lips, and the first swig of beer was a bitter comfort.

As soon as I set the glass down, I felt it—a pair of gentle hands gliding across my shoulder blades.

"Mind if I sit?" Without even glancing over, I knew who it was—Blair. I would recognize that voice anywhere, and just like that, irritation clawed its way up my spine.

"Even if I said no, you'd sit there regardless, Blair." My grip on the bottle tightened just enough to hide my irritation. Rather than sitting next to me, she slid right onto my lap.

"I like this seat better, and... I know you've missed me. Even if you won't admit it," she smiled softly, trailing her nails over the back of my neck.

With a flicker of a smirk, I took another pull from my beer. "If that's what you need to tell yourself."

"We used to be so good together." Blair's voice softened, but it wasn't genuine.

"Were we, though? And aren't you with that old guy?" I couldn't resist throwing that dig, despite my disinterest.

"He's not old," she snapped back. "He's a yacht captain, and for your information, we ended things."

"Why? His wife finally caught on?" I tossed out, barely interested at this point, wondering why I was even still entertaining her.

"Can we just skip over this and get to the make-up sex part of the night?" she purred. "It's been way too damn long."

"This is getting old, Blair." I took another sip, as I slowly scanned the bar wondering where the fuck my friends were. I could kill them right now.

"Remember that time I brought you to your knees, down into the dirt at the ball field?" Blair whispered into my ear. "You tasted so good."

"Blair," I breathed, trying my damn hardest to push away the mental images resurfacing. I could still feel the roughness of the chain-link fence against my palms that day. The excitement of knowing we could get caught at any moment.

"I'll never forget how your head rolled back." Her breath was hot against my ear, her tongue slowly stroking and nibbling.

"That was a long time ago," I managed to say, tilting my head away just enough to break free from the grip her tongue had on my ear.

"Why don't I remind you?" she suggested, lashes fluttering with hope. "In the bathroom?"

Fuck. Bathroom head? She was pulling out all the stops now. But this was Blair. If I gave her an inch, she'd take a fucking mile, and I didn't have a mile to give. This would lead nowhere good. Giving into Blair would end in disaster. I bit my knuckle, looking away from her, and carefully thinking about my next words, my next decision. Blair's fingers trailed down my shirt, making a path down from my chest toward the ridges of my abs.

Surprised by my own indifference, I caught her wrist gently but firmly, stopping her before she landed on her target. "I appreciate the offer. Tempting, but no," I said, and her eyes met mine with a mix of surprise and confusion.

"Reese, really?" she murmured.

"Really, I'm good, Blair." Disappointment flickered across her face before she hid it with a forced pout.

With a huff, she slid off my lap and crossed her arms defiantly across her chest. "Fine, but my drinks are on you tonight."

I didn't miss the bartender's knowing glance our way. He'd been an audience to Blair's failed attempt at seducing me. Without breaking eye contact with her, I gave him a subtle nod, agreeing to the transactional peace offering. It seemed like a small price to pay for ruining whatever plan she had for tonight.

Finally, the door swung open as Bailey and Crew walked in. They both grabbed a stool and took a place at the bar.

"Alright, chat... we made it to the bar so you have ten seconds to throw any last minute gifts at me before I log off for the night," Bailey said, smirking into his phone like an idiot. Lately he was obsessed with making as much money as he could talking to what he called "his fans" online.

"What's up, bud?" Crew greeted me first with a nod as he took a seat.

Bailey turned off his phone and leaned back in a relaxed manner, casually draping an arm over the top of the tall bar stool. His grin widened as he looked at Blair. "Well, well, look who's here. The devil herself."

Blair squinted at him. "And you'd be the first person I'd send straight to hell," she fired back. It brought back memories of the constant jabs they'd exchange when Blair and I were together—they never got along. Crew caught the bartender's attention with a lazy flick of his wrist. "On that note, we'll take some shots over here."

"Getting bored now," Blair announced abruptly, pushing away from her stool. Her eyes locked onto mine for a moment. "You boys enjoy your night. Reese, if you change your mind," she squeezed my arm, "you know my number."

The others didn't seem to notice her leave, already caught up in the anticipation of shots being lined up before us. Then I caught the tail end of Crew's sentence. "...Season is almost over."

Bailey leaned forward, resting his elbows on the bar. "Can't believe it's our last summer together."

"Let's make these next weeks count," I called out, lifting my shot into the air.

As the heat from the shot warmed my chest, I thought about these next few weeks with the boys. Constant laughter and reckless stupidity, the adrenaline of game days, chasing girls and random hook-ups—-it no longer had the same appeal it once did. And, I knew who shifted my outlook on it all. Chandler. As bittersweet as it was, last summer had been a turning point. I knew letting her go was the right move. For her, for me. But she showed me what I wanted in a relationship—substance, depth, something more meaningful. It was a glimpse into the future that I wanted, even if I may not be ready for it just yet. I was grateful for the lessons she'd taught me.

"Reese, you in there?" Crew's voice interrupted my thoughts, his hand waving in front of my face, snapping me back. "Wells Clark just walked in."

A loud sigh escaped me as I leaned back. He was almost as cocky as me, except I wasn't sure if he actually had a brain. He was a walking cliché in the form of a college football quarterback. Him and I had gotten into a little incident a while back, and let's just say my fist ended the night after connecting straight into his jaw.

"Hey, look, it's the soccer team," he drawled, a smirk plastered across his face as he approached us.

Bailey, who was on his second beer next to me, set his drink down. "Baseball," he corrected.

"Ah, you know what I mean." Wells shrugged off the correction with a nonchalant wave of his hand. "You play with balls, same thing." His attempt at humor fell flat.

I arched an eyebrow at Wells. "You do realize that the pigskin you toss around is called a ball too, right?" I had to hold back a smile at the flicker of confusion on his face.

His laughter was loud and abrupt, making Crew flinch. "Oh yeah, you're right," he conceded with a grin. "Guess I play with balls too, I mean... besides my own."

"Every word exchanged with you is a brain cell I will never get back," I whispered under my breath.

Wells, unfazed by my comment, leaned closer, the smell of his cheap cologne overpowering the stale beer smell. "By the way, I saw your little sister doing her thing at cheer camp while we were practicing on the field. She's a real looker—"

"If you speak about my little sister again, I promise you, you won't be able to walk out of here, let alone speak again."

"Damnit, I would have worn my other shoes tonight if I knew we were getting into a bar fight." Bailey crossed him arms. "Although, Reese didn't need any help beating your ass sophomore year."

Wells' smile faltered. His friend stepped in with hands raised. "Woah, woah," he said, trying to diffuse the situation. "We're all just here to have a good time."

The muscles in my jaw ticked with barely-restrained anger. "You've got about thirty seconds to get him out of my face before my fist ends up in his. Again."

The friend, eyes flickering between me and Wells, seemed to grasp the gravity of the threat. He tugged at Wells' sleeve, urging him away with a nervous glance in my direction.

"Alright, alright," Wells conceded with a dismissive wave of his hand, the cocky grin slipping back onto his face. "We'll continue this conversation another night."

"Yeah, get lost, Clark!" Crew yelled as he retreated.

"I'll be right back," I said, tossing my bear in the trash.

As I wandered back toward the bathroom, a sharp poke jolted me from behind. The annoyance came with a voice, grating yet familiar. "What the hell was that?" Caroline asked, accusingly.

I turned, the low flicker of an overhead light casting half her face in shadow, the other half illuminated just enough to reveal those piercing blue eyes. "What?"

She was small, but her presence filled the space like she could command the room with nothing more than her fiery spirit. "Why the hell did you pay for our dinner?"

The corners of my mouth twitched into a smirk. My eyes locked onto hers. "I guess that's one way to say thank you."

Caroline's lips parted, ready to launch another verbal missile. "Did you spit in the manicotti? Was that the joke?"

"We left before the chef even started making it," I shot back.

"Then why did you do it?" Caroline asked.

"I don't know," I said dryly, shrugging. "Consider it a birthday present. Trust me, it didn't hurt my pockets."

I saw Caroline's posture tense, her shoulders locking in like she was bracing for a battle she'd been through a hundred times. "We didn't need you to pay for us like we're some charity case," she snapped.

Whoa. What the hell is that response? Charity had never crossed my mind. "Charity?" I echoed, while a sly grin played at the corner of my mouth. "Nah, think of it more as... community service." I leaned against the rough brick wall behind me, hoping this would continue on. I had come to love these sparring matches with Caroline.

I could tell my words had hit their mark, ruffling her feathers just enough. We played this game well over the years. I annoy her to no end, and it somehow warmed my cold heart.

"Community service," she repeated. "You're such a prick. We don't want anything from you."

"Too late," I exhaled, sharply. "It's already done."

"How do you do that?" she asked, her voice sharp. "Just walk around being the most aggravating person that ever existed?"

"One of my many talents," I replied, the words rolling off my tongue effortlessly. "You should see what else I can do."

"What was the total?" Caroline asked, all serious and businesslike. "I'm paying you back right now."

There was something recklessly wild that always seemed to cling to her. I shook my head, the smirk never quite leaving my face. "Nah, I don't need your money." I paused, letting the anticipation build. "But you can pay me back in another way. I need a favor."

five

CAROLINE

"If you're about to ask me for a sexual favor, don't even waste your breath."

He leaned back, that infuriating smirk etching deeper into his tanned complexion. "Really?" he asked, the word oozing with sarcasm. "Because obviously, any person who buys you pasta expects you to get down on your knees."

"Fine then," I crossed my arms over my chest, preparing for whatever was coming. "Let's hear it. This"—I motioned at him with a flick of my wrist—"should be good."

"You teach cheerleading." The dim overhead lights cast a soft glow on his annoyingly perfect features as he studied me, searching for my reaction. Every move he made seemed intentional, from the way he adjusted his watch to the way his fingers tapped against his wrist.

"Well, thanks for that useful information," I said, matching my sarcasm with his. "Let me guess... you want to join the squad?"

He chuckled, the sound low and unexpectedly warm. It wasn't quite as annoying as the cocky grin of his—the one that had a way of getting on my last nerve.

"Actually," Reese said, leaning in closer, "my little sister needs to make the cheer team at Elite."

"Interesting," I said, tapping a finger against my lips.

"It means a lot to her," he said, before he took a sip of his drink. "Maybe you could help her out?" He smirked, thinking he was in control. "I would ask Blair but I'm sort of trying to avoid her at the moment."

Blair, with her perfect hair and movie star looks, had plastered photos of her and Reese together across every social media platform for years. His ex-girlfriend and I had never really got along, even when we cheered together, but now that I thought about it—I didn't think she really got along with anyone.

For barely a moment, I found it almost endearing that he would come to me for his sister, which meant he must really care about her. But the thought of doing him a favor? That was about as exciting as getting an elbow to the face during a failed cheer stunt.

"Wish I could help," I said innocently, shrugging. "But since she's related to you, I have to decline."

There was a subtle shift in his posture, a tightening around his eyes. "Oh, my bad," he drawled. "I was under the impression that you were one of the best."

"Your information is accurate. I am one the best—if not *the* best," I shot back, pride fueling my words. "But you'll need to look else-where for help."

"Fine by me," Reese shrugged, unfazed. "Got a few cheerleaders in my DMs, all begging to do me a favor." He punctuated his words with a wink.

"I wouldn't expect anything less," I said under my breath, knowing all the cheerleaders swooned over him. Except Sam, of course.

"There's a whole table back there with your friends, balloons, and everything anyone could ever want for their birthday. You might wanna ditch the ice queen act and, I don't know, enjoy it for once."

"As soon as I'm no longer in your presence, my night will immediately improve."

"Enjoy your night then," Reese said with an arrogance that prickled my skin. "Because after tonight, you have to spend the whole weekend with me."

Annoyingly, he was right. He was referring to the away tournament. It was in moments like these that I hated being President of The Blue Devils Committee—a title that had once been worn by my mother like a crown. I had taken the job to impress her, to make her proud of me for once, but she wasn't impressed. She also hated that I taught dance and cheer, and, well actually, it felt like she hated everything I did.

"Do your best to stay away," I said with a tight smile.

Reese's smile was slow, as if he savored the taste of my irritation. "Always do," he murmured before he turned and walked away, leaving behind the scent of his cologne—something woodsy and exclusive. The girl standing near us eyed him as she watched him go, her gaze lingering long after he'd disappeared into the crowd.

His cockiness gnawed at me—that lethal charm and the self-assurance with which he carried himself—as if he was the sole reason this world of ours spun around. He had this effortless power about him—probably a mix of old money and baseball—giving him access to people and places that only made his ego even bigger. Me agreeing to help him would mean that I'd also give in to that privilege of his that I've hated for so long. This small town might adore him, might lavish him with praise, but not me. He had everything at his fingertips, and I wasn't going to give him another thing he wanted.

The further I walked away from Reese, the more the atmosphere shifted. I was entering a different world now—one with happiness and excitement. My friends were orbiting around the table with drinks and balloons. They were singing "Happy Birthday" as loud as they could. Sam reached me first, squeezing me as tight as she could.

For a fleeting moment, I could breathe, the moment sweet and untainted by the bitter aftertaste of speaking to that asshat.

And as I took in the faces of my friends, their smiles and happiness all for me, I allowed myself to absorb the warmth of their affection. There was no pressure, no stress tonight. I was simply Caroline, surrounded by love and laughter.

A shot glass was shoved into my hand, the clear liquid sloshing a tad over the edge. Tequila and I had a love-hate relationship. I was happy and alive while drinking it, but those nights were also best left forgotten more often than not.

"Come on, birthday girl," they chanted, their faces expectant.

With a resigned breath, I tilted the glass to my lips, the liquid fire trailing down my throat, searing a path of warmth that settled uneasily in my stomach.

"Caroline," Sam nudged me. "Were you over there talking to Reese?"

My gaze flickered involuntarily toward the bar, where he was back with his friends. Even from this distance, I could see the casual way he leaned against the counter, like he didn't have a care in this world. But why would he? His life was perfect. I quickly averted my eyes, not wanting to betray any more of my turmoil.

"Unfortunately," I admitted, annoyed I was forced to think about him again.

I could feel Sam's gaze, heavy with questions because she was the only one here that went to middle school with me and Reese. She knew how much we hated—no, *despised*—each other.

"We had to suffer here staring at The Blue Devils while we waited to sing you "Happy Birthday." My friend Paisley said, swiveling on her stool at the table with a glass of wine cradled in her hand. Her red lips curved into a pout.

I slid onto the stool next to her. "You were suffering, huh?" I retorted, playfully. "That sounds awful."

"Not really," she murmured, her gaze drifting towards the bar. "I feel like every year they get hotter. And Reese has that new tattoo sleeve this summer... game over."

I couldn't help but cast a glance toward him, hating myself for knowing she was right. Why did everyone keep bringing him up? I wished the bouncer would yeet him out of here.

"Nah," Sam responded, eyes narrowing in thought as they scanned the dark bar. "Lately, Crew has been kind of doing something for me. He always looks like he just walked off the beach. I bet his skin is even salty."

Paisley's laughter was light. "You take Crew, I'll take Reese," she declared with a conspiratorial wink. "I'd never actually hook up with Reese, though."

"Why not?" I managed to ask.

Paisley leaned in so the others around us couldn't hear. "Haven't you ever heard what Blair has said about him? Or Wren, from my sorority?"

I shook my head—a little too eagerly, perhaps—and Paisley smiled, as if she was about to change my entire perspective on him. "Well, they both said he was the best sex they've ever had. Wren had three orgasms the night they hooked up."

"And?" I prodded, curious now.

"And, well Wren, she hasn't been able to have another orgasm ever since. He ruined her." She leaned back, with pity in her voice. "Poor thing got Reese'd and released."

She cannot be serious. Reese'd and Released? Oh, hell no. This guy was out here strutting around like he owned this town, crushing souls with that stupid, smug grin. And even worse—he was basking in it all, like leaving a trail of emotional devastation in his wake was just another accomplishment on his rich boy resume.

"That's probably why Blair's still hooked," Sam said, twirling a strand of hair around her finger. "She can't get over him, always trying to win him back."

I shifted uncomfortably. "That's really sad," I murmured aloud.

"But he is dreamy though," Paisley sighed. "Has everything you'd want in a man."

I rolled my eyes at her comment, even as a part of me secretly acknowledged the truth in her words. He was annoyingly good looking, and I hated that about him, too.

Sam finally spoke up again. "I guess," she said skeptically. "Lives off Daddy's money and status only to eventually have his own wealth and power when he goes pro."

"Anyway, what's the deal with you and Wells Clark, Caroline?" Paisley teased, layering on another shade of lipstick.

The murmur of conversation around us seemed to hush for a moment, waiting for my response. But I gave them nothing, just a sip of my drink and a shrug.

"I heard he's into you," Paisley continued, undeterred by my silence, "and probably coming tonight."

"Awesome," I said aloud, tracing the rim of my glass with a fingertip. "Please, for the love of sanity, don't let me drink enough to hook up with Wells Clark."

I understood the appeal. He was a cute quarterback and all, but he couldn't ever keep an actual conversation going. And after the way things ended with Boston and me last summer, I knew the risks of starting to have feelings for the wrong person.

"Got ya girl," Sam said, pulling me back from my thoughts. "You're going home with me tonight."

six

REESE

The snap of the ball hitting Parker's glove was the only sound I needed—a satisfying pop, another out. The game narrowed to the silent conversations between Parker and me. Each signal in his glove, each nod or head shake—a language only we understood. The world beyond the diamond faded. Even the batters didn't matter. It was just him and I playing catch—well that's how I saw it anyway. The batters on the other side might not agree.

The innings flew by. No runs had been scored against us, but we weren't making it happen either. We were well matched. It wasn't until the seventh inning that finally Boston tagged home. One to nothing. When the last batter struck out in the bottom of the ninth, our team erupted. We won. By one run, but I'd fucking take it. This weekend's tournament was finally over, and we'd won it all.

"Let's celebrate," Bailey yelled as he threw his arm around my shoulder.

Crew chimed in, pulling off his batting gloves. "Let's go to that country bar across the street," he hollered. "Best part is, we can walk there from the hotel." We were a few hours away from Bayside, and we didn't have to check out until tomorrow.

"Yeah, but we all know your ass will be crawling back drunk," Bailey joked.

I was all for celebrating the tournament win, but I also knew that Chandler—the girl I was kind of with last summer—was on the Blue Devils committee this year. Which meant she'd be around tonight. And while I'd been doing my best to steer clear of her, avoiding her completely? Yeah, that wasn't happening. She'd be there with the rest of the committee members, looking gorgeous, laughing like nothing ever happened between us. And Boston would be doing everything he could to pursue her while I had to act like that shit wasn't getting to me.

We headed to our rooms to shower, and just as I slid open the bathroom door, a knock sounded. Parker, sprawled on his bed, didn't so much as flinch—completely ignoring it. Basically naked, with the exception of the towel wrapped around my waist, I yanked the hotel room door open. Outside, a train wreck of whistles and catcalls awaited me, led by my best friend himself, Bailey.

"What the hell do you want?" I barked, glaring at their grinning faces.

"Hurry your ass up and get down to the lobby," Bailey said, emphasizing every word with a finger jab to my chest. "We're grab-bing some appetizers and drinks before we hit the bar."

I glanced back at Parker, still lounging on his bed, hat no longer hiding his face. He rolled his eyes and muttered something about how a guy can't ever get some quick beauty rest in.

I sighed, shutting the door on the commotion. I turned to glare at my weekend tourney roommate. "Parker, in your case, I think we can drop the 'beauty' and just call it rest."

Parker shrugged, swinging his legs off the bed. "You're right. These good looks are natural. No sleep needed." He tilted his head in my direction. "But, you might want to change out of your birthday suit because girls won't even look my way if you're dressed like that."

I shot him a wink and stalked back into the bathroom, shutting the door behind me. When I stepped out, I was freshly dressed in jeans and a casual black fitted tee. I shot Parker a sideways glance as I adjusted the pendant necklace around my neck then grabbed a hat off the desk to throw on. "Ready, Sleeping Beauty?"

Parker grinned, adjusting his cap. "Let's do it."

The dimly-lit hotel bar was packed with the team and other guests. I spotted Crew, Bailey, and Boston at a table in the corner.

"Over here!" Bailey waved me over, almost spilling his drink in the process.

Just then, the elevator doors swung open, as Chandler and Willow made their entrance.

Boston was practically drooling over Chandler in her little black dress, and I understood the reaction—she could pull off fucking anything. Bailey caught me staring. He knew the situation between us. He wrapped his arm around my shoulder and steered me away from the group before she reached us.

"Let's go check out these cowgirls," he slurred, gesturing to the lobby doors.

I downed my drink and followed him, knowing everyone else would slowly make their way across the street. I needed distance from Chandler. I knew I'd done the right thing. Hadn't I? Being the bigger person to let her explore her connection with Boston was supposed to feel good... so why did it feel like I was the one who'd lost something? Maybe because I had. Not just her—I lost the chance, the possibility of what we could have been. And now, all I was left with was the question: what if? Maybe she wouldn't have picked me anyway. Maybe I was torturing myself over something that was never meant to be.

The scent of spilled whiskey and worn leather filled the bar. Bailey waved down the bartender with that familiar mischievous smirk tugging at his lips. He ordered shots as more of the guys started to join us.

"Alright," he said, sliding a row of glasses towards our newly formed huddle. "We're taking this shot, and there's a group of girls on our left. We're all gonna pick one to slide next to on the count of three."

I shook my head. "Why do we go along with this shit?" I asked, but Bailey was already counting, his voice carrying over the pulsing music.

"One, two, three..."

The sharp sting of tequila hit the back of my throat, a fiery reminder to never let Bailey pick the shots again. Then, we let him lead the way. He dove into conversation with a girl whose laughter sounded more donkey than human.

Crew and I drifted over to two brunettes nearby. The girl closest to me glanced up, her eyes searching me closely. "Well, hello gorgeous," she purred.

"Hi," I replied, flashing her a dimple. Before I could ask her name, Bailey's voice interrupted with our prearranged code word. "Blue Devils, fire drill!"

Fire Drill was code for "let's switch girls"—a douchey-yet-effective tactic to remove ourselves from conversation we didn't want to be in, and have someone else take over and distract. It was shitty, but here I was, always backing up Bailey, even when he was an idiot.

"Excuse me, it's been great," I murmured just before the annoyance flared in her eyes.

"Where are you going?" she called out as I slipped past her, Bailey and Crew shadowing my movements, an orchestrated shift down the line.

As I moved toward the next person, I noticed a pair of sexy tan legs and a glimpse of blonde hair. Blondes weren't my preference, but it was just a chat, right? Then she turned around, and instantly, I realized my mistake. It was the one and only, Caroline Matthews.

"Caroline," I said, making a sad attempt to hide my disappointment. My gaze landed on the two shots lined up in front of her. "Double fisting? Classy. Really setting the bar high."

She grabbed one without hesitation. "What can I say? I aim low

—survival was the only goal this week." Then she tossed it back like a pro.

I leaned against the cool wood of the bar. "I know that feeling."

She turned, her glare sharp. "I doubt you've ever had a rough week in your life."

A mirthless laugh escaped me. "You have no idea."

Caroline's attention snapped away, drawn to something, or someone, across the room. I followed her gaze to Boston and Chandler, all over each other on the dance floor. I winced, the image burning my retinas, overwhelmingly unwanted. In a strange way, I knew Caroline was feeling the same discomfort I was.

"Another shot," Caroline commanded the bartender.

"Shouldn't you finish that—" Before I could finish my sentence, she swept up the second shot glass and downed it—making it disappear in an instant.

"Nevermind," I shook my head. "Guess you know what you're doing."

The bartender slid another whiskey my way, the ice clinking against the glass. Before my fingers could wrap around it, Caroline's hand darted out, snatching it from me.

"I'll take that, too," Caroline declared.

"Of course you will," I shook my head as I looked down at her. I had a significant height advantage over her—a fact I never failed to enjoy. Her long blonde hair framed her face in effortless waves, and those cowboy boots she wore only made her look even more defiant.

"Need this more than you do," she snapped back, blue eyes flashing.

"Maybe you've had enough," I added, dryly.

"I didn't come to the bar for judgment," she shot back, slamming the empty glass onto the bar with satisfying finality.

I signaled to the bartender to get me another drink, and he nodded.

Then Bailey's voice carried over with another "fire drill" call, and I felt an uncharacteristic resistance. My feet remained planted on the sticky bar floor, and beside me, Crew didn't budge either. We formed a silent pact, turning our backs to Bailey. For once, I wasn't going along with it—maybe it was the gravity in Caroline's gaze that anchored me. Or maybe it was my curiosity about her that kept me there.

"Fire drill!" Bailey bellowed, throwing his hands up in distress.

The bartender closer to him raised an unamused brow at Bailey. And before any of us saw it coming, she grabbed the water tap and aimed it with precision at her target, drenching him.

"What the hell?" Bailey spluttered, water dripping from his hair, down to the collar of his shirt.

"Sorry," the bartender said, though the smirk playing on her lips spoke volumes to her lack of remorse. "I thought you said there was a fire."

Bailey grinned like a fool and shook his head as he wiped the water out of his face. Caroline threw her head back in a loud, infectious laugh. I couldn't hold back either. We both sat there snickering uncontrollably while Bailey looked like a soggy cat, trying to regain his dignity.

"Did Bailey just try to fire drill you?" Caroline laughed, wiping a tear from the corner of her eye. "Because that went terribly wrong."

"Yeah, it's Bails," I admitted, still chuckling. "Would you expect anything less?"

"Not at all," she shot back, still trying to fight the laughter.

"You better stop laughing like that, or I might think you're actually enjoying my company."

She turned to me, those sky-colored eyes holding mine. A taunting smirk played on her lips. "Trust me, I'm not enjoying your company." The way she said that didn't sound all that convincing.

Then it hit me that it wasn't just some girl at the bar Crew was talking to—it was Sam, Caroline's best friend. "Is Crew talking to...?" I started, turning toward Caroline.

"Sam?" she confirmed, rolling her eyes. "Yeah, and she hasn't stopped smiling from the moment they started talking."

As if feeling our eyes on her, Sam turned our way. "Caroline," she called out. "Will you go back to the hotel room with Crew and me? Please!" Her smile widened with hope. "Maybe we can drink a little more and relax? I'm ready to get outta this bar."

I glanced at Caroline, anticipating her fiery spirit to challenge the suggestion, but instead, she seemed to consider it. "Ugh, fine," she relented with a sigh, giving in quicker than I expected.

Crew threw an arm over my shoulder. "Reese is coming too!"

Caroline barely talked to me most days, barely gave me the time of day. When she did, it was pure, unfiltered hatred. Us getting along? That seemed borderline impossible—unheard of. Most women were drawn to me—I hardly had to try—but never Caroline. No, she didn't swoon, didn't blush, didn't so much as flicker an eyelash in my direction. Why was she immune to my charm when it worked so well on others?

Honestly, I didn't know whether to be impressed or offended by her ability to see right through my bullshit. But one thing was certain: She had my attention. Every move she made, every sharp remark, every damn time she didn't give me the reaction I wanted—I wanted to know more. *Needed* to.

I leaned closer to Caroline, her perfume mingling with the smoky ambiance of the place. It was now or never. "Can we have a truce for one night?" My voice was barely above a whisper, but the intensity behind the words was unmistakable. "Put our differences aside for our friends? You can go back to hating me tomorrow."

Those dangerous eyes twinkled with a playful fire—one that could warm you up just as easily as it could burn you down. Possibly both.

She took a slow sip of her drink, buying time, calculating.

"I'll take that deal... for my friend, and because I've had a few too many." She paused, her tongue darting out to wet her lips. "Which may be clouding my judgment, but we'll go with it."

I leaned against the bar and caught the bartender's eye. "I'll take the tab for everyone over here," I said, pointing from Sam and Caroline to the Blue Devil athletes.

The bartender reached under the counter, and passed me a long strip of paper that made me immediately regret my decision. "Here you go," he said, a lopsided smile playing across his face.

As I scanned the textbook sized bill, one item snagged my attention—a fifty dollar charge for water. My brow creased. "What's with the water tax?"

He tilted his head toward Bailey, who was engaged in an intense discussion with the bartender who sprayed him, droplets still glistening on his shirt. "For the fire drill game that one was playing. Had half the bar believing it was a genuine emergency."

I shook my head at the absurdity. Only Bailey. I paid the bill and tipped with appreciation, but when the bartender cracked open a bottle and set it next to him on the bar, I grabbed it up in one swift motion, bringing the whiskey bottle to my lips.

"This is coming with me."

"Considering your generosity, take it as a parting gift," the bartender replied.

I held the bottle tightly in my grasp as I left the bar, the entourage trailing behind me.

seven

CAROLINE

The green light flickered when I swiped my keycard, and I nudged the door open with my shoulder. Sam and Crew stumbled past me, Crew's arm slung possessively around her waist. It was night and day compared to the obvious distance between Reese and me.

"Damn, how did you guys get a suite?" Crew asked, his eyes going wide as he checked out the room, like it was the first time he'd seen one.

"I mean, I'm committee president," I said with a slight shrug. "Of course I was going to get myself a suite."

"You even got a balcony." With a flick of his wrist, he pointed toward the sliding glass door.

Meanwhile, Reese looked unimpressed by the room and its amenities. Typical. He was probably the richest person in Bayside, of course no amount of luxury could faze him. His fingers, decorated with a few large rings, curled possessively around the neck of his whiskey bottle. Then he brought it to his lips, taking a pull.

Crew looked down through the floor-to-ceiling windows. "This view is insane," he said in awe before he moved around checking out the rest of the suite. He wandered into the large bathroom, and yelled, "Is that a jacuzzi? We gotta do that!"

Sam chuckled from beside me. "Luckily, Caroline and I have our swimsuits," she said playfully, before she glanced at Reese and Crew. "But what are you two going to wear?"

"You know," Crew drawled, his voice carrying a hint of mischief, "skinny dipping is usually a second date kind of thing for me." He winked at Sam. "But I'm willing to compromise for you."

Reese threw an arm around Crew's shoulders. "I don't think either of them want to see that, buddy." His gaze flicked our way briefly, like he was helping us out. "So we'll keep on the boxers."

"Yes, let's do that," Sam said, pulling out a can of sparkling seltzer from the mini fridge. She handed me one before she grabbed one for herself. The seltzers hissed as we popped them open, a momentary distraction.

Crew and Reese slid open the glass door and walked out onto the balcony, leaving Sam and I alone in the room to change.

"Can you believe Crew? He's acting like he's into me tonight." Sam smoothed down the sides of her swimsuit, settling on her hips. "But I don't want to go all the way with him. Not when he's hooked up with everyone and might go party with those twins later."

I paused, shimmying into the straps of my bikini, the stretchy fabric clinging to every curve. "Then don't," I whispered, my eyes meeting hers in the mirror. "Just do what you're comfortable with."

"I always do," she replied with a faint smile.

"Just enjoy the moment, Sammy," I added. "Flirt, get to know him better, kiss if it feels right in the moment. But remember, he's lucky to even have your attention, not the other way around."

She caught my gaze in the mirror, a flicker of resolve igniting in her eyes. "I know," she said, and then her voice dropped, wearily. "And hey, I'm sorry about Reese being here. I just... I couldn't find the words to tell Crew no."

I turned away from our reflection, my gaze dropping to the knot on my swimsuit bottoms secured with a quick twist. "It's fine," I assured her, the lie slipping from my lips. "I'm a big girl. I can handle one evening playing nice."

For Sam, I could handle one night of not murdering him for what he did to me in sixth grade. I could do my best to keep the anger to myself, to not let him get to me.

She handed me one of the hotel robes with a small smile. "Seriously, you're the best for doing this."

"Anything for you," I said, honestly. I really would do anything for her, and I knew she'd do the same for me.

"I owe you," Sam replied, as she bent down to turn on the jacuzzi.

Together, we stepped through the sliding glass doors onto the balcony where Reese and Crew were mid-laugh, both carefree—completely opposite of the turmoil churning beneath my calm facade. But the moment their eyes landed on us, the laughter died.

"Jaccuzi is ready to go," Sam said, sliding in next to Crew.

"Red bikini... nice choice," Crew murmured, his grin almost on the verge of creepy.

I turned away from everyone, ignoring Reese's smoldering presence. Instead, I took a breath and leaned over the balcony, gazing down into the below.

"Alright, let's get this party started then," Reese said as he began to strip off his shirt and pants on his way inside. Soon he was standing there in nothing but his low-slung, brand-name boxers. Crew scooped Sam into his arms. She laughed and held on tight, as they followed behind Reese.

I trailed behind them, my gaze inexplicably drawn to Reese's retreating form. His back was a canvas of defined, tanned muscles shifting and flexing with each step—obvious proof of how hard he worked on and off the pitcher's mound. When he turned, the sight of his sculpted torso sent an unbidden surge of heat through me. His six-pack was infuriatingly perfect, and I caught myself staring, transfixed by the hard lines that seemed to lead—*sinfully*—down to his waistband.

Oh, no not the fanny flutters. What was wrong with me? I silently scolded myself until they disappeared. Reese was trouble—every woman in Bayside knew that. I had personally experienced my own trauma from this jerk. And worse, he knew what he was doing when he set me up to be the punchline of a cruel joke. My first dance should have been magical, but I was humiliated. The laughter still echoed in my mind, a tormenting sound that played on repeat. It was more than just a prank or a momentary lapse of judgment on his part. He had stolen something from me that night, took away some of my innocence and trust. He wasn't the only reason I kept most people at arm's length, but he was part of the reason I was colder. And here I was, struggling to remember why I should look away.

Reese slid into the steaming bath effortlessly, setting the whiskey bottle on the narrow shelf just behind him. He leaned back, arms draped casually over the edge. Sam and Crew were still focused on each other as she slipped off her robe. Their contagious laughter filled the small space as they sank into the bubbling water. They seemed lost in their own little universe, nestled together in the corner.

I slid the hotel robe off, hanging it on the wall hook. Reese's gaze lingered on me, heavy and intense, like a palpable thing that seemed to draw all heat in the room toward me. There was a quiet sort of shock there, like he hadn't expected me to actually pull off a swim-suit. He grabbed the whisky bottle slowly, eyes still on me. He swallowed hard after taking a sip, the gulping sound obvious in the suffocating stillness. His Adam's apple bobbed, annoying me even more. Why did I think that was so hot?

"Wow," he breathed in a husky whisper, almost like he was holding something back.

With deliberate nonchalance, I descended into the jacuzzi, his gaze still assaulting me. "What?" I asked, melting into the water. "You act like this is the first time you've seen a woman in a bikini."

His lips parted in a slow grin, his tongue teasingly sweeping across them. "Not the first time," he drawled. "Just the first time seeing *you* in one."

A fluttering broke free in my chest, I couldn't stop it. *Don't let those green eyes fool you, don't fall for the charm or the dimples.* This was Bayside's most notorious bad boy, and I knew it.

My skin prickled, and not just from the bubbling jets. "Well, it's just a bikini," I said, aiming for casualness, though my voice weakened just a little under his stare.

"Maybe on the hanger," he drawled, his lips curving into a devilish grin. "On you? It's something else entirely."

"We're just keeping the peace tonight," I snapped, watching his eyes dip below the water. "You don't have to overdo it."

"Chaos," he murmured, his voice a sinful rumble, "when I agree to something, I go all in."

I turned my attention back to Sam and Crew, catching the tail end of what seemed to be a heated debate.

"She was in a happy relationship," Sam insisted, sliding back against one of the jets.

"But she had no girl code, so why would the girls keep her safe?" Crew questioned, arguing back.

"Because she was in love and that should matter most." Sam flicked water at Crew, and he grabbed her hand to stop her.

"The trick to winning Love Mountain is the friendships... you just hope to find love in the process," Reese said, surprising everyone. He didn't seem like the type to sit and watch a reality show.

Before I could comment, the disturbing sound of intense kissing took over. Out of nowhere, Crew and Sam were lip-locked in a kiss, suddenly making me feel like an intruder.

Reese must have felt it, too, because he glanced at them before turning back to me. "Balcony?" he asked, creating an escape plan from this awkwardness.

I nodded, wordless, and followed him out. Slipping the robe over my damp skin, I felt it cling to every curve, a soft cover that did little to shield me from Reese's unrelenting gaze. He casually draped Sam's robe over his shoulders to cover himself up.

The night air brushed against my skin as we stepped out onto the balcony, the door shutting behind us with a click. Underneath the dark sky, the town stretched out before us. Reese stood close—too close. But, his presence wasn't as unsettling as it usually was. For a fleeting second, I allowed myself to relish the tranquility of the elevated view, the soft breeze that played with strands of my hair, trying my best to forget about the man I was stuck here with. I leaned against the cool metal railing of the balcony, people watching. Reese—the definition of walking trouble—was momentarily lost in the view below, too.

"Watch that one." Reese nodded towards a girl teetering carefully on high heels, trying her best to find any balance she could. "She's going down."

She wobbled like a newborn deer on ice as I snickered at the scene below us.

"Three... two... one..." And just like a scripted fall, her heels betrayed her, snagging on a sidewalk crack. She slowly fell to the ground. Her friends' screams were over-dramatic before they erupted into a chorus of giggles, helping her back to her unsteady feet.

"Spot on," I admitted, though it irked me to do so.

"Always am," Reese replied, with that cocky arrogance that infuriated me. A dimple flashed in his cheek, an unfair addition to his charm.

A hush fell over us punctuated only by the distant murmur of nightlife and the occasional laughter below. Then our gaze shifted downwards again in unison as two figures drew our attention. Boston and Chandler, hand in hand, their fingers laced together in a way that was grossly intimate, but somehow it still felt like a slap to the face. We watched them until they disappeared into the hotel lobby beneath us. Something neither of us should have seen.

There had been something between Boston and me last summer

—a real connection, even if it was never given the chance to fully bloom. It stung more than I cared to admit—the realization that I had gambled on a nice guy, only to find myself discarded for someone else, someone who perhaps fit more seamlessly into his world.

Boston was the wrong choice, a huge misstep. He was the kind of hurt I didn't anticipate because I believed he wasn't capable of inflicting it. He was the nice guy, yes—but the wrong one for me.

"Does that upset you?" I ventured, carefully. "I know she was with you last summer... and now she's with your brother."

His hand paused, the bottle neck halted halfway to his lips. Then, with a slow, deliberate movement, he took another long pull from it. There was a practiced ease to his nonchalance, but the tension in his posture betrayed him.

"Nah," Reese said finally. "Those two have always been together. Just took me a minute to catch on." My gaze flickered back to where they had been just moments ago as he continued. "Shit, I think it's taken them a while to realize it, too. But trust me, there was never any space for anyone else. You try to get in their way, it'll just end up backfiring."

"I mean it would have been nice to know that information last summer."

"Maybe," he said, raising a brow. "But then I wouldn't get the pleasure of seeing you so miserable."

"Have I told you that I hate you yet?" I asked, leaning in slightly.

"You've mentioned it... why do you even hate me so much, though?"

I shook my head, feeling the past claw its way up my throat, but I swallowed it back down. He knew what he did in sixth grade—the whispers, the laughter, the humiliation that lingered like a stain on my soul. I let out a humorless laugh, one I had no control of.

"Is that a joke?" My words were a whisper, but they had an impact. "I've always just been a joke to you, haven't I?"

Viscous silence followed my accusation, wrapping around us like the creeping ivy on my parents porch. Confusion flickered across his face, an expression I read as clear as day despite the dimness. He was either reveling in the cruelty of it and playing dumb or he completely forgot. Which would be even worse. The most traumatizing moment of my life—just slipped his mind.

"You've never been a joke to me." He didn't flinch as he said that, didn't even have the decency to look away. Instead, he held my gaze, unwavering.

I narrowed my eyes at him, searching those fathomless green pools for a flicker of deceit. "Really?" I countered, folding my arms. "I always knew you were an ass, but a liar, too?"

Reese's gaze swept away from me for an instant, drifting behind him to where Crew and Sam were wrapped up in their own private world. "I have no idea what you're talking about," he said, turning back to face me, his green eyes sharp, searching for something I wasn't willing to give. "When have I ever lied?" he asked softly. That tone in his voice dismantled me. I wasn't ready to dissect this—not here, not now.

Setting my drink on the railing next to me, the words came out slurred and heavier than I intended. "I've had way too many drinks tonight for this conversation."

As I turned toward him, my elbow caught the edge of the seltzer. It slowly tilted, headed for a disaster. Time seemed to stutter as we both lunged, our bodies synchronized in desperation to catch the falling drink. But it was Reese's hands that closed around it first, snatching it from the air inches above the ground.

"Nice catch," I breathed, suddenly aware of how close we were— just inches apart, my hand gripping his elbow for balance, caught in a moment of accidental closeness.

"I'm a pitcher," he said, his voice dripping with that cocky edge, "you didn't think I'd be good with my hands?"

"You're a pitcher?" I asked, sarcastically. "I had no idea."

"One of the best," he lifted his chin, "but that's just one of my many talents."

"Don't hold back now. Your modesty is so inspiring."

A single strand of hair blown by the wind fell over my face. Time seemed to slow as Reese reached out that toned, veiny arm of his. His fingers lightly brushed against my cheek as he tucked the stray hair behind my ear. "Being this humble is tough, but I manage." His eyes lingered on my lips before our eyes locked again.

That gaze of his, those vivid, almost magical eyes, drilled into me with an intensity that I couldn't turn away from. I was caught in the gravity of him for a moment, I'd never anticipated that. He did something awful to me—I knew exactly who he was. This man should be dead to me, but that didn't stop the pull. It was like being a kid again, staring at a rose covered in thorns, knowing it was dangerous but still dying to reach out. Too beautiful to ignore, too dangerous to touch but completely irresistible.

My hand had yet to release its grip on his elbow. The proximity was intoxicating, confusing. This didn't feel like the Reese Carrington who had made me a punchline years ago. But it was, and it had to be the alcohol painting him in shades less cruel. Maybe he was just setting me up to be another pawn in some twisted game of his. Another girl to cross off on his Reese'd and Released list.

"I should go... check on Sam," I stammered abruptly, the moment shattering as I forced myself to retreat, to stand up straight and put distance between us.

eight

REESE

Pulling my phone from my pocket, I glanced down at the last text message, at the words from my birth mom on the screen.

CINDEE

I'll be at the diner again after the game this week. No pressure but I just wanted to let you know in case you're ready to talk. Always thinking about you.

Each letter tugged at me, toward a complicated and fucked up situation I wasn't sure I wanted to think about or deal with—ever. She had sent this text almost every week this summer, but I couldn't bring myself to respond.

The bus came to a halt, and we rushed out. My feet hit the pavement with relief. We were back in Bayside. Bailey was grinning like an idiot beside me.

"I'm just saying, I thought that bartender was into me last night," he claimed, oblivious to the skeptical looks we all shot him.

"The one who sprayed you in the face with water?" My voice was flat, but I couldn't hold back a smile.

"Hey," Bailey protested, flicking his hair out of his eyes, "Some might say she was putting out a fire, you know—because she thought I was so hot." Bailey's knack for spinning every situation into self-flattery was as impressive as it was exasperating.

I snatched my duffel from the luggage hold as I turned to Bailey. "Bails," I began, hoisting the bag over one shoulder, "has anyone ever told you something is wrong with you?"

"Only every person I've ever met," he retorted, oddly proud of that fact.

Crew walked over and plucked his duffle from the bus after me."Oh he's always known something is wrong with him," he said, shouldering his bag. "Just doesn't care."

The moment I saw Caroline headed in our direction, I snatched her luggage for her, setting it down so she could grab it.

"I could've done that," she said, her icy blue eyes meeting mine.

"I know," I said with a wink, watching as she extended the collapsible handle of her suitcase and pulled it upright. "But I got it." She turned on her heel and walked away without a backward glance.

Crew's voice broke the stillness. "She still hates you, huh?"

"Like always," I nodded, but I sensed something different about her after this weekend. I was seeing her in a different light. The way her hair fell around her face, the way her eyes softened when no one was looking—I swore I almost saw something warm behind that cold exterior of hers.

Bailey leaned against the side of the bus. "That's because Caroline is evil."

"People say that about me too," I confessed.

Bailey scoffed, folding his arms. "Yeah, but deep down you're soft and squishy. And her, she's sugar, spice, and emotional damage in a cheer skirt. Those pom-poms of hers sparkle, alright... but they also destroy lives. Probably come with a restraining order, too."

I watched her slip into her car. I wasn't sure I believed that anymore—that Caroline was pure evil. Caroline and I had never gotten along. We didn't mix—like fire and ice. But this weekend, I saw a glimpse of something else—maybe a tiny sliver of vulnerability. It was there in some way, even if she shut it down almost immediately. There had to be more to her than people thought, and I was determined to find out what she was hiding.

"Reese," Bailey's voice pulled me back from my thoughts. "You're staring."

"Am I?" The admission was half-hearted, my focus fracturing as she pulled away.

Bailey shook his head in disapproval as we made our way to our cars. "Don't do it, man."

"I'll see you both at Gin & Jerry's later," I said, giving them each a handshake and pat on the back.

I climbed into my truck then twisted the key. I drove back home, back to reality. But as I rounded the corner and into my driveway, I saw her. My sister, her petite form curled on the front steps. Her long blonde hair covered her face, but even from a distance, I could see the tremors of her sobs. My heart clenched—anger seizing me—as I pulled up.

The door shuddered on its hinges as I tore it open then slammed it shut. Each step toward her crackled with the electricity of my mounting fury.

"Explain. Now." The words were a growl, torn from a place deep within me. Lo was sixteen now, but she'd forever be my baby sister and the little girl I'd once taught to throw a baseball.

She turned, and then I saw her tears, trailing down her cheeks. "It's nothing," she whimpered.

"Tell me his name," I demanded, muscles tensing as I sat down next to her.

"His name?" Confusion laced her quivering voice, as she looked up at me.

"Whoever made you cry," I answered. "I'll go handle it." And I meant every fucking syllable.

A smile cracked on her face as she brushed away a stubborn tear.

"It's not a he," she murmured, her voice still shaking from the sobs. "Her name is Wendy Clark."

"Clark?" I echoed, my tone sharpening. "As in Wells Clark's little sister?" She gave a small, defeated nod. A smirk tugged at my lips. "Even better. I'll go beat his ass right now for whatever she did."

But Lo's laughter was soft, and she reached out, her fingers grabbing my bicep with surprising strength. "Don't, Reese."

"What did she do?" I demanded, shaking my head, pulse pounding.

Lo let out a reluctant breath, like even saying it out loud would make it worse. "She posted a list on her story today—everyone she thinks will make the cheer team. I wasn't on it. And she's got some top secret connection that's teaching her and her friends the routines early. They'll have an upper hand at tryouts."

I let out a sharp exhale, my jaw tightening. "Cheating her way to the top. Typical Clark move. Why do you even want this so bad?"

She leaned back, looking anywhere but at me. "I don't know. Why have you always wanted to play baseball?"

I shrugged, trying to calm myself down. "Because I'm good at it."

She nodded slowly. "Well, I want this really bad. I want to be good at it. I want to be good at something like you are."

There was something raw in her voice, something that made my stomach twist. I'd seen Lo excited before, passionate about things, but this—this was different. This was her putting herself out there, risking something. And I hated that a fucking Clark was the one trying to take it from her. Truthfully, there was nothing I wouldn't do for Lo. If I could have gift-wrapped her dreams and dropped them in her lap, I would've—no hesitation.

"Then practice," I said, my voice firm, like it was the easiest thing in the world. This was the best option I could give her, because it was true. "You'll be fine."

She slumped her shoulders. "But I don't have an advantage."

I huffed, dragging a hand down my face before leaning in,

leveling my gaze with hers. "Hey, you're a Carrington. We always have an advantage."

But doubt lingered in her eyes, and it hit me like a punch to the gut. She didn't believe me. And I hated that I couldn't solve her problems as easy as I could when she was younger.

I swallowed hard, trying to shove down the frustration and helplessness clawing at my chest. "You're going to be fine," I assured her, forcing the words past the lump in my throat. "We have some time to figure this out. And Lo," I added, reaching for her hand, "don't ever let a fucking Clark make you cry. Pinky promise me."

A shaky giggle escaped her, and she looped her pinky around mine, sealing the promise with a wobbly smile. It wasn't enough. But it was something.

We stood together, and she made her way inside, leaving me alone on the porch, my hands braced on my hips as I stared out into the night, my jaw tight.

This wasn't just her problem anymore. It was now mine.

And for his sake, Wells fucking Clark better pray I didn't run into him tonight.

I let out a dry laugh, shaking my head. "Cheerleading," I muttered under my breath, "is going to be the fucking death of me."

nine

CAROLINE

A row of cars sat in my driveway, leaving me no choice but to park on the curb. I killed the engine and sat there for a moment before I pushed open the car door and stepped out. I immediately smelled the grill my dad must have set up. Once I got inside, I could see my family was on our back deck.

I moved slowly, hoping no one would notice me escape up the stairs to the sanctuary of my room. But just as I placed my foot on the second step, a deliberate cough came from behind me.

"Caroline," my mother's voice floated up to me. "Wasn't sure what time you'd be home. Put your things away and come have dinner with the family."

"Actually," I descended further up the stairs, "I'm not all that hungry, and I'm meeting Sam at Gin & Jerry's soon."

"Then you can just sit with us and enjoy the company of your family before you go," she said, more a demand than a request.

"Be right down, Mother."

I let out a long breath as I made my way back downstairs and then outside. I slid into a seat, my presence barely registering with my family. I wondered, not for the first time, why my mother insisted I be here, like I was some sort of centerpiece or table setting.

Across from me, my cousin fluttered her lashes, basking in the glow of attention as she captivated the audience with tales of her millionaire fiancé and his real estate empire. She went on about the blueprints of her future home.

"Caroline," my mother's elbow nudged me with enough force to pull me from my boredom. "You see that? You should be more like your cousin. She's going to have a great future."

I grabbed a dinner roll, its flaky remnants spilling on the plate in front of me. I brought it to my lips as I rolled my eyes.

My sister's phone vibrated on the table, rattling her plate. She barely glanced at the screen before saying, "It's the Barn," and lifting it to her ear.

"Hello?" she said, curiously. The barn used to be our refuge in Bayside, where we'd spent countless days helping with the animals. The owners eventually gave us our first jobs there because we loved volunteering. It blossomed into the most popular venue for events, and now they could hardly keep up with the demand.

Charlotte stood abruptly. "A month? And the next opening you have is still a five-year waitlist?"

She gripped her phone tighter, listening before she shook her head. "No, I don't even need to think about it. I'll take it." The words tumbled with urgency, and the realization hit me.

Oh no. Please tell me she's not doing what I think she is.

"We're moving up the wedding," she said softly, easing back into her seat.

My mother's hands flew to her mouth, tears welling in her eyes. "Is this really happening?" she asked in awe.

I found myself leaning forward, elbows resting on the table. "You're going to plan a wedding in four weeks? I thought you didn't want to get married until you were done with medical school."

"This is the only place I want to get married," she hissed, pushing her plate away from her like she was no longer able to eat. "They never have any openings... I put my name on the list years ago. We can make this work, right, Mom?"

Mom turned, her eyes crinkling at the corners just before a small smile played on her lips, the kind that held more love and understanding than I could ever know.

"Oh, honey," Mom said, "of course we can make this work. The grandparents are going to be so excited," she continued, already reaching for her phone. "I need to tell them first to get their flights scheduled."

As our mom called everyone she knew, I felt the ground shift beneath me. Four weeks. That was how long I had to find a wedding date. I should have had years—years to find someone worthy to stand by my side, someone who could withstand the scrutiny of my old school Greek family.

My Dad continued turning the sizzling meats on the grill nearby. Dan, oblivious to what just happened, stood beside him.

"Dan!" My sister yelled, and he pivoted towards us, holding a half-eaten chicken wing between his teeth. "We're moving up the wedding. A spot for us opened up so we're doing this thing in four weeks!"

I watched him, the gears turning as he processed the unexpected news. The chicken wing, now dangled limply from his mouth. Dan's eyes widened in sheer surprise.

Charlotte shrugged off his reaction. "He'll be excited," she declared, more to herself than us. "Once the shock wears off."

My entire life, all I'd ever wanted was to feel included in this family—to impress, to belong, to be enough for them. Soon all of my family would be here, and I wasn't ready to face their judgment. To be the one who failed them at not being on the right path to marriage and whatever else success meant to them.

This was ridiculous. Charlotte couldn't be serious. I sank in my seat, feeling like a ghost around my own family. Of course. Another summer where I'd fade into the background while she took center stage. Would the universe ever let me have my own moment? Mom was probably already creating a mental checklist. Dad was probably writing speeches in his head. And me? I'd be the only one without a date—basically human foliage. Present, mildly helpful, and completely overlooked. She was the favorite, the one who always found a way to shine. I should be happy for her. I was happy for her. But was it selfish to wish, just once, that someone looked at me the way they look at her?

"Oh, Charlotte, we're going to have so much fun planning your dream wedding," my mother breathed out, leaning in to give her a hug.

Yaya chimed in from where she sat, still eating. "I'm so happy for you," she declared. "You're both going to be doctors soon and now married... you go, girl."

"Caroline," a voice whispered, tugging at my sleeve. My cousin, Kim, drew me away from listening ears. "Can you believe that? A couple weeks. Crazy."

"Yeah. Seems out of character for Charlotte," I said absent-mindedly.

"I wouldn't blame you at all for finding a reason not to be there," she said, giving me a skeptical look.

"Why would I skip my sister's wedding?"

"Because..." she hesitated, her glance darting back to the crowd before settling on me once more. "You've never brought a guy around, and you cannot show up alone. Our family will never let you live it down."

I stiffened, knowing the weight of their expectations too well.

"Of course I'm going," I said with more conviction than I felt. My cousin's eyes widened slightly before she quipped, "You have more balls than I do."

The backyard began to empty, laughter and excitement vanishing as family and friends departed. In the dimming light, I felt the hollowness creep in—a shell of a person who never had a purpose. My sister had the perfect life, while I continued to be Char-lotte's shadow. Her light would always cast me further into darkness. I used to hope that one day we could both shine, but in this family it was just her or Cooper who were allowed to be in the spotlight.

"Nights like tonight should be a wake-up call for you. Life is short, and you"—Mom paused, picking up plates on the table—"need to start getting your life together. You don't want to be single and teaching cheerleading forever, do you?"

Her words stung, burrowing beneath my skin and nestling next to the insecurities that whispered incessantly in the darkest corners of my mind. I was never good enough—she took every opportunity she could to let me know.

"I don't know, Mom," I said as I turned away from her judgmental gaze. Every step felt heavier than the last as I made my way to my room. I had to get ready and leave this house, escape the stifling air thick with expectations and disappointment.

Life had to get better than this, I thought as I turned on my vanity lights. I was Caroline Matthews—Blue Devils committee president, the best cheer and dance instructor in town. I commanded rooms, choreographed routines. And yet, here I was nothing more than a failure; my accomplishments dimmed by the unrelenting comparison of Charlotte.

"This won't define me," I murmured to my reflection, a silent vow that felt both fragile and fierce. There was a world beyond this, one where I wasn't just the woman without a date or one with a disappointing career, but a force to be reckoned with—a bad ass dressed in blonde waves and determination.

The neon sign of Gin & Jerry's buzzed in the dark, its glow guiding me forward. I shoved the door open and slipped inside, scanning the bar for the familiar faces I desperately needed tonight. There—in the back corner—were my friends. Relief flickered through me, but between them and me sat the last people I wanted to see. Reese and his teammates were posted up at the bar. I ducked my chin, pushing through the crowd as I hurried past them, praying

I'd go unnoticed. I just wanted to get to my friends and let this awful day morph into something remotely salvageable.

"Care!" Sam called as I approached, snatching up her purse from the empty seat next to her.

"By the way, don't let me forget to tell you. My sister is going to be your newest bride," I whispered to Sam, and her eyes widened. I knew my sister was probably going to take advantage of her and be extremely overbearring, but Sam would be more upset if she wasn't the one who got to be her wedding planner.

Piper was mid-story. "...So we went out on a first date," she said, as she applied more lipgloss, "and then when he got up to use the bathroom, I realized he had an ankle monitor on." A collective gasp rippled around our group, followed by a hush of anticipation as Piper went on. "And when he got back to the table, he said he forgot his wallet at home. Therefore, I have officially given up on dating."

Laughter erupted. My eyes drifted away from our table. They landed on the entrance just as Chandler Hartford sauntered into the bar. And I watched as her eyes scanned, then locked on a target. Reese, who was leaning against the bar.

"Have you guys heard about what's going on between them?" Kim asked, our entire group now watching the same show I was. My curiosity piqued as I watched Chandler's delicate fingers curl around the stem of a wine glass. Reese didn't turn, his attention still on Bailey, but the slight shift in his posture gave away that he was fully aware of how close she was.

"What's going on between them?" I asked, unsure if I even wanted to know—although I could never resist any gossip bait. It was my weakness.

Kim's dark eyes flickered with the thrill of another story, and she leaned in. "Boston and Reese are waiting for her to make a decision between them," she pulled out the lipgloss again. "They've left the ball in her court, and she's been stringing them both along."

"Th-that's just awful. How can she string along two brothers?" stuttered a voice from our cluster of friends.

"That family has enough problems, and she's just dividing them even more," Sam added.

Kim nodded, and her lips twisted into a frown. "It's just not fair," she agreed. "Those brothers are gorgeous. And every girl in Bayside has been trying to snatch up Reese since he and Blair broke up. I heard he actually wants to date Chandler, not even make her a 'Reesed and released' victim." Her tone slipped out of sadness and dipped more into envy.

Did everyone know about this Reese'd and Released thing? My gaze drifted back to Reese, to the casual way he leaned against the bar, how even though I couldn't stand him, he did have one of those faces you could stare at for hours. Like those videos of handsome men on social media you can't help but keep watching on repeat, and it's almost painful when you have to scroll away.

I wasn't sure why hearing all this upset me, but it did. It wasn't just that I was still nursing a bruise from the Boston situation. No, this felt like much more than that. She came to Bayside, effortlessly drawing everyone into her orbit. And they loved her for it. I've been here my whole life, and still—never good enough. Not for any of the guys here, not even for my own family.

"Can I get two tequila shots, please?" I flagged down the wait-ress. "Make them doubles." I needed them. Not just one—two. Pronto.

ten

REESE

Bailey's phone buzzed against the bar top. He glanced down, tapped the screen, and whatever he saw made his lips twist into that grin—the cocky, shit-eating kind. He shot me a knowing look.

"Should I even ask?"

He leaned back in his seat. "I just got a for-my-eyes-only text from the baker girl of my dreams," he said, running a hand through his hair.

Bakergirl. It was the username of a girl he'd met on a dating app. They hadn't met in person yet, but he was utterly captivated, snatched by the balls at just the idea of her.

"For your sake, I hope she's exactly who you think she is and not, you know... some person named Earl or Bertha who wants to lure you into their sketchy stalker van," I said, under my breath.

"Don't tempt me with a good time... but trust me, she's definitely a hot college girl who bakes."

"Right. Well, good luck with that." I chuckled, taking a slow sip of my drink, already mentally preparing for the inevitable "I got catfished" meltdown.

The moment Chandler Hartford came over with Willow trailing just a step behind, I felt the atmosphere shift. Bailey leaned against the bar, his eyes narrowing in playful foreboding as he murmured, "Uh oh, here's trouble."

Willow, always the whirlwind, who happened to be the coach's daughter, circled around to Bailey's other side with a mischievous grin and gave him an affectionate shove that nearly made him spill his drink.

Chandler drifted closer with an empty wine glass. Waiting for the bartender to take notice, she turned those hazel eyes toward me.

"Didn't get to talk to you much at the tournament," she said, softly. "But you killed it out there. Like always."

A small smirk toyed at the corner of my lips. "Would you expect anything less?"

"There's never a day I don't expect you to be the very best," Chandler replied, her sarcasm so sweet it was almost sincere.

"As long as you know." I chuckled, glad we could still joke around. I still cared about her, but I wasn't sure how to navigate being around her. With everything going on in my life, especially the situation with Boston, I couldn't quite figure out where she fit into it all. I had a strong suspicion that she knew she belonged with him. And where exactly did that leave me?

As the evening went on, we found ourselves on the back patio. A large group had congregated there—my teammates, Caroline, and other members from the committee all seated at the back tables. They were in the middle of playing truth or dare.

I hung back, observing as I looked at the lake. Caroline was at the heart of it all, taking charge of the game. She had always been fierce, but tonight there was a colder edge to her. Something seemed off about her. I noticed the empty shot glasses near her elbow, which probably had something to do with it.

"Alright, alright, settle down!" Sam called out to the group, giggling. "Who's next? Bailey!"

"You know I always take the dare, baby girl," he said, taking a sip of his drink.

"Dare you to try to get the hot bartender's phone number," she said with a devilish grin.

Bailey stood up from his seat, a smile spread across his face. We all watched as he disappeared into the bar. Moments later, he emerged, phone held high.

"Got them digits, baby!" Bailey shouted, winking at the round of applause that greeted him.

It wasn't long before Caroline's gaze landed on the one person I'd hoped she wouldn't go after.

"Chandler, truth or dare?" she asked with an impish smile.

"Truth," Chandler responded.

"Who do you like more, Reese or Boston?" Her question hung in the air, halting any chatter or laughter.

Every eye turned to Chandler. Boston and I looked at each other, and he paused mid-sip. I'd had enough of this stupid game. The Chandler situation wasn't a game to me, and I knew it wasn't to Boston either.

"Caroline, stop," I demanded.

"What? What's the problem?" Caroline never took her eyes off Chandler. "Didn't you hook up with Reese last summer? How far did you get? First base? Second? Did you go all the way?"

"Caroline!" Boston growled, heavy with anger. "What the fuck?"

"What's the matter, Boston? Was she doing the same thing with you?" Caroline retorted.

Chandler's hazel eyes flickered with hurt before she turned in retreat. Boston followed after her, not looking back.

Willow and Parker, their faces etched with disapproval, turned to let Caroline know how wrong she was. Caroline stood defiantly, almost amused as they spoke, and I couldn't stand back anymore. When I reached her, I didn't hesitate. My hand found the bend of her elbow, grip firm but not rough as I commanded, "Come with me."

She didn't resist, which surprised me more than her earlier outburst. Caroline allowed herself to be steered away from the chaos she had stirred. We came to a stop at the side of the building.

"What the fuck was that?" I asked, my voice low but edged with enough intensity to let her know I was serious.

Caroline leaned back against the brick wall, her fingers found their way into her hair, sifting through the strands. Without a word, she slid down the wall until she was sitting on the ground, knees drawn up. "I don't know," she whispered and damnit, why did seeing her like this make me want to knock out whoever put that look in her eyes? I was so sure she didn't have a soft side... but maybe I was wrong.

I crouched down before her, so we were face-to-face at her level "No, tell me," I insisted. "What was that?"

Her blue eyes, shifting shades in the darkness, captured mine. I saw something flicker—a small glance of vulnerability. "Everyone was wondering it but was too scared to ask," she said, with a shrug so casual it could have been rehearsed. "Everyone thinks I'm evil anyway, so why not be the one to find out the truth for you and Boston."

How could she think that about herself? How many people had put that in her head? Had I? There was an ache of sadness that settled heavy in my chest from the thought alone.

"Why though?" I asked, searching her face. "Do you get off on making her cry? On knowing that you're bigger and better or some-thing? Because you play the evil queen part well and all, but I don't think that's really you."

"I am evil," Caroline admitted. "I think it's in my blood, and I was destined to be this way. And no..." She hesitated, her gaze flickering away and then back to mine. "I don't think I'm better than her... I know I'm not."

In that moment, I saw past the icy exterior, past her actions, to something deeper—something she kept locked behind those steely blue eyes. Moved by an impulse that was part instinct, part curiosity, I shifted to the ground, caging her in with my legs, one on either side of her.

"Talk to me," I said, resting an arm on my knee—leaving no space for her to shut me out.

"Why?" she asked, softly.

"You made that scene. You brought me into this, so help me understand." The heat between us was undeniable, her body caught between my legs and the rough brick wall, trapping her into having this conversation. I wasn't just boxing her in with my arms—I was trying to break through the icy fortress she'd built around herself. She's always been snarky, a firecracker, but right now? She looked... breakable. And I didn't like it. Something about this—about her right now—hit differently. If she'd just let me, maybe I could shoulder some of the weight she carried, take away some of the burden she refused to share. She didn't have to battle whatever she was dealing with alone, not when I was right here. But I was last person she'd let in. And fuck, I wanted in.

She looked away for a moment, lost in thought or maybe just unwilling to look me in the eye. "Maybe I'm jealous of her," she admitted, and it was like that admission cost her a piece of her soul. "How easy she has things. How everyone, including you, thinks she's so beautiful."

I processed her words, letting them sink in. "What is it you want to hear, Caroline? That you're fucking hot? Do you want me to tell you that my dick gets hard anytime I'm around you?" The words just came out, surprising even me.

Her lips parted slightly, a sharp inhale the only sound between us. I leaned closer, letting my hand hover near her jaw before trailing my fingers along the column of her throat, slow and deliberate, until they rested just below her ear.

"Because you're hot as fuck," I added, my voice nearly a growl as my thumb brushed the curve of her neck. A lazy smirk tugged at my lips. "Not exactly a ray of sunshine... but hey, some of us like a challenge."

In the dim light, I saw her breath catch before she swallowed it. "I think you are probably trying to make me feel better, but I know what's going on," she said, looking down at her hands. "You're waiting for her to pick you. Just like Boston is. And he chose her, whether she picks him or not. He's fully in when it comes to her, regardless of anything else."

I caught the pain in her words, and it struck me harder than I expected. Did I look this pathetic? That I'd just wait around for someone to decide between me and someone else? I had a soft spot for Chandler, I always would—and maybe some part of me hoped she'd realize there was nothing between her and Boston, and I was the one for her. But that wasn't reality, and even I could see it now. Those two? They were always meant to be together.

"I'm not anyone's second choice, and you shouldn't be either," I said, casually shifting the watch on my arm.

Her posture seemed to deflate ever so slightly, but the lift of her chin told me she wasn't about to show any more weakness. "I don't even know why we're talking about this, like we're friends or some-thing," she spat out. "We're more enemies than anything else."

"We don't have to be," I confessed, my gaze locked on hers, unwilling to be the first to look away.

Caroline chuckled, but it was humorless. "Even if that were true..." She paused, and for a moment, she almost seemed hurt. "I still can't ever forget about what happened."

She pushed herself off the ground slowly until she stood over me.

"What happened? What are you talking about?" I asked, confused as fuck. Why was this woman so damn confusing? And once again, why did I even care?

"I'll apologize, okay?" Caroline stepped over my right leg. "I'll tell Chandler that I'm sorry, and I won't get in your business anymore. But please," she paused then continued, "don't try to pretend that you care about me."

As she walked away, I tracked every movement until she was gone from sight. But she was etched in my mind. My arms rested heavily on my knees, more confused than ever. All I knew was that there was a moment tonight when our eyes collided that something shifted, at least for me. I wanted to understand her, to keep finding ways to see glimpses of whoever Caroline really was.

eleven

CAROLINE

"Big night ahead, huh?" Sam nudged me playfully, misinterpreting my frown. "Your sister's final fling before the ring!"

The pace of this wedding was dizzying, each event blurring into the next as we raced through the festivities for Charlotte. The relentless planning that was in overdrive, the bachelorette party today, the shower coming up—was enough to give anyone whiplash. In this madness, how could it possibly feel right to Charlotte? How could she enjoy blazing through all of this?

"Something like that," I muttered, forcing a smile. "I'll catch up with you later if you decide to go out though."

"Sounds good," she said, quickly fixing her hair before following me out of the bathroom.

I rushed out of the Blue Devils facility and sped over to my sister's house, knowing she would be furious if I was even a minute late. Just as I arrived, the limousine, which felt more suited for prom night than a bachelorette party, pulled up with all the subtlety of a marching band. It was just for the four of us—my sister, her best friend and maid of honor, my brother's wife, and me.

"Cheers to the bride-to-be!" I raised my glass, the liquid sloshing dangerously close to the rim as the vehicle navigated the streets. The ride over was a blur, punctuated by the pop of another cork. I matched their enthusiasm drink for drink, the annoyance of tonight dissolving with each sip.

The limo slowed to a stop outside Gin and Jerry's. The bass was thumping from within, and as the limo door opened, I peered out cautiously, hoping to go unnoticed. Relief washed over me as I stepped onto the pavement—no prying eyes, no whispers. I was happily in the clear.

"Come on, Caroline!" My sister's voice, bubbly with excitement, urged me forward.

The bar swallowed us whole, the bodies all around jostled and swayed to the music. My gaze landed on the familiar faces of the Blue Devils. The whole baseball squad was clustered around the pool table.

"Let's do shots!" My brother's wife, Kay suggested, her voice rising over the music.

"Definitely," I yelled, feeling the need to keep drinking to get through this night. We moved our way through the crowd, shoulders brushing against strangers, until we reached the bar. The bartender nodded in recognition at my sister, already lining up glasses.

"Four of the usual, coming right up," he called out, reaching for the liquor bottles behind him.

"Make them strong," my sister added, throwing a flirtatious wink his way.

I tapped my fingers on the bar, watching the bartender pour our shots with practiced ease.

"Here's to new beginnings," I said, raising mine in the air.

"Here's to being the future Mrs. Penny," my sister's maid of honor, Stella cheered, and we all downed the shots in unison.

The opening chords of a song shattered conversations, drawing all eyes to the bartenders who suddenly vaulted onto the bar. The nearest one grinned and gestured wildly at our little bachelorette party. "Ladies, your stage awaits!" she shouted over the music.

"Go on! I've got your stuff," I urged the group, shoving their purses into my arms as they squealed with delight.

Standing back, I fumbled with my phone, trying to capture the moment as they began dancing, laughing hysterically. I found myself grinning—even snickering—as I snapped photo after photo.

"Looking good tonight, Matthews."

I turned as Wells Clark's lopsided grin slid into view. He leaned against the bar with an ease that was both irritating and endearing, the glow of the neon lights catching the mischief in his eyes. Wells and I had always had a flirty relationship. More than once, I'd thought about possibly taking things further, but there was a slight problem—his intelligence wasn't quite on par with his charm.

"Thanks Clark, but you said that the last time I saw you."

He chuckled and scratched the back of his neck. "Can't believe you remembered that. I don't even remember what I did ten minutes ago," he replied.

"Guess you'll have to come up with a better compliment," I said as I tapped him on the back. Wells just laughed, and even though it wasn't actually funny, for a moment, it was enough—to distract me from having to celebrate my sister and her perfect life.

But then, I noticed it like an unwelcome intruder, my gaze inadvertently drifted over Wells' broad shoulder. Reese was with his entourage, Bailey babbling something in his ear while Crew chimed in. But Reese's eyes were locked onto mine, their intensity sending a shiver down my spine. Quickly, I shifted my attention back to Wells, pretending to be fascinated with his latest anecdote. It was a performance, a signal to Reese that he had absolutely no impact on me.

The truth? Giving into Reese in any capacity would be dangerous—the kind of danger I might never recover from. He was everything I stood against: privileged, adored, and so effortlessly perfect it made my teeth clench. No, I wouldn't be "Reese'd and released," and I'd never let him have the power to hurt me ever again.

"Matthews? You still with me?" Wells asked, bringing my focus back to him again.

"Still here," I lied because I wasn't really. Wells' words had long since faded into the background. "It's been great, but I should probably get back to my sister."

He leaned in, his grin hopeful and a little too eager. "Well, save me a dance for later?"

"I'll think about it," I said with a soft smile.

My sister was no longer dancing but now sipping her drink. Her hair was messy, and she was glassy-eyed and giggling to herself.

"What's so funny?" I asked, as I slid into the seat beside her.

"Life," she slurred, waving her hand dramatically, "is just amazing right now."

"It's always amazing for you," I retorted, unable to mask the skepticism in my voice. "And if Dan's so flawless, why do you need a shotgun wedding?"

Her laughter died, eyes narrowed into slits. "How dare you call it that? Who are you to judge me, Caroline?" Charlotte used that tone —the one that meant her words were about to cut like a knife, twisting just enough to make sure I felt every bit of it. "You're nobody. An underpaid cheer coach, useless committee president— big deal... and don't even get me started on your dating life. We all know it's non-existent because no one wants you. You're pathetic."

"I'm pathetic?" Out of everything she said, the single word —*pathetic*—latched on tight, hitting me harder than I expected. The bar's smoky haze curled around us, but not enough to hide the hurt and humiliation written all over my face.

"Yes, you're pathetic, and the entire family is ashamed of you. Marriage, financial security, children, none of that is in the cards for you, and you know how important that is to them. You're embarrassing our family."

She didn't stop there. She kept spitting more and more terrible things. Each whispered insult from Charlotte took on a life of its own, echoing off the dark wood walls, while the bottles lining the shelves stood like silent judges behind the bar.

I wanted to lash out, to let my normally quick tongue shield me from the pain, but the words were somehow lodged in my throat, stubborn and immovable. I could only stand there, held captive by the weight of Charlotte's condemnation, feeling every bit the failure she painted me as.

Stella swiveled on her stool, holding her drink in mid-sip—before chiming in. "Didn't your mother once say she never stood a chance from the start?"

Charlotte let out the fakest chuckle I'd ever heard. "Oh, you mean because she was a mistake? Mom and Dad only wanted two perfect children, and then along came Caroline, the constant failure. The fuck-up."

I should've been used to cruelty—familiar with it, maybe even numb to it. But it never got easier. Every time cut a little deeper, leaving me exposed, feeling the same hurt from old memories I never wanted to keep. Charlotte's mocking voice dragged me straight back to childhood, when her constant ridicule always made me feel so small.

* * *

My favorite little stuffed horse peeked out from the top of my backpack. I named him Sir Trotty-Trot. Charlotte spotted it one afternoon, her laugh piercing as she pointed it out to her friends so they could collectively laugh and judge me.

"Caroline still carries around her stuffed toys like a baby," she teased, loving any opportunity to make fun of her baby sister.

In a desperate attempt for acceptance, I plucked Sir Trotty-Trot from the warmth of my backpack and tossed him into a bush, abandoning my only ally in the hopes of gaining entry into a club that would never truly open its doors to me. My heart shattered with each step I took away from him, my sister never even noticing how painful it was for me.

That night, as I laid in bed, staring at the empty space on my pillow where Sir Trotty-Trot should have been, the ache in my chest felt too big for my small body to hold.

Then, soft footsteps echoed from beneath my door before there was a quiet shuffle. A moment later, Cooper slipped inside—my first hero.

"Here," he whispered, tucking the worn stuffed animal into the empty spot beside me, his touch careful, like he knew how much it mattered. Like he knew I needed saving. "He missed you."

And just like that, the world wasn't so broken anymore. Even if only for a moment. As I clutched my little mini horse to my chest, the bond between me and my brother tightened, forming an understanding that no amount of cruelty from Charlotte could ever sever.

* * *

But he wasn't here to rescue me now. I was all alone.

I clung to the memory of Cooper's kindness, using it like armor against her onslaught. I stood there, rooted to the grimy floor as each insult embedded itself deeper. The urge to flee was overwhelming, a primal scream building within the confines of my chest, yet I remained motionless, a statue built by years of enduring this torment.

"...And can we just talk about how we don't even need to *think* about her having a plus one to the wedding?" Charlotte continued. "She'll be the only one in my family again without a date, but no surprise there."

"Who can she date? No man in Bayside can stand her. She's like boyfriend repellent or something." Stella laughed, and my vision blurred as tears threatened to take over. All I wanted was to run away, but that would mean victory for Charlotte, and I refused to give her the satisfaction. My fingers twitched at my sides, desperate to grasp onto something, anything, that could keep me strong, keep me standing.

"I don't even know how she can stand herself," Charlotte snarled, holding up an empty glass and shaking it rudely at the bartender.

I couldn't hold back the tears any longer. The overwhelming

humiliation was suffocating, and all I could think about was how to make my escape, how to bolt from this stupid bachelorette party before my last shred of dignity snapped. The last thing I could do was let them see me cry. Just as I silently begged for an out, for someone—*anyone*—to pull the damn fire alarm, salvation arrived. In the form of someone I never expected.

"There you are, baby. You look beautiful."

Time stalled. The room blurred. A long arm slid around me like the man it belonged to had done it a thousand times before. His presence was solid, confident, an unexpected lifeline. His large hand gripped my waist firmly, grounding me at the exact moment I needed it most. Then, he turned to Charlotte, calm and composed, like this was just another effortless move in his playbook as he extended a hand. "I don't think we've formally met. I'm Reese."

My sister's jaw hit the floor, her tipsy haze vanishing in an instant as she gawked at the man next to me. Reese, with his effortless charm and those swoon-worthy green eyes, was practically a celebrity in our small town—he definitely wasn't intimidated by my sister. She knew exactly who he was—the whole town did.

She stuttered out a response, her voice trembling. "I-I know who you are... everyone knows who you are." She looked from him to me, her eyes narrowing ever so slightly. "What's happening right now?"

"We're together," he announced casually. "She didn't tell you I was her date to your wedding?"

Charlotte's glare, icy and accusing, shifted to me. "No," she spat out, the single syllable laced with venomous disbelief. "It must have slipped her mind because she never once mentioned that."

Reese's hand was still steady on my hip, and it was somehow calming me. "Well now you know," I added, watching her process the information. "Didn't want to steal any of the excitement away from celebrating you."

The lie rolled off my tongue smoother than I'd expected. My heart hammered, not from deception, but from the realization that Reese had just stepped in to save me. But why? He must have overheard my sister's harsh words, and out of pity, he stepped in. Whatever the reason, I accepted without hesitation.

"So you've been dating... *him?* Really?" The words tumbled out of her mouth. Her gaze flicked between Reese and me again, like she couldn't solve this equation, like it couldn't possibly add up. It hurt more than I cared to admit, the insinuation that it was hard to believe Reese would ever date someone like me. But it never surprised me how low she thought of me.

"Lucky me, right? She's way out of my league," he confirmed, taking me by surprise again.

Reese set down his empty glass on the bar top. Then flashed that panty dropping dimple of his as he turned toward me, rolling up his sleeve. The movement drew attention to his tattoos that slid down his arm, coming to a stop around the luxe watch on his wrist, giving off a hint of rebellion but also class at the same time. I strangely found myself staring a bit too long.

Oh, no—not these uncalled for and rebellious fanny flutters again. I scolded myself internally. Why did that simple gesture make me react that way? Don't go there, Caroline. Don't even think about it. Before I could gather my thoughts, he took my hand, pulling me away.

"Well, if you'll excuse us," he said, turning his back to Charlotte, "I'm stealing her for a dance."

My sister's eyes widened, a flicker of something I had never seen before crossing her face—was it jealousy? I didn't think that was possible. For the first time in our lives, was she envious of me?

The dance floor was packed around us, full of couples swaying to the slow beat. As we moved, those around us blurred. I caught the scent of his cologne—a mix of cedarwood and something dangerously intoxicating. Each step drew us closer together, his grip on my hand firm but also gentle. Reese pulled me into him, and suddenly, there were no more worries, no more stress—just this calm and dangerously captivating feeling he left me with. His chest pressed against mine as I could feel every line of muscle beneath his shirt, his body hard and warm.

"Come here," he demanded, placing my hand up around the nape of his neck. I'd never been this attracted to anyone before—it was intense, unsettling.

"Why did you do that?" I whispered, my voice barely steady—caught somewhere between confusion and curiosity. His unsolicited rescue couldn't have been better timed. But why?

Reese's hand slid lower down my back, sending shivers up my spine that had nothing to do with the large ceiling fans above us. "Figured you needed the save," he said, simply. "And selfishly figured if I help you, you'd help me."

"Should have known there was a motive. Help you how?"

In that moment, as his eyes held mine captive in a way that felt like falling off a cliff, I knew I was in dangerous territory. Still, here I was, drawn to him, finally giving him all my attention—an inch away from doing anything he wanted. My senses were heightened, aware of every point of contact, every brush of his breath against my cheek.

"I'll be your date to that wedding," he growled into my ear. "Be your fake boyfriend until the big day is over." I felt the brush of his calloused thumb against the small of my back. "In exchange," he continued, "you help my sister."

The idea of pretending to be with Reese Carrington, of all people, was absurd. And still part of me was intrigued by the thought of defying expectations and watching the world react.

As we continued to move to the music together in a way that almost felt too natural, a reckless part of me wanted to say yes, to dive headfirst into the unknown for a chance at pulling the idea of this off.

"You want to fake date me," I thought out loud, "and in return, all I have to do is get your sister on the cheer team?"

"That simple," he said, but it wasn't simple at all. My mind spun with the implications, the power plays hidden beneath the surface of his casual assurance. Could I really do something like this, and do it with him?

I could easily get lost in those green eyes if I wasn't careful. I could tell he was trying to read every one of my thoughts. I could see the darkness lurking in his eyes, a challenge he didn't need to voice. There was only one thing I could do, make a safe decision—I couldn't trust him.

"We can't do this," I whispered. "No one would buy it—not for a second. My mom..." I cut off the sentence. My mom knew who he was, how powerful he was, that his family is in a tax bracket we'd never even dream about. She would never believe that he'd date me.

His hand shifted, not leaving its place but pulling me in a little closer, holding me in this dance of deception. "Think about it and get back to me."

"I'm telling you we could never get away with it." I said, not quite understanding how he could be so casual about this.

His eyes were focused on something past my shoulder. "From the looks of it, she already believes it," he smirked, turning me enough to see my sister's jaw still on the floor, still frozen in place where we left her.

"Honestly? I'd pay someone good money right now for a picture of her face—framed and mounted, right on my bedroom wall." I snickered, turning away to hide my grin.

When I looked back up at him, his expression had turned serious. "If you were really mine, I'd never let anyone speak to you that way," he said, matter-of-factly. "And you shouldn't either."

My heart skipped a beat, not from the proximity of him but from the unexpected protectiveness in his words.

"I only allow family to speak to me that way, it's just the way we are."

"Even with family," he replied, like what I'd said was useless information, "you need to draw your boundaries. And I can tell you this... when I'm around, no one will talk to you that way. I don't care if that is your sister."

I should have recoiled at his words, at the brazen implication that he could, or would, step into my life with such audacity. He didn't know me, and he didn't know my family. But somehow what he said was oddly charming. I wasn't used to anyone standing up for me—especially not when it came to my sister or mother. In fact, the only person who ever had was Cooper.

"So," he continued, "you might want to take that into consideration before you make your decision."

I laid my head on his shoulder as we finished the dance. Giving my sister one last show. I loathed myself for loving the way I felt in his arms, for the warmth that spread through my veins, the electricity that danced along my skin where he held me close.

I was actually considering his offer—his ridiculous idea. Not for the allure of being Reese Carrington's girlfriend, but for the leverage it granted. Just the thought of shocking my family and causing the same reaction in them that Reese had on my sister was almost too tempting to resist. But the real question was, could I actually do this? Could I bury the grudge I had against him until my sister's wedding? At the end of the day, it would just be a business arrangement, nothing more.

twelve

REESE

"Where do you want this?" the man at my door asked, looking down at the keg on his dolly.

"The bar area is fine," I grumbled, pointing toward the family room where the bar was set up. He nodded and maneuvered past me.

"Okay, cool. I have three more coming in," he called over his shoulder.

"Are you having a party?" my sister asked, standing behind me with her hands on her hips. "Is this what you do when we're gone for summer?"

"Yes," I said, rubbing the back of my neck. "Don't you have a best friend's house you can stay at tonight?"

"I'm sixteen, Reese," she shot back. "I'm old enough to hang out with you."

I looked at her, deadpan. "Like hell you are," I said. "Especially not around my shithead teammates."

"Why don't I just tell mom and dad and see what they think about your little gathering?"

"Nice try," I shrugged. "I could give a damn if they know."

"Fine," Lo broke the standoff, "but if I'm exiling myself to

Breana's for the night, then I need extra cash. They're hitting the mall and I refuse to be the only one just window shopping."

"Here," I sighed, pulling out my wallet and thrusting money into her outstretched palm.

"Always a pleasure doing business with you, brother."

After Lo left the front door swung open repeatedly, bringing in more guests until they were everywhere—some talking, others dancing. And then of course, in walked Chandler with Willow at her side.

"Carrington," a voice called, as a cluster of my teammates walked over to me.

"Hey," I managed, my eyes locked onto Chandler as I patted them on the back. She looked good like always. I was still a little fucked up about her, still a little bitter about stepping aside for Boston. I still thought I'd made the right decision, but I was doing my best to relinquish my feelings for her, and things with women were strange at best lately.

"Everything cool?" one of the guys nudged me.

"Never better," I lied, the words as hollow as the bottle I tipped to my lips. Pretending not to give a shit came easy to me at this point.

A yell made us all turn to look, "The champ is in the house!" Some guy at the party leapt onto our unsuspecting left fielder. The two of them hit the floor, their limbs entwined as they began to wrestle.

"Hey—" My voice sliced through their grunts. "If you fuckers break that table, you can pay to have the next one shipped in from Italy."

They paused, one mid-headlock, eyes locking with mine. For a brief second they silenced. Then, a burst of laughter erupted from them, and they resumed their wrestling match. I shook my head with a grin. Sipping on my Jack & Coke, I made my way through the pulsing bodies that filled my house. These parties always ended up being bigger than I anticipated, word spreads like wildfire in Bayside. But I was not expecting to see the second baseman from one of our rival teams—one who'd tried to start a fight with me last week.

"You've got to be fucking kidding me," I said, jaw twitching. His eyes widened as he froze in place like I caught him red handed.

"H-Hey, man," he stuttered, "just here to chill, not start any drama."

"Chill elsewhere," I replied, my tone was dark. "Or I can make sure you can't ever walk in here again." Then my eyes shifted to the girl with him as I took another sip of my drink. "But she can stay."

He scoffed, his ego bruised. "No fucking way. If I go, she's going with me."

"You can leave with that loser or stay," I drawed, locking eyes on the girl still standing by him. "Choice is yours."

He fumbled for composure, but she paused, her gaze flickering from him to me. Slowly, she licked her lips, and her cheeks flushed with color.

"Well," she hesitated, her voice barely rising above the music, "I'm not ready to go home yet."

His response was immediate rage. "What the fuck?"

Without missing a beat, I gave a subtle nod to my teammates. They were standing nearby watching. In one fluid motion, their hands were firm on his collar as they marched him toward the door. The scrape of his heels against my hardwood floor was satisfying.

As he struggled, having no power against the two kicking him out, I slipped my arm around the girl's slender shoulders. "Have fun," I called out, just loud enough for him to hear as the door swung shut in his face.

The girl I had my arm around tilted her head up to me, a curious gleam in her eye. "You must be Reese," she ventured.

I flashed her a half-smile. "Guilty," I admitted. My eyes locked onto hers just long enough to let the connection simmer. "Treat yourself to whatever you like." I gave her a quick wink as I nodded toward the bar.

I made my escape to the backyard, needing to get out of this crowded space inside. But before I could push open the door, a firm grip on my arm yanked me off course. The bedroom door slammed shut behind me, and I found myself staring down at Blair, a devilish look on her face.

"Blair, what are you—" I started, but she cut me off, her hands pushing against my chest until I fell backward onto the bed.

"Shut up and just listen," she demanded, her fingers tracing the line of my jaw as she straddled me. The alcohol in my system had dulled my reflexes, and although I didn't feel the way I used to about her, I was all too familiar with this move of hers. She kissed my neck, sending a familiar heat coursing through me. "I really miss you," she whispered, her lips grazing my skin with every word.

"Miss me, or miss me fucking you?" I asked, keeping my voice casual—even if my body was fighting the urge to react.

Her response came with an intentional roll of her hips, emphasizing my point.

"Does it matter?" she breathed as she continued to grind against me. Just as her mouth hovered over mine, about to lean in to kiss me, the door flung open.

"Sorry to interrupt whatever is about to happen here, but could you please get out? Reese and I have an urgent matter to discuss." Caroline stood there, dressed in a bright pink top and tight ripped jeans that screamed peppy—an obvious contrast to the annoyance in her voice.

"Can you give us forty-five minutes?" Blair snapped, irritation clear in her tone.

"Try forty-five seconds," Caroline shot back, arms folded across her chest.

"Buzz kill," Blair muttered under her breath as she climbed off me.

"She's stubborn. You should probably go unless you want an audience," I said to Blair, half-amused by the situation.

"Should've locked the damn door," Blair huffed, exiting the room with a dramatic slam.

Left alone with Caroline, I couldn't help but appreciate the irony of the situation. The look she gave me was calm, collected, but possibly ready to unleash havoc at any moment.

"What?" I asked, playing dumb. "You miss me?"

Caroline settled herself beside me on the bed. "Forty-five minutes, huh?" she quipped, an impressed look on her face.

I leaned back, propping myself up with my elbows, the mattress sinking slightly under my weight. "Not including the foreplay, Blondie," I winked.

"Touché," she conceded with a roll of those striking eyes, her expression shifting. She bit her lip, hesitation flickering across her face, as if she wasn't sure how to say what was on her mind.

"What's up, Caroline?"

"Were you really about to hook up with Blair?"

"Nah," I said casually, the corner of my mouth twitching upwards. "I was just about to ask her to leave."

"I'm sure," she replied, her eyes narrowing in disbelief.

"Her and I don't work," I confessed. "She just hasn't realized it yet... but you and I, we can make that happen if you want."

"Reese, can we be serious for a minute?"

My posture shifted, spine straightening as I met her gaze head-on.

"I'm always serious," I said, my tone suggesting amusement, but I kept my eyes focused on her.

"Whatever," she dismissed, rolling her eyes. "You know that arrangement you propositioned me with?"

"Yes... I have Maggie Little helping my sister at the moment, she jumped right on it. Unlike you."

"No way," she shot back. "You cannot have Maggie helping your sister."

"Why can't I?"

"Because she's terrible." She folded her arms across her chest. "She barely made the team and isn't even a cheerleader anymore. I'll make sure she gets on the cheer team."

"Oh, you will?" I asked, intrigued. I couldn't help but raise an eyebrow. "Which means you want me to be your date to your sister's wedding?"

"Let's call it a mutually beneficial arrangement," she replied, unable to say the actual words. "But we have to make this believable. We need to convince them we're together, or they would think you being my date to the wedding is suspicious."

"Knew you'd come around," I said with a smirk.

"Even though you're probably the last person I'd ever expect to go with," she said, as she flicked an imaginary piece of lint off her top, "I do need a date to the wedding, and I know you can impress my family."

"Is that so?"

"If anyone is confident enough, maybe too confident about themselves, it's you. And I know you could handle them. I'll get your sister on the team, we will make it to the wedding, and then we can break up right after."

I flashed her a dimple. "So, you think I'm impressive?"

"That's what you took from what I just said?" she asked, dropping her hands to her side.

"No, while you were talking I was actually wondering if this deal comes with any benefits." The words slipped from my lips, knowing I was pushing it now.

"You mean the benefit of getting to fake date me and be my date to the wedding?"

I swung my legs off the bed and inched closer, my feet silent on the carpet. "That's not what I mean."

"No benefits, Reese." Caroline's slender body tensed, like she was preparing to fight off an active threat. "Nothing changes between us."

This was a challenge, then. One she laid before me with a shiny red bow attached to it.

"What's the fun in that?" I let out a small chuckle. "If we're going to act like we're dating, we might as well enjoy the fun part of dating."

The look she gave me then was almost worth the words—her blue eyes flared, daring and defiant, but something else was going on with her. Some sort of battle was happening in her mind. Her lips parted, but it wasn't just any response that escaped them—it was pure Caroline, and the force of nature that she was.

"I'd never date you under normal circumstances," she declared, but her voice held a softness that betrayed her, a vulnerability she couldn't quite hide. "And I definitely would never hook up with you." The defiance was there, yes, but so was the uncertainty—a fleeting glance, the hitch in her breath, her shaky voice that told a different story.

She was seated on the edge of the bed, her hands fidgeting with the rings on her fingers—had to be a nervous habit. The scent of her perfume, a blend of vanilla and something wild, like a forest after rain, filled my nostrils and clouded my senses.

"Why don't I believe you?"

She swallowed hard at my question, the delicate movement of her throat drawing my attention momentarily. When she spoke, her voice was stronger than before, but I sensed the effort it took to maintain that composure. "This is just an agreement, Reese. When we get what we both need, this is over."

"Whatever you say, Chaos."

Her eyes sparked with that familiar glare. There was always a fire in her that never seemed to burn out where I was involved. "You think you're so irresistible but there are women in the world who aren't obsessed with you, you know."

There was no missing my grin. Not from her words but at the frustration behind them. Even when she was angry, I could feel the air between us crackling with electricity, and I was drawn closer to the flame of her spirit more than ever before.

"I know," I drawled, a small smile still on my face. "And maybe those are the kind of women I'm into. I like the challenge."

Caroline was still for a second, and then she turned. "Well, this isn't some game you can win," she retorted as she got up and walked to the door. That spark in her eyes, the quickened pulse at the base of her throat, they told me everything she refused to confess.

"You must not know who I am," I shot back, and only silence answered. The door clicked shut, soft but final, the sound echoing with more conviction than any of her previous protests.

I remained perched on the edge of the bed, running a hand through my hair as I gathered my thoughts. That woman had no idea what she had just done. By walking out that door, by trying to keep me at a distance. Caroline Matthews was a mystery to me, and I was now fully committed to figuring her out. To finding out what made her the way she is—to understand the unwavering stance she always took against me, the vulnerability she thought she hid so well.

"Challenge accepted," I whispered to the empty room. The thrill of the chase pulsed through my veins.

She was one hell of a firecracker, and I so badly wanted to unravel her. Not because I couldn't resist a challenge, but because for the first time, I couldn't resist her.

And she had no idea.

thirteen

CAROLINE

"Okay, I've had enough. Time for carbs." Sam panted, her face flushed as she turned down her speed on the treadmill.

"I'll never understand your nutrition plan," I said, breathlessly. "But it works because you're always in such good shape."

"Thank you. I take pride in my eat-whatever-I-want diet. But, I'll see you later?" she asked, stepping off the machine.

"Yeah," I answered, my breath catching as I slowed the pace on my treadmill. "I'm going to run a bit longer, but I'll get out of here soon."

She nodded and grabbed her water bottle, then turned away. I let my focus narrow back to the screen in front of me, hoping to beat the goal I reached yesterday.

And then *he* came.

It was subtle at first—the sly way he slid into place on the machine next to mine. He wore a simple black hoodie pulled over his head, and still somehow it accentuated his broad shoulders. His dark sweatpants clung to the contours of his legs. And as he began to walk, I didn't even have to see his face to know who it was.

"What are you doing here, Reese?"

When I side eyed him, I saw that the hair peeking out of his hood was damp, like he'd just been through some intense workout. "You're in the Blue Devils' gym," he said, smugly. "You know I work out here."

"Well, the committee gets to work out here too, but why are you at the treadmill next to me when there's a dozen others?"

"Aren't we dating?" His large hand gripped the side of his machine. "Or has it not started yet? How does this work exactly?"

"I don't know," I admitted. "I've never fake dated anyone before."

"Well," he began, his voice smooth for being on a treadmill, "shouldn't I have your number at least?"

He flashed that dangerous grin of his. A part of me wanted to tell him hell no, to guard the sanctity of my private life from the intrusion of this man who was never up to any good. But another part of me—the one that recognized I would probably need his number at some point knew he was right.

"Do you really need it?" I countered, my breath uneven. "I'll be training your sister every Tuesday and Thursday. I can keep you updated on our arrangement when I see you."

Reese's stride didn't falter next to me; the slow, confident way he walked was aggravatingly composed. He turned his head, green eyes catching the fluorescent lights overhead, making them glow emerald.

"Did you tell your parents about 'us' yet?"

"I was actually going to talk to them when I got home... but knowing my sister, I'm sure she already told them something, and they're definitely going to want to meet you."

"Lucky for you, parents love me," he said, casually. And of course they did. Reese had the kind of charm that could disarm a Navy SEAL.

"We'll see. You've never met mine."

"Stop underestimating me," he said, narrowing his eyes. He stretched his long arm across my machine, slamming his fist down on one of the control buttons. The belt jerked to a halt beneath my feet, forcing me to grab onto the handrails to keep from stumbling forward.

"What the hell?" I blurted out, my balance wavering as much as my composure. But Reese, unfazed by my annoyance, simply slid his phone out of his hoodie pocket and held it out.

"Number," he demanded.

I snatched the phone from him, my fingers tapping aggressively on the screen. My frustration clawed its way up my throat as I punched in the digits. "Here," I said, shoving the phone back into his hand, our fingers brushing for a moment. "But I don't know if I can actually go through with this."

He pocketed his phone, his eyes locked on mine. For a fleeting second, I allowed myself to really look at him—to take in the sharp jawline and the intense green eyes that seemed to see right through me.

The flash of dimple in a self-assured grin was the last thing I expected. "You'll be alright," Reese said, the words rolling off his tongue with that hint of humor. With a tilt of his head, he added, "I'll text you later."

Without waiting for my response, he brought his water bottle to his lips, tilting it back as he gave me a final glance. The muscles in his throat worked as he swallowed, a simple act that somehow captured the essence of him—smooth, controlled, effortlessly powerful.

As he walked away, I was struck by the way he just... got exactly what he wanted. And I was powerless against it.

At home, I stepped through the front door and tossed my keys onto the keyholder. My mother was nestled in her favorite armchair, the soft glow from her reading lamp hovered over her as she read her latest romantasy novel. My father's attention was consumed by the TV screen.

"We haven't seen much of you lately," my mother said without looking up.

"I know," I confessed, adjusting the purse on my shoulder. "I've had committee stuff. And my schedule is full at the dance center."

She sipped her tea, and I could feel the weight of her gaze, ponderous and assessing, even as she maintained her focus on the book before her. The dance center had become my sanctuary, a place where rhythm and movement drowned out anything else.

"Uh huh," she murmured, her response carrying a note of skepticism. "Your sister seems to think something is going on with you and Reese Carrington," she said casually. "But I told her there's no way that's true."

"Why can't it be true, Mom?"

"Reese is always on the sports highlights, in the paper. That boy is destined for big things." She paused, finally looking up at me. "He's going far away from this place. His father, one of the richest in Bayside... they're nothing like us, dear. I know you aren't getting mixed up with someone like him."

My father, blissfully unaware of the conversation my mother and I were having, let out an absentminded grunt at the tv—the left fielder missed a routine ground ball.

"What if I was?"

I knew Reese was wild and untamable. His presence in Bayside felt almost too vibrant, too volatile for the small town life here. I knew he wouldn't be here after this summer. His future was larger than Bayside, and I couldn't blame him for wanting to escape. But that didn't matter, our fake relationship would end at my sister's wedding.

"Then it would be a mistake," she said, simply.

"You're the one who wants me to be with someone rich and successful. You always say you want me to have a better life than you and Dad."

"I do want you to be with someone successful, like a local doctor or a business owner... but there is no way that boy is taking you seriously."

A small, bitter laugh escaped me. "Is that what you think of me? That I'm... what? Not good enough for him? Aren't parents supposed to think *their* children aren't good enough for anyone?"

The silence that followed answered my question. I watched the steam curling up from the teacup in my mother's hands. "Caroline, you're always so sensitive," she said with a dismissive flick of her wrist, settling back into her armchair. Her gaze returned to her book.

I felt the familiar sting, but stings associated with my mother always felt fresh, no matter how often it happened.

"Well," I began, not able to resist proving her wrong. "We're dating. And I'm bringing him to the wedding."

Her tea cup halted mid-sip, and the porcelain clinked softly as it touched down on the saucer. My mother's jaw hung slack, disbelief etched into every crease of her usually composed face. "Did you hear that?" she said to my father. "Your daughter is delusional."

fourteen

REESE

"Alright, you wanna see some abs, Chat?" I heard Bailey ask, his phone propped up against a sports drink, capturing himself on camera. "Let's see those gifts, and I'll take the shirt off."

I shook my head in disbelief that he was going live before the biggest game of our entire season. A few of the other guys were cackling as they brushed past Bailey and his online audience, the sound of velcro straps being ripped open and protective gear snapping into place filling the space as we prepped for the championship game. Each one of us was busy wrapping our wrists, changing, starting to get focused as we usually did before each game.

"Oh, the guy behind me?" Bailey taunted his phone's lens with a devilish smirk. "That is Reese, Chat. He's our starting pitcher."

A few heads turned, their expressions a mix of amusement and annoyance, but none more so than mine as Bailey said, "Bro. Take off your shirt. I need six more magical creature gifts and I have enough to get my mom the Bronco she wants for her birthday."

My steps faltered for a heartbeat as I actually considered it. I shot him an icy glare. Under normal circumstances I would never, but for Bailey's mom, there wasn't much I wouldn't do.

"Not taking my shirt off, but I'll do the dance," I offered. Bailey's eyes narrowed with the fire of a man who knew he got exactly what he wanted.

"Alright, Chat," he inched closer to the camera. "I'll do you one better. How about we show you our pre-championship game dance? You gotta send us lots of good luck though."

The suggestion sent a ripple through my teammates—a mix of groans and grins—and suddenly the space around us became a stage. Lockers became drums as palms slapped against cold steel. Howls erupted from the other players as we pumped each other up.

With a flick of his wrist, Bailey cranked up the volume on his portable speaker, and a bass-heavy beat spilled out. He started off the dance, and made a motion with his hands, signaling for more of us to enter the frame. One by one, the guys lined up before the camera, their bodies beginning to sway, each of us letting loose.

We snickered, losing it at our wild, made up choreography. Bailey's mouth dropped open—not in surprise, but at a few of the virtual gifts floating across his screen. The guys kept dancing, caught up in the moment—totally unaware of how epic this show for social media was.

"I'm going to regret this," I said to Boston, who just jumped on Parker's back. The crowd of dancing bodies parted, granting me passage to the phone and center stage.

Positioned before the eager audience beyond the screen, I moved to the beat in a quick dance. I lifted up the fabric of my shirt in a slow teasing motion. Then, I showed off my abs to whoever the hell was on this live. A chorus of whoops and hollers erupted around me as my teammates all jumped on me at once.

Dragons, unicorns, and every magical creature you could think of burst across his phone screen. The chat blurred into an indecipherable stream of letters and emoji moving too fast to see.

"Reese, look!" Bailey shouted. He was pointing at a particular icon on the screen—a shooting star that left a comet trail of dollar signs in its path. "That's two thousand dollars by itself!" he screamed.

The locker room was alive with the kind of laughter that made us all forget the nerves and the pressure of this game. This feeling of Blue Devils brotherhood was something I would miss, no matter where life led me after it.

"Alright, alright, let's get our head in the game," Coach bellowed, his words grounding us and bringing us back to the seriousness of this game.

"We take this championship game, do you understand me?" Coach continued, his eyes sweeping over us as he adjusted his hat. "It is ours, and we protect it at all costs."

In that moment, the mood shifted palpably. Any playfulness before was replaced with tension and focus. Coach's words hung heavy; we all knew winning this one wouldn't be easy.

When I got to the field, my eyes filtered through our home side section, searching for one face, one pair of eyes that could unravel me. There she was—Caroline. Seated between her sister and parents.

Raising my arm, I waved her over. Our eyes locked across the distance. Her expression was curious and maybe even a bit hesitant. When she got closer, I reached up and gave her what I'd been holding in my left hand.

"What's this?" she asked, looking down.

"What's it look like?"

Caroline hesitated, holding it up. "You want me to wear your jersey?"

I couldn't help but chuckle as I spit out a couple of sunflower seeds onto the dusty ground. "You're my girlfriend." I glanced past her shoulder, noticing her family. Their attention was fixated on us. "Also, kiss me because your parents are watching."

She leaned in, and I stretched up from my concrete pedestal as our lips met in a quick peck. Her lips were so soft and her gloss was fruity on my tongue. "Put me out of my misery already," she said softly. With a long exhale, she tossed my jersey over her shoulders and it draped over her tank top.

The fabric settled around her, and the sight of her in it made the stadium lights burn a little brighter, made the night air feel a little heavier. There was something intimate—possessive, even—about seeing her in it.

"Alright, get out of here," I teased with a small grin. "Because you putting that jersey on just makes me wanna take it off you."

Caroline's eyes rolled skyward.

"You're already sounding like my next ex-boyfriend."

"You can't get rid of me yet," I said, shooting her a wink.

"I might if you don't win this game," she tossed over her shoulder as she walked back to her seat. The sight of my jersey hanging off her frame hit me like a punch to the gut—I liked my name on her way more than I should. "Oh, and good luck!"

"Don't need luck," I yelled back.

My gaze flicked to her family. They looked like they'd just seen a unicorn do a backflip—mouths open, eyes wide, completely short-circuited by the fact that she was kissing me.

I couldn't help it—I grinned slowly at their astonishment. We had just sent a message and if it wasn't clear enough, then it was also written in the lines of my name across her back.

"Come on, Reese! Bring the heat!" Someone shouted from the stands as I took my place on the mound.

I nodded subtly, my gaze locked onto Parker behind the plate. With a fluid motion, I wound up and unleashed a bullet straight into Parker's mitt. "Strike!" the umpire bellowed.

The innings flew by, each team's defense refusing to give in. Third inning, nothing. Fourth, zip. The fifth rolled around, and suddenly we found our rhythm. A double here, a stolen base there, and before the other team knew what hit them, we'd racked up two runs.

"Keep it up, boys!" Coach commanded. "Don't let up!"

We couldn't hold them off, though. They evened the score in the sixth. Our advantage slipped through our fingers, and the pressure began to mount. Heading into the ninth inning, we were deadlocked.

"Last chance," Coach said as we gathered our batting gear. "This is where legends are made. Let's make sure they remember us."

Bailey was up. He hit a ground ball and just barely made it to first base.

"Reese, let's go," someone yelled as I stepped up to the plate, taking position. Everyone was on edge as I kicked the dirt, eyeing the pitcher with a cocky tilt to my head that said I wasn't worried for a second. My swing connected and the ball soared high and deep, right past the outstretched glove of the right fielder.

"Run, damn it, run!" The cheers erupted from our dugout as I tagged first and rounded towards second base, sliding in with a cloud of dust. Bailey rocketed to third.

Boston stepped up to the plate. His first swing sent the ball foul. On his second swing, the bat connected, sending a line drive zipping past the shortstop and deep into left field. Bailey, me, and Boston sprinted home and scored before the other team could get the ball back to the catcher.

Fireworks exploded overhead. We fucking did it. The stadium roared to life, a sea of cheers and flashing banners, my teammates flooding the field in a blur of triumph. Adrenaline surged through me, grounding me in the moment. This wasn't just a win—it was *the* win. The dream. The kind you never want to wake up from. We shook hands, grabbed our gear, and took one last walk off that field, the summer sun setting on a season we'd never forget.

fifteen

CAROLINE

A shrill squeal pierced the silence, shattering the concentration in the room. I turned just in time to see a whirlwind of elation in a sparkly leotard hurtling towards me.

"See! I told you you could do it!" I caught the little girl mid-flight, her tiny arms cinching around my neck in a victorious embrace. Her cheeks were flushed with triumph, eyes glimmering brighter than the sequins on her outfit.

"I expect all of them to look like that from now on," I said, setting her down.

"You're the best," she breathed out.

"You did it all by yourself. Remember, control is key." I ruffled her hair as she scooped up her backpack, and skipped out of the room.

Just as I took a sip from my water bottle, footsteps entered the room behind me.

"Do you believe in lost causes?" The words came out hesitant, with a trace of sadness.

I turned, finding Reese's little sister, Lola, standing timidly. Her gaze held a flicker of hope.

"Lost causes?" I asked curiously.

"Th-that's what the other girls are saying," Lola stammered, her fingers fiddling with the hem of her top. It was completely opposite of the confidence her brother exuded. "That I shouldn't even try out because I'm a lost cause."

I could feel the weight of her insecurities threatening to suffocate her potential, but lucky for her, she had me. I knew I'd be able to help her make the team, and we were definitely going to work on her confidence—although her brother surely had enough for both of them. It wasn't just because of the deal I had with Reese but because she reminded me of a young me in a way. I was always underestimated; I always felt as if I needed to work harder than others.

"Lost cause, huh?" My voice was a whisper as I tapped on my chin. "Well, they obviously don't know who they're dealing with."

"Let's get started, Lola. We have work to do." I motioned her forward into the heart of the studio room where I liked to believe miracles happened.

"You really think I can make the team?" Her words were a fragile hope wrapped in vulnerability.

"Absolutely. I have no doubt," I confessed, taking a few steps closer to her. My shadow stretched across the floor like a dark promise. "And now you have me in your corner. We'll prove them all wrong—you're going to make the team."

Her smile, hesitant at first, eventually widened. "Thanks." She tucked a strand of hair behind her ear. "You don't seem the way Reese described."

"And what exactly did your brother say about me?" I asked, beginning to stretch an arm behind my head.

She mirrored the stretch I was doing. "He said you were a firecracker," she began, "looked like a Barbie but would probably act like a drill sergeant."

"Let's keep him thinking that," I murmured, my voice low with mischief. She nodded, acknowledging our unspoken pact. "It seems like he cares a lot about you. Who would have known he'd have such a soft spot for his little sister."

"Reese is complicated," she said suddenly, fixing her hair in the mirror. "People don't get him. They see the surface, how arrogant and bold he is, but beneath that, he's... different."

"Different how?"

"He actually has this really big heart," she continued. "It's like he's better when no one's watching. When the eyes are on him, the mask goes up, you know?"

"Sounds familiar." I smiled, my mind drifting to the countless times I'd hidden behind a mask too. "Well... let's get to work."

"Why are you helping me, though?" Lola asked.

"Because it's what I do," I answered smoothly, even though it was more a lie than not. I couldn't exactly tell her about this crazy deal her brother and I had. "I love teaching."

We started with the basics. With each jump and motion, I saw her confidence rising just a tad. She was building trust in me with every corrected posture and softened landing.

"Point your toes," I instructed. "Yes, just like that."

An hour vanished before I knew it, leaving us both breathless. Lola's grip tightened around her water bottle, her face flushed.

"Listen, this weekend, stretch—a lot," I said, eyes locking onto hers. "And come back with those jumps you've been practicing. That's all I want you to focus on."

A smooth voice with a hint of mockery intruded from behind me. "Giving homework on the first day, are we?”

I spun around on my heel, and there was Reese, leaning against the doorframe like he owned it. He wore his casual arrogance effortlessly, his sleeveless shirt showing off his broad shoulders and the curves of his biceps. Everything about him seemed dark—his hair that was a tousled mess, his sun-kissed skin—everything except for those vivid green eyes. They locked onto me, bright and knowing, making it impossible to look away from.

And seriously, why did he have to look like some rebel sculpted for the sole purpose of testing my self-control? I hated how he owned the room so easily, with that effortless charm dripping from his lips like sweet, deadly poison. I could smell his delicious scent from where I stood, and he looked every bit the man too handsome for his own good.

"It's not homework. Just something to practice," I said firmly. "You of all people should know—practice makes perfect."

"And here I thought perfection was unattainable," he drawled.

"Only to those who don't practice enough," I shot back.

From the corner of my eye, I caught Lola's approving nod. "I like her," she declared to Reese.

I turned to Lola, with a satisfied smile. "Don't forget to keep those toes pointed. Good job today."

"Will do!" she chirped before slinging her dance bag over her shoulder and skipping towards the door. "Gonna refill my water bottle before we go," she called back to Reese, her ponytail bouncing with each step as she disappeared into the hallway.

Reese pushed off from the door frame as he rubbed his chin. "Weird," he mused, "didn't think you'd win over Lo already."

"Guess it just means she's a good judge of character," I replied.

"I don't know about that," he spoke, then paused, his eyes cutting to me with a sharp, assessing look as he inched closer. "Will I see you at Gin & Jerry's tonight?"

"Guess so," I said, starting to roll up the cheer mat.

"And for the record," his voice was smooth as silk, "you didn't look too bad in my jersey."

I smirked, not even glancing up. "I'd look good in any jersey."

His tone dropped as he helped me carry the rolled up mat to the side of the room. "Nah," he murmured, tilting his head just enough to catch my eye. "Only mine."

"You and that oversized ego of yours," I shot back.

"I never leave home without it," he said, a grin spreading across his face. "And do you always bring that with you?"

"Bring what with me?" I snapped, already annoyed.

"The lettuce stuck in your teeth," he replied, his grin widening with pure amusement.

A flush of embarrassment crept up my neck, staining my skin a rosy shade of mortification. "Oh my god, what?" I turned as I stumbled toward the mirror, which reflected back the truth.

Fuck my life. I grimaced. There it was, the bitch ass intruder sticking out like a weed in the white picket fence of my teeth. I had a salad at lunch. How had I gotten through three lessons oblivious to the giant leaf wedged between my teeth? My cheeks flamed with the thought of all the eyes—students, co-workers. Had they noticed? And out of all people, of course Reese would be the one to point it out.

"I'll save your little friend a seat at the bar," he snickered.

"You're such a jerk!" The words escaped before I could stop them, filled with defensiveness and embarrassment. But he didn't even glance back, that cocky grin never wavering as he disappeared from view.

A few hours later, the bar's door swung open, cheers erupted, reverberating against the walls and filling the bar with energy. The Blue Devils, still riding the high of their epic championship win, entered the room to an eruption of applause, the excitement following them wherever they went. I watched from my corner as whistles pierced through the drone and hands slapped backs as they made their way to the bar.

"Wild, isn't it? We just have to get through the Bayside Ball and then we're all done with anything Blue Devils." Sam spoke up through all the cheers.

I turned to her, still unsure of how to tell her about the situation I found myself in with Reese, because I wasn't going to be completely done with the Blue Devils after the ball. I had a little bit more of an attachment to one of them. "Really wild."

So what are your plans after summer?" Sam asked, leaning in closer.

"I'm not sure," I admitted, my gaze drifting to Reese who was signing championship hats. "I love being an instructor. There's just something about the excitement on someone's face after they've worked so hard—about watching how far they come. It brings me so much happiness."

Sam nodded. "Well, it sounds like you've found your passion," she said, understanding flickering across her face.

"Passion, yes," I murmured, "but will that passion impress my parents? Not in the slightest."

"Who cares?" Sam shot back, rolling her eyes. "It's your life, not theirs."

"If only it was that easy," I sighed, really wishing it was. My dreams came in second, right after doing everything I could to make my family proud of me. "What about you?" I asked, eager to escape my own thoughts. "How is everything going with bridezilla?"

"Well, she's actually not the worst bride I'm dealing with right now, but don't worry. I'll be able to breathe a little more after wedding season." She shrugged.

"Well any bride is so lucky to have you, Sam."

Sam and I drifted through the bar, toward the back where most of our friends usually lounged around. The back of the bar was quieter, darker, its brick walls covered in posters and records on display. There was a back wall of games and a music player that connected to an app on our phones we all often fought over.

"Is the lighting different in here, or do you just get prettier every time I see you?" Wells Clark stepped in front of me. It felt too rehearsed to be sincere, but his effort was noted.

"I'd prefer the second."

His grin widened as he leaned in closer. "So when are you going to let me take you on that date?"

Sam snickered behind me. "Yeah, when are you doing that, Caroline?" Her gaze swung between me and Wells with mischief. "And while you decide, I'm going to use the ladies' room."

The echoes of Sam's laughter lingered as she walked away, and I fired a glare at her retreating back. The moment she disappeared to the restrooms, I turned back to Wells, feeling the sudden gravity of his expectation.

"I don't know," I began, stirring my drink. "I'm pretty busy these days." The idea of a real date with Wells Clark didn't sound *too* bad. It had been over a year since I had hooked up with anyone—since I had allowed myself the vulnerability of any connection. And not only were my hormones doing cartwheels, but I'd been craving attention harder than my 2 p.m. Diet Coke fix.

Wells leaned in, his eyes dark. "Well, I can work around your schedule," he said with a half-smile. "We can get out of here right now if you want. Go back to my place."

Was I actually considering this right now? The moment of silence between Wells and me was quickly shattered by an unmistakable raspy voice. "Not happening tonight, quarterback," Reese drawled, smirking as he fixed Wells with a look that could make hell freeze over.

The shift in atmosphere was instantaneous. Wells let out a low chuckle, but it was dark. "If not tonight, then soon," he said confidently, throwing me a wink. "You let me know when."

He turned to Reese, his gaze turning from playful to pointed, like there was some sort of silent conversation passing between them. Wells stepped back, like he was surrendering in the moment but there was still unfinished business between them.

Reese stood in front of me, his towering frame boxing me in. "Really?" I scoffed, trying to ignore how the dim lighting cast shadows across his sculpted features, giving him an almost predatory look. "You don't need to act like my boyfriend tonight, none of my family is here."

"I wasn't acting." he said, casually running his fingers through his hair.

"Well then, why interrupt, Reese? Maybe I did want to go home with him. Maybe I haven't hooked up with anyone in over a year. I could have been considering it."

His eyebrow arched slowly as he leaned in, his breath a warm whisper against my cheek. "And you're considering that with Wells

Clark?" The name rolled off his tongue tainted with disdain, like just saying it left a bad taste in his mouth.

"Why not?"

His half-smirk twisted into something more evil as he inched even closer, forcing me to retreat step by step until my back collided with the cold brick wall beside the music machine. Reese loomed over me, a tower of temptation, and casually rested an arm above my head. "You don't need some boy who just gives you attention until he gets off."

"What do I need then?" I asked, knowing exactly what I was walking into.

The air between us grew thick, saturated with desire and the scent of his masculine cologne. He placed his other hand on my neck, his thumb resting on my racing pulse point. He leaned in, his grip gentle but commanding.

"You should only spread your legs for someone who can give you exactly what you want," he growled.

"And you know what I want?"

He clenched his jaw and carefully drew out his next words. "I think what you really crave is a man who adores you... but fucks you like he doesn't. And after you have it once... you feel like you might die without it."

In that moment, Reese wasn't just the bad boy with a reputation that preceded him. He was the embodiment of every fantasy I'd ever had—the tall dark and handsome danger that was in all my dreams. My chest constricted like he had stolen the air from me as I forced out, "Too bad you and I... we can't go there."

He didn't flinch. Didn't pull away. Instead, Reese's thumb kept moving—slow, gentle strokes against my skin. Feather-light, but intentional. Dangerous. My breath caught, the warmth of his touch unraveling every reason I had to resist.

"Why can't we?" He asked softly, but there was something else beneath it. Something that made my pulse stutter.

I swallowed hard, forcing myself to remember. "We need to stick to the plan," I said, my voice barely above a whisper. "We have to make it to my sister's wedding, and I've heard rumors about you."

The rumors everyone knew, that I'd become another name on his stupid R&R list. A list that forever ruined you for anyone else after him.

His thumb never stopped as he exhaled a quiet laugh, but his eyes, dark and unreadable, stayed locked on mine. "Do you believe them?"

"I have no reason not to." I admitted, but I didn't know. I *wanted* to. Because believing them was easier than admitting the truth—that I was already losing this fight.

He flashed a dimple, narrowing his eyes on my lips now. "We'll make it to your sister's wedding," he assured me. "You'd just be more satisfied when it happens." His close proximity felt like an intoxicating danger. "And those rumors?" he added, "they're all true."

"There's a possibility you don't really live up to all the hype," I said, not able to give his ego the satisfaction.

Reese's gaze didn't waver. His eyes locked onto mine with an intensity that felt like it could set the air on fire. His voice dropped to a husky whisper. "You wanna test that theory?"

sixteen

REESE

I slouched in the booth, fingers tracing the sleeve on my coffee cup while I tried not to focus on her intense eyes, the same ones that sort of reminded me of my own. I took my time with each sip, waiting for her to start the conversation.

"Reese," she finally began. "Oh, hunny, I never get tired of seeing your beautiful face." Her kindness was almost suffocating. "I am still in shock that you came to the diner the other night, and that you're willing to meet me here."

I knew my dad hadn't been completely honest with me when it came to her, but none of that did anything to dull the sting of her absence.

"You've been coming to the games, waiting for me at the diner most of the summer. Figured I'd hear you out."

She fidgeted with a sugar packet on the table. "I'm so sorry it's taken this long for me to come around," she whispered. "I'm sorry I haven't been around most of your life."

"It's fine," I murmured. But it wasn't fine, and we both knew it.

"For so many years, I just felt so helpless. I was told that I had no chance against your father, that I was nobody compared to him...

after a while, you start to believe it," she whispered, sorrow in her eyes. "I didn't have the money that your father had, Reese. I didn't have the justice system in the palm of my hand like he did."

I looked away from her, focusing on the steam rising from my cup, unable to look at the sadness in her eyes any longer. I'm not the person who feels remorse, I'm not the guy who comforts people, but maybe it was because at the end of the day she was still the person who birthed me.

"Look," I said, my voice hoarse with the effort of keeping it level, "I didn't know any of that. I just know I was a kid who needed his mom, but you... you weren't there." I was searching for something—anything—that might help me with the animosity I felt from years spent wondering if she'd ever come back for me. "I appreciate this, you coming to me now, now that I'm an adult who can sort of understand. But understanding doesn't erase anything."

There was a silence then, punctuated only by the soft clink of silverware from a nearby booth and a distant cash register.

"I know." The words were barely louder than the sound of sugar packets still being shuffled by her anxious fingers. "I'm sorry for that, Reese." She folded her hands on the table, knuckles whitening with the grip of her own regret. "Every single day I wondered how I could rewind time, rewrite our history. How I could have changed it all." Her voice cracked.

The ache in my chest tightened knowing there was nothing either of us could do now. But it all still fucking hurt, every missed birthday, game, and milestone in my life. I was who I was now because of all of it. I was hardened by it. Somehow, I found a way to channel that pain and inadequacy into baseball. I made sure I wasn't just good enough but the best pitcher there was, and I'd gotten where I was because of her in some twisted way.

The silence stretched between us. Too much time, too many years were now lost. She waited for some sign of forgiveness—a sign I wasn't sure I had in me.

"Time travel," I said finally, "it's the only way." The corner of my mouth lifted upward in a small smile because sarcasm was clearly the best option in these situations.

She caught the smirk and, surprisingly, she let out a gentle laugh. It was what we both needed in such a heavy moment. Her eyes crinkled at the edges, reflecting back a history of pain that we were both carefully trying to navigate.

A warm smile spread across her face. "You're funny. I should have known." She leaned forward slightly, her gaze softening as she took in my features. "Not just that, but you're handsome. And those dimples..." A hand fluttered to her chest, fingers brushing the gold necklace she was wearing. "I'm sure you have every woman in the world after you."

I swirled the remnants of my coffee. "Women," I chuckled, "they haven't exactly been my area of expertise." The steam rose from my cup, disappearing into the void above us—much like the years we'd never get back. "Might be the abandonment issues I have," I added, letting the dig at her slip before I realized it.

Her reaction was a soft sigh. She fumbled with a napkin, twisting it between anxious fingers. "Reese," she began, still sounding strange coming from her. "I can tell you this..." she paused, searching for the right words. "I've spent so many years wondering how to get you back. And if you allow me"—her breath hitched—"I will be in your life every day until the last day of mine. In any capacity you allow."

For a moment, I considered the possibility of letting her in. Could I forgive her? Could I trust her? I wasn't sure, but I knew the feeling of not having her in my life, and having the choice to allow her back in, and how much, had to be better than that.

"Alright," I murmured, giving a slow wary nod. "I guess coffee is a good start then."

There was an almost imperceptible pause as the moment hung suspended, and then she wiped a tear just as quickly as it fell—relief marking her face. I lifted my cup with a steady hand. "Cheers," I said, the word slipping out.

"I do have something I want to ask you before we go," I said, curiously.

"Ask away," she murmured, sliding her purse onto her shoulder.

"After all this time," I began, "why are you finally trying now?"

She exhaled slowly. "Honestly, I had given up hope for a long time." Her hands, once steady, now shook as she clasped them tightly together. "I thought you wanted nothing to do with me, hated me even. But when I finally came back to Bayside and saw you pitching last summer, I saw it."

"Saw what?"

She reached across the table, her fingers brushing against the pendant on my chest—it had become as much a part of me as my own skin.

"This. It was my father's," she said softly as she traced the outline of it. "I hoped... I hoped that maybe it meant a part of you was still holding on."

"I've hardly ever taken it off since I was younger... I've never really known why it means so much to me."

Across from me, she smiled as she said, "you're a lot like him, you know—my father. He loved Bayside, grew up here too." She looked out the window. "He had this charm about him; you couldn't help but love him—the whole town did."

"Sounds like someone I'd get along well with," I said, now under-standing my attachment to it.

We rose from our table, and she gave me a hesitant hug. "I'll text you tomorrow," she murmured. "To see if you'd like to meet up again soon." I held open the door and nodded as she made her way to the parking lot.

I lingered for a moment, gathering my thoughts. I was turning to leave when she walked. Caroline, with her mother and sister. Her sister carried a binder with colorful tabs peeking out from the edge.

"Caroline, you didn't tell us Reese was joining us," Her mom said accusingly.

I caught her faltering step. Our eyes locked for a split second, panic flaring across her face.

"Oh," she stammered, voice cracking, "must have slipped my mind."

I stepped back aside as Caroline and her family traipsed in.

"After you," I murmured, gesturing toward the vacant tables with a flick of my wrist.

Caroline's mother halted mid-stride, her gaze lifting to meet mine. "I still can't get over this." She looked up at me. "Reese, I've been telling Caroline to bring you by the house."

We drifted toward a booth bathed in the soft glow of afternoon light, which filtered through half-drawn blinds. I slid into the space next to Caroline, our elbows brushing. Before I could respond to Mrs. Matthews, Caroline responded for me. "Mom, I told you. He's been so busy—you know, winning championship games and Blue Devils stuff."

"I'm never too busy for you, Care Bear."

Caroline reacted exactly how I thought she would, in the form of a discreet kick under the table. And it took every ounce of restraint not to let out the laugh I was holding. I caught the deadly glint in her eyes as she hit me with her best glare, but it only fired me up. There was a thrill in the deception of this whole thing, in seeing her react. With a slow grin, I reached across the table and took Caroline's hand in mine. She stiffened, knowing she couldn't pull away without raising suspicion, not with her mother's hawk-like gaze tracing our every movement.

What I didn't see coming? The warmth. The softness of her skin. There was this undeniable tension between us. Holding her hand, I couldn't ignore how effortlessly hers fit in mine, how smooth her skin felt against the roughness of my calloused fingers. This was supposed to be just an act, but damn... it was already affecting me more than I realized.

"Reese," Charlotte said, opening her binder. "The whole town is talking about how amazing you were. They needed that championship win."

"I'm glad we could make them proud."

Caroline's mother fixed her eyes on me before she said, "You must have every major league team interested in you."

"I don't know about that," I answered, giving my best attempt at modesty.

"By the way, if you want to get to that thing you had to do today, you're totally welcome to leave here early, Reese," Caroline said earnestly. "I know you don't want to sit around for wedding talk."

"Actually," I said, the words slipping out with ease, "I happen to love wedding talk." It wasn't true, but I couldn't pass up any opportunity to aggravate her.

"Oh, do you now?" Caroline glared, and I squeezed her thigh in response.

Charlotte reached into her purse and pulled out a pile of papers before she laid them in front of their mother.

"Dan said his parents want me to sign this," she said with a sigh, her voice lacking the usual confidence.

"Don't tell me he wants a prenup?" Their mom asked without even looking down at the stack.

"Yeah," Charlotte replied, her fingers traced the edge of the paper. "Do I sign it? Do I need to have someone look at it?"

As her mom held up the contract, my eyes scanned every line as fast as I could. Every clause, every line, all tailored to protect him. It might look fair to the average person, but it was one-sided, every word safeguarding his interests, his future. Not hers.

"Wait," I said, holding up a hand. "Don't sign that. That... That is lopsided."

Three pairs of eyes snapped to me, wide with surprise. Their expressions were pure shock. Maybe they figured I was just another jock, all athlete and no brains. I wasn't sure what was going through their minds.

Charlotte's eyes were wide with a mixture of confusion and realization. I could almost hear the wheels turning in their minds, skeptical but trusting as she said curiously, "Lopsided?"

"Look here," I said, pointing to a certain section. "And here. This is all for him. You need clauses that protect your savings, your future, even your time—if you take a break to raise kids, you should be compensated for that. It's not just his contract," I continued, searching their faces to see if they were following. "It's yours, too. You need to re-work this. To make it fair."

Caroline's mother was the first to break the silence that stretched, her voice laced with amusement and maybe even respect. "You really are a lawyer's kid, aren't you?"

"Guilty," I admitted. "Law has always been a bit of a fascination. My dad had a library filled with all his law books. Couldn't help but get sucked into it."

I glanced at Caroline. Her expression had crystallized into intrigue. Her mother and sister, meanwhile, seemed to be under some sort of spell, both finding a new energy.

"If you email it to my dad," I offered, "he can easily re-work it for you."

"Okay, can we keep you instead of Caroline?" Charlotte joked. Well, I wasn't sure if she was actually joking.

Caroline's family continued to hang on my every word as if I was some strange otherworldly creature. Caroline sat there, her gaze flitting between me and her family.

"Wait a minute," Caroline's mom changed the subject. "Isn't tomorrow the Bayside Ball?"

I turned toward Caroline. A sudden panic had taken over her features. Her mouth opened, a stuttering half-breath escaped, "Yeah but—"

"Surely you two are going together, aren't you?" Her sister interrupted with a judgy look.

"Of course we are," I said, the words slipping out before I had a chance to think about it. But the truth was, the Bayside Ball had been so far removed from my cluttered thoughts, buried deep underneath the championship game, shit with my mom, the upcoming draft, and everything else lately.

Caroline leaned back, with a weak smile as she nodded in agreement. But that look on her face did not escape me—there was a sadness in her eyes. Was it reluctance or regret? Did she not want to go with me? Did she want to go with someone else? My mind raced, but I held back the flood of questions.

"Oh good," Charlotte added, her shoulders relaxing just a bit. "You two are going to be the talk of the town."

Eventually, we all rose from our seats. Caroline's mother and sister strode off toward their cars as we said our goodbyes, and I walked Caroline to her car.

"Your mom seems... nice," I ventured, not taking my eyes off her for a second. I didn't really sense the whole mother-daughter bond, but Caroline's mom and sister both had the same cold and distant thing going on.

She clenched her firsts, holding her keychain in one hand. "It's... been like this for as long as I can remember. My mom—" Caroline's fists unclenched, and her hands trembled slightly. "It feels like she's always hated me. My sister always went along with it because they loved her more, gave her more attention. And my dad? He never stood up for me. Didn't even notice that he should."

"That's tough," I said, slowly starting to understand her a little more. Caroline wasn't evil. She was guarded because she'd learned to be, to protect herself.

"The only person I ever had was my brother." Her eyes searched mine for something, maybe understanding. "He was nice to me. But my mom hates that I'm a cheerleader, and despises that I still have anything to do with it." She paused, a bitter laugh escaping her lips. "And I don't even know why I'm telling you this."

"Was your mom a cheerleader?"

She shook her head. "No. She tried out every year and never made the team. Loves reminding me how ungrateful I am for being one. Says I take it for granted," she spat out with a humorless laugh.

I closed the gap between us, wrapping my arms around her. She stiffened for a second—then sank into me, like she was finally letting go. Her body fit against mine like it belonged there, the scent of peach shampoo and rain wrapping around me, making it impossible to think about anything else.

"Why are we hugging?" Her voice was muffled against my chest. The last time we were this close, I felt her wild pulse beneath my fingertips, our bodies no more than a breath apart. Since that moment, I'd been practically praying for another chance to be this close to her again. As her head rested against me, I felt the tension in her muscles slowly start to unravel.

"Because," I said, pulling back an arm and tilting her chin up, forcing her to meet my eyes. "You looked like you needed one."

She froze, her breath hitching as she kept her eyes locked on mine.

"Listen to me. Your mom... she's jealous. You're everything she wanted to be. And instead of dealing with that, she's taking it out on you."

Her expression flickered—sadness twisting into something uncertain, like she was turning my words over in her head. Then, finally, she nodded. And damn, if it didn't feel like a punch to the gut.

"I never thought about it that way," she murmured. "Even if it's not true... thank you for saying it."

Then, just like that, she let go. Stepped back. The walls snapped back into place like she'd realized I'd seen too much. And I hated that she thought she had to do that.

"Caroline," I began, the words coming out softer than I expected, "are you okay with us going to the ball together?"

For a moment, she paused, her hand lingering on the door handle before she finally opened it. "You and I..." she repeated slowly like she was processing the thought. "Go together?"

A chuckle escaped me as I leaned against her car, my arm casually resting on the edge of the open door as she slid into the driver's seat.

"Yeah, that's normally how it works," I said, trying to hide my confusion in humor. Why was she acting so strange about this? Why was she so hesitant? It was just a dance.

She hesitated, not looking me in the eye. "You don't already have a date?" she asked, her voice quivering slightly. "I figured you'd have a lineup of women."

She looked like some adorable creature in the woods, caught in the glare of headlights, ready to bolt but carefully staying put. And there was something about the way she framed the question, like she was searching for an excuse, any reason to not go with me.

"Nah," I said, pushing back. "The girl I wanna take is right in front of me."

The silence stretched taut between us before she smiled, but it held no joy. Her fingers rested lightly on the ignition, hesitating just long enough to make my chest tighten. "How about I meet you there?"

Something wasn't right about the way she said that, and it sent a prickle down my spine. I caught the sadness lurking behind those lashes. What was she hiding?

"Why wouldn't I come pick you up?"

She dragged her teeth across her lower lip. "I have committee stuff to do," she murmured, dragging her seatbelt slowly across her body. "I have to give out the awards, set up some things, so... I'll just meet you there."

It was a good excuse—practical, believable. But it still didn't sit right.

Her voice was too soft, her words too carefully chosen, like she planned them.

I leaned in slightly, studying her, watching as her fingers gripped the steering wheel again just a little too tightly. "You sure about that?"

Her shoulders stiffened, but she forced a quick nod, keeping her eyes on the dashboard like looking at me would somehow give something away.

My jaw twitched, the unease growing. "Did I do something?" I asked, softer this time. "Because it kind of feels like I did."

She shook her head too quickly. "No. Nothing at all."

She was a terrible liar. But I knew her well enough to know that she didn't want me to push further. And when her mind was set on something, she didn't seem like the type to let anyone change it. But not knowing what I'd done to make her pull away? That was the worst part.

"Alright, I'll see you there," I finally said, playing along, and gently pushed her car door until it clicked shut.

seventeen

CAROLINE

Clutching my tiny purse, my fingers instinctively found my favorite lipstick—a soft pink shade I always reached for in moments like this. I needed the familiarity, the comfort. Slipping past the heavy curtain that separated me from the ballroom, I exhaled, stepping into the quiet sanctuary beyond. A stolen moment to breathe, to gather my thoughts, to brace myself for the speech and the ceremony waiting on the other side. I sorted through the envelopes, each holding inside them the names of each winner.

For other women, going to this ball with Reese might have sent them spiraling into a highlight reel of heart eyes and swoon-worthy daydreams, but not me. What he'd put me through in the past hovered over me like a dark cloud, threatening to burst open and drench me in the pain I couldn't get away from. He had the power once, to crush a more vulnerable version of me, but I was smarter now. I knew exactly what I could expect from him.

I was tuned in to the voices on the other side of the curtain as guests arrived—laughter, the clinking of dishes, the subtle shifting of feet. Most of the voices I recognized, players or Bayside locals. But none of them belonged to Reese. Each second that ticked by without the sound of his voice was a silent confirmation of my fears.

"We're starting, everyone," a committee member yelled from behind me.

I closed my eyes for a moment, attempting to shut out the thoughts in my head. When I opened them, I was still there, doing my best to stay together. What if he decided not to come? Or worse, what if he arrived hand-in-hand with someone else, a more beautiful, drop-dead gorgeous kind of someone? How would I face the questioning eyes of my family? Our plan—the one thing we had painstakingly constructed—would crumble.

With a trembling hand, I fished my phone from the clutch, and big surprise, no new alerts. No messages. No missed calls. Not a single word from Reese. Tossing it aside, I positioned myself behind the podium. The murmurs from the crowd beyond grew louder, teasing at my heightened senses.

"You got this," I whispered to the empty space, the words barely a breath.

With a hiss, the curtain began its slow retreat, revealing the ballroom inch by inch. I forced a smile as I peered into the audience. My skin prickled with heat as the voices started to silence, the faces blurred together. And then my gaze found him—Reese. The world narrowed to nothing more than the distance between us, every sound fading into the background. He was sitting at a table, his posture relaxed. The seat beside him, blatantly vacant. I froze for a moment, feeling lightheaded from the rush of adrenaline and relief that flooded my veins. Reese was here. And he was here alone.

"Good evening, all. Welcome to this year's Bayside Ball," I began, still distracted by him. By Reese, sharp and smoldering. He owned the room in that suit. The way it hugged his broad shoulders, how it fit his tall, muscular body so well. His intimidating green eyes locked onto mine, and for a moment, the room fell away. He looked so at ease, the epitome of nonchalance. Still, there was something undeniably masculine about him that sent a shiver down my spine, making me feel confused. Why did he affect me so much?

I continued speaking, doing my best to focus. Awards were handed out, applause rose and fell. "And now, for Most Valuable Player," I announced, opening up the envelope. "This year, the award goes to... Boston Riley."

A murmur rippled through the room, and I felt the weight of surprise settle over the crowd. I figured this was going to Reese, but there it was, Boston written in blank ink, undeniable.

"Unfortunately, Boston couldn't be here tonight," I continued, striving for poise as I searched for a sign of him. Then, Reese rose from his seat, every muscle beneath that suit coiled with tension as he made his way out of the ballroom, his expression unreadable. Was he upset Boston had won MVP, or was it something else?

And then she moved—Chandler, her steps moving after Reese. My stomach dropped as I watched them both disappear.

The last of the awards were handed out as applause swelled around me. I stepped back, relieved to be done with my duties for the night. The curtains closed, and with the finality of that heavy drape, the music began—the signal that everyone could now enjoy the night and relax.

As I joined the ballroom, couples found each other, the slow song bringing them all to the dance floor. Where did he go? Why did the sight of Chandler going after him make me feel sick?

"Caroline, you did great," Sam said, her tone earnest, eyes bright with pride. "I may be partial," Sam continued, her hand lightly brushing my arm, "but I think you were the best committee president Bayside has ever seen."

"Thank you," I gleamed, offering a smirk. "I couldn't have done it without you."

"Oh, they're playing another good slow song," she murmured, looking around. "I'm going to go find Crew. Just ran into twin sisters who said they're here for him."

"Oh, no! Go get him, girl," I encouraged, grimacing.

Sam squeezed me, then she was gone. There I stood. Alone. Surrounded by couples drifting across the ballroom floor.

"Are we allowed to dance together? Or should I keep my distance?" Reese's voice slipped through the music, smooth and teasing, but there was an undertone of something deeper. I froze, the air catching in my lungs. There was a raw, unspoken question in his voice that dared me to turn around, to let the relief flood in, to admit how much I wanted him here.

I turned. Reese stood there, so calm, with his hands casually tucked in his pockets. The sight of him—so tall, so unavoidably perfect—nearly made me forget how to breathe. The dimmed lights seemed to highlight the firm set of his jaw and the unruly, sexy way his dark hair refused to stay in place.

"I'll allow it," I said, a smile teasing at the corners of my lips.

Reese didn't hesitate. He stepped forward, extending his hand confidently. His warm fingers wrapped around mine, and the dance floor opened up before us.

My hand traced the line of Reese's shoulder, skimming over the fabric of his suit. His fingers found the small of my back, pressing gently, pulling me closer until the space between us vanished.

"Chaos," he rumbled. His warm breath fanned across my ear as we swayed, and I had never liked hearing that nickname more than the way he'd just said it. "You in this dress... it's going to bring me to my knees."

A shiver raced down my spine at the heat of his words. In his arms, I could almost believe in the possibility of *us*—that there might be something real between us.

"Thank you," I whispered. "You look handsome." The words felt inadequate for the way the suit clung to his form, turning every head in the room.

Reese licked his lips before giving a half-smile. His hand was steady on my back. "I can pull off a suit," he admitted, the playful arrogance in his tone softened by something more tender. "But you're wearing that dress like it was made for you."

There was a serious danger in those eyes of his. They pulled you in even as his gaze warned you to stay away. My breath caught, hitching on the edge of a sensation too potent to name. This dance with Reese was more than just movement to music; it was intimate, intense, each step and sway was something much more than I could understand.

"Thank you." I said, looking up at him towering over me. "I thought maybe you took off."

"Nah," he said simply. "Just needed to step outside and think for a moment."

"Think?" The word drifted between us carefully. "With Chandler?" I asked, unsure if I wanted to know what they were doing together.

"Yeah," he admitted, his voice a rumble deep in his chest. "We talked on the dock outside. I think we both got the clarity we needed." There was something in the way he said those words, a finality, a realization, that told me all I didn't want to know.

I knew he had history with her. There was a possibility something had happened between them, but I continued to pry, anyway. "What kind of clarity?"

Reese's hand found mine, turning me in a slow circle. His fingers applied gentle pressure at my waist, guiding me with ease. As we spun, his head tilted toward the back of the room, drawing my gaze to where Chandler and Boston slow danced together.

"Things are exactly how they should be, and Boston made it back just in time. I'm happy for them," he murmured.

"Me too," I whispered back, my smile fragile.

"Besides," he murmured, his voice vibrating against the shell of my ear, "I could never leave without dancing with you first."

I found myself leaning closer, drawn in by his gravity. "Well," I started, my voice barely above a whisper, "I could deal with you leaving or not showing up tonight, but I really need you there for my sister's wedding. I need to be able to rely on you. They already think I'm a joke, like everyone else."

There was a flicker of confusion on his face, like he didn't understand what I had just said. "Why wouldn't I be there?" he asked. "Why do you think you can't rely on me?"

I stepped back, gathering the right words to tell him how bad he had hurt me in the past, to bring up something I never wanted to talk about ever again.

"Sorry, Reese, I hate to interrupt," a photographer said, holding up the camera hanging around his neck. "But could I get some photos of you? You weren't here at the end of the award ceremony," he asked apologetically.

Reese released his gaze from mine and nodded. I let him go.

I caught fragments of their conversation. "You're going big places, man," the photographer said. "I see you going in the top five of the draft."

It was true. Reese was bigger than this town, and we all knew he'd make it big one day. That thought shouldn't have mattered to me, but hearing it made my chest feel heavy and tight. Why did the thought of Reese leaving us all behind make me feel unsettled? We were nothing more than two people who had found a mutual benefit in each other. I reminded myself of the role I had to play—the fiery, untouchable Caroline Matthews.

"Appreciate that," came Reese's voice.

With every click, I was reminded that he was out of reach, still in his own world while I remained in mine. We were on separate paths, just as we had always been.

Top five—on the path to becoming a legend. A professional athlete. A life I couldn't even imagine.

"We'll see, they never go how you think," Reese said casually.

REESE

The sharp ding of my phone pierced the quiet as I sat on the boat, taking in my favorite view. This was my favorite place to be when I needed to clear my mind. With a long sigh, I pulled my phone out of my pocket to see messages coming through from the group chat.

BAILEY

One last end of summer celebration?

CREW

I call the twins

PARKER

Once again, no one wants that freak show.

CREW

As long as you know that freak show is
all mine

BAILEY

What kind of celebration are you guys
talking about? A fucking orgy? I just want to
drink together. You know, hang out, maybe.

ME

Like you'd ever say no to an orgy

BAILEY

Can one of you idiots just answer my
question?

ME

Where at?

PARKER

Let's do it at Willow's.

BAILEY

Bet

A few hours later, I pulled up to the party, and Bailey was waiting by his truck for me.

"Went on a date with Bakergirl last week. She's actually hilarious, man," Bailey said, grinning like an idiot as I shut my truck door.

We strolled toward the entrance. "Is that so?"

"Swear, bro. It's not often I'm around someone who's funny like I am." He laughed.

"Glad things are going so smoothly for you," Crew added as he slid up next to me. "Sam wants to make things exclusive, which means I'd have to cut off the twins." He shook his head, a wry smile playing on his lips.

I couldn't help but snicker. "You? Exclusive?" I arched an eyebrow, leaning against the wall. Crew with only one girl—that was something I had never seen. "Do you even do that?"

Crew rubbed the back of his neck. "You know, that's a great question," he mused. "I always thought I'd never be a one-woman type of guy," he continued, his gaze drifting across the party. "I just have so much love to give... but maybe I should give the girlfriend thing a try?"

"Finally growing up, huh?" Parker asked as he clapped us both on the shoulder. "I'm so proud of you assholes."

"Cheers to that," I said, my voice a low drawl, not entirely sure if I was toasting to the sentiment or the notion that maybe we were all actually growing this summer.

"Didn't you and Willow just happen like ten minutes ago?" Bailey asked Parker, giving him shit.

"This coffee has been brewing for a while, my man," he replied, his grin flashing. It was obvious the entire summer that those two were into each other.

Boston turned to me after grabbing a beer from the cooler. "Hey man," he said.

"Hey," I nodded back. The simplicity of the greeting was a lot for us. We shook up, a casual collision of hands that we didn't often do.

"I'm glad you've been spending some time with Mom," he added.

"Taking it slow with her, but things are okay."

"I get it," he replied, nodding. "I also never got a chance to tell you—thank you."

"For what?"

"For stepping aside when it came to Chandler," he said, and though the words were simple, they were heavy. "You could've made things a lot more difficult for us. I know you have your own history."

"Nah," I murmured. "I should've never stepped in the way to begin with. But I'm happy for you two."

He gave me a nod, and it almost felt like the grudges between us were beginning to dissolve. I reached out and clapped him on the back as we navigated through the bodies.

My attention skimmed over all the faces. Then, Caroline.

I watched as she mingled, her blonde hair bouncing as she was in motion. The tank top and shorts she was wearing hugged her in all the right places. Had she always been this beautiful? Or was I just seeing her differently lately?

I leaned against the wall, taking a sip of my drink, my gaze tethered to her every move as she laughed with her friends—and that's when it happened. Some guy slid up beside her. His hand found her waist—an annoying gesture that almost broke my composure. He whispered something in her ear, and she pulled away slightly, looking uncomfortable. Something inside me twisted. He didn't move, didn't take the hint.

Pushing off from the wall, I set my glass down on the table, harder than intended.

"Be right back," I told the guys. They barely glanced up from their conversation. With an eerie calmness, I approached Caroline, determined to cut in before I came to my senses.

"Leave." My voice was low and lethal as I closed the distance between us. The guy still had his hands on Caroline, but the moment he heard me, he stiffened. His steps faltered, eyes going wide as recognition dawned.

"Shit—Reese, man, I-I'm so sorry," he stammered, hands flying up in surrender. He backed away fast, like my words had shoved him straight into whatever hole he'd crawled out of.

"What the hell are you doing?" Caroline angrily whispered.

"What's it look like?" I shot back, barely sparing her a glance.

She folded her arms, eyes blazing. "Like you still don't get that I can take care of myself."

I exhaled, leveling her with a look. "I'm not half-assing this, Caroline. If I'm playing the role of your fake boyfriend, I'm doing it my way—take it or leave it. I told you before, when I do something, I go all in."

"Come with me," Caroline demanded, her fingers latching onto mine. She tugged me away from the party, away from prying eyes. Her friends watched us leave, their expressions full of surprise and speculation. Their stares clung to me, but I couldn't care less.

She pulled me into a secluded bedroom. The door clicked shut behind us, shutting out everyone else. The room was dimly lit by the soft glow of a bedside lamp.

"Reese, you can't do that," she breathed heavily. "What if our friends saw that?"

I didn't hesitate. "I don't care."

I stepped closer, closing the space between us. Her scent

wrapped around me—something soft, like daisies or wildflowers. But there was nothing soft about the way my pulse pounded.

"I only care what you think," I said honestly, my voice low, steady.

She turned, her eyes wide and incredulous. "Why? We hate each other?"

"Do we?"

"Obviously," she said, her voice a whisper. Her hand felt small and defiant in mine as I drew her closer to me.

"You sure about that?" My voice came out raw, edged with vulnerability I hadn't meant to show. I searched her face for signs, reading the flicker of doubt in those icy blue eyes that were becoming my undoing. "Because I don't hate you."

I knew what was happening with me. The more I was around her, the more I wanted her. Every glance, each intentional touch under false pretenses, had built up something undeniable—something I couldn't ignore anymore. Caroline liked to pretend she was unreadable, but she wasn't as untouchable as she thought. Beneath that cool indifference, I caught glimpses of something real—something waiting to break through.

"Reese," she started, lips parted slightly, a silent struggle written all over her face. "If you know something I don't, then please, enlighten me."

Her grip on my hand tightened, like she was cracking ever so slightly.

"Caroline," I murmured, leaning in so close that our foreheads nearly touched. I could feel her uneven breaths against my skin, see the flicker of conflict. "I think deep down, you know exactly what's happening."

"Reese," she whispered, her voice cracking, "I don't..."

"Shh," I soothed, placing a finger gently over her lips. "Don't try to deny it. The way you look at me when you think I'm not watching, your laugh when it's real and unhinged, the heat in your cheeks right now. You want me. And I'm fighting it just as hard because I want you, too."

For a moment, the world seemed to stop spinning, and all that existed was the two of us. No raging party just on the other side of the door.

"Even if that were true," Caroline said softly, "this can't go anywhere. Are you tempting at times? Maybe... but that changes nothing." She paused, her breath hitching slightly as if admitting this was the last thing she wanted.

"Tell me," I murmured, my tone low and dangerous, "how tempting am I?"

She hesitated for a second—maybe two. Then her lips parted into a small smile. "Not that tempting," she breathed, a lie so blatant it was almost endearing. "Just sort of." Her teeth caught her lower lip, holding it prisoner for a brief, heart-stopping moment before releasing it. "It doesn't mean I hate you any less."

My fingers brushed through her hair as I firmly pulled it away to expose her neck.

"Chaos," I whispered against the warmth of her collarbone, pressing a kiss there, feeling her pulse race under the pressure of my mouth. "We both know you don't hate me."

A shiver ran through her, either from my words or the touch of my lips, I couldn't tell. And then she looked up at me, her eyes two blue flames flickering with the small sliver of defiance she had left.

"Then you don't know me," she said with a shaky breath.

But oh, how little she understood. I was beginning to read her like my favorite book. Each breath she took was a sentence; every glance told me exactly what I needed to know.

"Are you wet for me right now?" I drew out the question, the words covered in an intimacy that neither of us could deny. "Are you fucking soaking?"

She drew in a breath, steady and controlled, but I could see the faint tremble in her posture.

"Not at all," she said, lip caught between her teeth.

I let out a low chuckle, pushing this just enough to shove her over the edge. "Why is it so damn hard for you to admit the truth? Just tell me the truth. If you want me to walk away, if you really feel nothing... then say it. End this."

She took a step back. The silence stretched between us, thick and charged, but I didn't back down. I searched her eyes, daring her, my voice rough with something real. "I can take it. I'm a big fucking boy." Yes, I was challenging her, begging her at this point—hell, maybe both. Because I might be wrong about everything, but I'd been as clear as I could be with her. "Maybe I'll even just do the wedding—"

I didn't get the chance to finish.

Because Caroline snapped.

One second she was standing there, rigid, battling whatever war raged inside her. The next, she was gone—no, not gone—moving, colliding, breaking. She launched herself at me, her hands fisting into my shirt, her lips crashing into mine like she was done fighting, done pretending, done holding back.

Her legs wrapped around my waist, locking behind my back with sudden, uncontrollable force. My arms wrapped around her instinctively, holding her tight as our mouths collided in an explosive kiss that was both electric and intoxicating. My hands gripped her tight ass, feeling the soft flesh give beneath my fingers. She tasted so sweet, like candy. And fuck, she was needy. I could feel it in every inch of her body as she grinded herself against me. It was a collision of everything we'd been holding back, this long-awaited release that had been building between us for what felt like fucking eternity.

Her heart pounded against my chest as I pushed her against the wall and used one hand to support us both. A picture frame rattled next to us before it crashed to the floor. Her high heels followed, slipping from her feet and thudding onto the carpet. Each movement between us was more desperate than the last, like we were both drowning and only the other could offer the air to breathe. Her fingers tangled in my hair, legs tightened around my waist, pulling me closer, deeper. I obliged without hesitation, my hands roaming across her back, tracing those curves that had taunted me for far too long.

Then, as abruptly as it began, she paused with a sudden release of my lips. Our foreheads remained together.

"I shouldn't have done that," she breathed. I released her and she turned and walked into the connected bathroom.

"Caroline," I called softly, following her into the dimly lit area. "Why are you fighting this so badly?"

She stood with her back to me in front of the mirror. Her hands moved to her hair, fingers combing through the blonde strands, trying to smooth out the evidence of what just happened.

I edged closer, watching the rise and fall of her shoulders with each breath she took. I reached out, hesitating for just a fraction of a second before my hand found the bend of her elbow.

"Let me in," I murmured, my voice barely above a whisper.

She didn't turn, but her reflection met mine in the mirror. Those striking blue eyes, now stormy, were filled with thoughts she wasn't ready to voice. I could feel the heat radiating from where my fingers grazed her skin.

Then in a raw, almost wounded whisper she asked, "How can I trust you, Reese?"

I could have laughed—should have, maybe—at the irony. Trust was something I didn't have much of myself, and here she was, demanding it from me. Her gaze didn't waver in the mirror, challenging, expectant, maybe almost lost.

"Because," I started, "I know you feel what I feel." I stepped closer. I let my lips graze her exposed shoulder, tender and possessive all at once. She leaned into me then, the last of her resistance melting away. Our eyes met—heavy, unguarded, filled with everything we weren't saying. That look said it all.

I had my answer. And hopefully she had hers too.

"Trust this," I whispered against her skin.

"This is so wrong," she exhaled, spinning around.

I reached out, fingers gentle but insistent, tilting her chin upward. "How can it be wrong when it feels so good?"

I wrapped one arm around her waist to pull her into me, while the other slid up the smooth expanse of her back under her shirt. A soft moan escaped her as my fingers traced the contours of her back, the sound reverberating through me like the sweetest music.

Any remaining resistance evaporated like mist in the heat of our embrace, and I felt her fingers slide under my shirt, tracing the lines of my abs. In that small, secluded room, nothing else mattered. There was an undeniable rightness in the wrong we were committing, and I lost myself in the taste of her lips and the feel of her against me.

And then, as if reality had decided to crash through the walls we'd just built around ourselves, the bathroom door swung open with a resounding thud. Time stopped as Caroline and I turned in unison toward the intrusion.

Boston stood there, his eyes wide, mirroring the shock that rippled through us. Beside him, Chandler's gaze darted between us in disbelief.

nineteen

CAROLINE

"Damnit," Reese muttered, raking a hand through his dark hair as he shifted uncomfortably, trying to regain some semblance of composure.

That was humiliating. I covered my eyes, horrified, the heat from the intensity of the moment lingering on my skin. "I knew I shouldn't have done that," I muffled the words into my palms. "They already hate me, now they're really going to hate me."

Reese exhaled, a sound caught somewhere between frustration and reassurance. "It's fine," he said, his voice low and surprisingly steady. His glowing eyes locked onto mine as I dared to peek through my fingers. "Boston and Chandler are together now. Why would they care?"

His casual dismissal was meant to comfort me, but he didn't sound as confident as he usually did. Even so, there was something in the way he held my gaze that told me no matter the fallout, we were in this together.

"I was with Boston last summer, who is your brother, and you were with Chandler. None of this is fine," I whispered. With trembling hands, I smoothed down the fabric of my tank top before I twisted the door handle. Recently, it seemed like there had been this subtle shift between Boston and Reese, like they were just starting to move in a good direction. Did this just ruin the progress they were making?

And then there was the kiss that was still tingling my lips. The incendiary, mind-blowing kiss that had my entire body on fire. It was more than just a kiss; it was that moment of pure, unfiltered passion that I knew people spent a lifetime chasing.

As I treaded the dimly lit hallway, I could hear the whispers, see the judgment in their eyes. Chandler and Boston were in the middle of it all, their heads close together, all eyes on me as I approached. A knot had formed in my stomach as heat crept up my neck, spreading across my cheeks. I felt exposed under the harsh, unforgiving light of scrutiny. Chandler's lips moved in conversation, and I couldn't hear her, but the message was clear—I was the topic of the hour, another joke to everyone here.

I was frozen to the spot, a deer caught in the headlights of their mocking amusement. Then Reese approached. The whispers ceased the moment his arm draped across my shoulders, possessive and protective all at once, like a silent declaration that dared anyone to try him.

"If anyone's got something to say, now's your chance," Reese growled, his voice dark and dangerous. He intimidated everyone just as effectively as he commanded my racing pulse. He scanned the crowd, daring anyone to step forward. No one moved; not a single pair of eyes met his.

At that moment, I realized how the room held its breath. The power Reese wielded was not just in his status, or being the star pitcher—it was in the certainty that he wouldn't back down to anyone. I knew he was trying to defend me, but I still felt the scrutiny and the accusations.

The crowd slowly shifted back into normalcy. I caught Willow's voice, trying to lighten the mood.

"Am I the only one who hasn't hooked up in my own bathroom?" she said, opening her fridge and grabbing a can.

"Well, baby girl, you're in luck," Parker quipped. "I'm willing to be the man who steps up to take that bullet."

Willow gave Parker a playful shove. "How honorable," she tossed back at him. "You're practically a knight in shining armor."

Their lighthearted exchange loosened a tightness in my chest, which I hadn't noticed until it eased. I turned to Reese, the press of his arm a reminder that I wasn't alone in this fishbowl. "I have to get out of here," I murmured, my voice barely a whisper.

I passed the threshold of the front door and kept walking. My house was a ten minute walk, perfect for clearing my head,

"Where are you going?" Reese yelled.

"Out of here," I tossed back, not slowing my pace. I needed space, air that wasn't thick with tension and the lingering confusion.

"You're walking?"

I glanced over my shoulder. "No. I'm taking the spaceship."

A chuckle escaped him. It was a dangerous thing, that laugh—a reminder of how easily Reese could make you melt. With his charm, his annoying good looks, and that laugh.

"Are you being funny right now?" Reese questioned. "Is there actually a sense of humor in there?"

I stopped dead in my tracks, turning on my heel, allowing him to see the frustration on my face. "Why are you following me, Reese?"

"I'm walking you home... or at least to your spaceship," he said, matter-of-factly.

"Fine." I relented. "But the second you do that eye thing you do, you need to turn around and go back."

Reese chuckled again. "What eye thing?" he asked, feigning innocence.

"You know exactly what eye thing you do," I said. It was more than his gaze—it was the intensity behind it, a fire that seemed to burn behind them. "The one that tells me all the dirty thoughts you're having."

"Okay, no eye thing," he agreed. "But are you okay?" he asked, his tone more serious now.

I swallowed the knot of emotions lodged in my throat and managed to murmur, "I don't know."

There was truth in those three words—a confession of confusion, an admission that despite how others saw me, I did have feelings deep down. "I know I seem like I don't care what any of them think, but I do."

Reese's eyes narrowed slightly, his gaze probing. "Why? You don't even like them."

"That's not true," I said, my voice steadier than I felt. "I just don't let a lot of people get close to me. I prefer it that way."

That was something I rarely acknowledged, let alone shared. I was Caroline Matthews—untouchable, unbreakable—yet here I stood, moments away from shattering the illusion I'd worked so hard to portray.

"Yeah, I noticed," he drawled. "Why is that?"

"It's just easier," I murmured. "People can disappoint you when you let them get too close or expect too much."

There was a pause, a moment stretched thin as if the world itself were waiting for his response. Then, in a voice that rumbled through the stillness like distant thunder, he said, "People can disappoint you no matter what."

I wasn't just thinking about the people here in Bayside. No, it was him too—Reese Carrington. If I allowed him to get too close, if I allowed his magnetism to draw me in... he had the power to devastate me, utterly and completely. Like he had in the past.

"Keeping them at a distance means it doesn't hurt as bad," I said aloud.

Reese didn't reply immediately, but when he did, there was something new in the calmness of his voice. "Maybe so," he finally said. "And maybe some people are worth taking that risk for."

"I don't know, but I do know we can't let what happened tonight happen again," I found myself saying, knowing I was shifting the topic.

"Come on, Caroline," Reese said, putting his hands in his pockets. "I know you liked it. You were the one who kissed me in there."

I was desperately trying to push that fact into the shadows. The sensation of his lips against mine lingered, a permanent imprint that refused to fade with the darkness around us. I touched my lips involuntarily, the memory igniting a warmth that spread through my chest and settled deep in my belly.

"Can you not be cocky right now? I'm in a very sensitive state." My attempt to deflect was sad, and I knew it. Reese had this infuriating way of stripping down my defenses, leaving me feeling exposed.

Reese's smirk lingered in the half-light. "Sorry," he said with a tilt of his head, miming the action of shoving something into his pocket. "I'll tuck that away for now."

I rolled my eyes at him, well aware of how cheesy that was. Even if I did like it—and god, every cell in my body screamed that I did—it was wrong on a myriad of levels. "Even if I liked it, and if I did, it's probably because it's been way too long since I have hooked up with anyone."

"Use me then, Chaos," he said, a rough whisper that sent shivers down my spine.

Use him? I swallowed hard, unable to think or respond. And despite myself, despite every rational thought that screamed *caution!*, I couldn't shake the image of his hands—those strong, assured hands that were all over me—the way he clenched his jaw and looked down at me.

"Think about it—it's perfect. Your family thinks we're together, the whole party probably does now, too." He let the moment stretch. "So why not make the most of it? Use me to take that ache away. I know you want to."

"Use you?"

Reese stood there, effortlessly commanding the space around us.

"I'm happily volunteering," he said, his voice low and smooth. He leaned in, just enough for me to smell that delicious scent of his. "Until the wedding, I'm all yours—boyfriend, fuck buddy, whatever you want me to be."

My steps faltered on the quiet street. Each word unfurled within me, painting images that should have been blurred by doubt but instead made my knees weak. For some reason—no, for *every* reason—what he offered sounded incredible. My mind reeled at the thought of taking what he presented so freely. I wanted him more than I wanted to admit.

"Fuck buddy," I whispered to myself, letting the idea wash over me in waves.

"Just sleep on it, let me know," Reese said, his tone casual like he was offering me snacks.

I turned on my heel, the gravel beneath my feet crunching like static as we approached my home—a sanctuary that felt too small to contain the breadth of my thoughts. "How are you getting home?"

Reese gestured behind us, and I glanced back to find a sleek black SUV idling at the curb. It was the same SUV that usually drove his dad around town, and sometimes picked and dropped Reese off.

"You had your driver following us this whole time? We didn't have to walk?"

A smirk tugged at his lips, easing the sharp edge of his jaw.

"What fun would that be?"

I let out a huff as I marched toward my house. The staccato beat of my heels on the concrete punctuated the silence.

"Hey, you going to Taillight Tapout tomorrow?" Reese yelled after me.

"Only if you aren't," I yelled back, not bothering to look at him.

"See you there," he called out, the amusement clear in his tone. I didn't need to look to know he was smiling that half-cocked grin that threatened to unravel me.

twenty

REESE

My truck rolled slowly through the field of people and other trucks when I arrived. I slid out, opened my tailgate and grabbed a beer from my cooler. Taking a seat, my gaze skimmed over the crowd as I watched the pre-show rituals. Country music played through speakers, and laughter echoed through the field.

Crew ran over and took a seat next to me, already with a beer in hand. He flicked a glance toward the assembling crowd. "So, who's your money on for snatching up the crown this year?"

"Couldn't tell you," I shrugged. "Just here to watch it all go down." And we knew the first match would begin any minute as the last rays of sunlight began to fade. Taillight Tapout was one of my favorite rituals. Drunk men wrestle, we drink beer out of our tailgates, and women dance. What else could you ask for?

Bailey pulled in and parked next to me, settling in. And just when I didn't expect it, Caroline came into view. The fading light framed her as she stepped out of the passenger seat of Sam's car, almost making her glow. My eyes were drawn to her rhinestone-studded cowgirl boots and the way her hips swayed in those perfectly fitted denim shorts—almost like there was no one in the world that could fit into them the way she did. The top she wore hugged her curves, and I took a long sip, trying to process the sight of her. She was stunning, and it made my mind incapable of forming coherent thoughts. In all the years I'd known her, I had never truly realized how beautiful she was.

I tried to keep my breathing steady as she embraced her friends, fighting off a smile on my own face as she laughed. Without my approval, heat seemed to be traveling south from her presence.

"Reese, you alright there, man?" Crew nudged me, but his voice sounded miles away. I nodded absentmindedly, my attention still clinging to Caroline as she brushed strands of blonde hair out of her face.

"Damn, Reese," Bailey added "You've got that look on your face —It's the same way I look at pizza. It's adorable, really... but spill it. Who the fuck are you looking at like that?" Both of them narrowed their eyes trying to figure it out.

"No idea what you're talking about," I smirked, my focus unwavering. Each pull from my beer was an attempt to quench a thirst that had nothing to do with dehydration.

"Can I get your attention, please?" A loud, deep voice grabbed our attention. He stood in the center. "Let the annual Tail Light Tapout begin," he bellowed. "Last man standing at the end of the night will be crowned Taillight King."

Excitement crackled through the field with hollers and cheers as two girls strutted into the circle. They wore tiny outfits, almost like swimsuits. They hoisted signs above their heads with the names of the first contenders.

"First up is Hunter the Havoc against The Angry Ben-ver!" the announcer added. The wrestlers entered the middle. Bodies clashed with grunts and thuds beneath the stars. Parker and Bailey surged closer to the chaos, but I stayed back watching, detached but still somewhat entertained.

Then I noticed Caroline again as she hurried past me, on her way to speak to a group of her friends parked on the other side of Bailey's truck.

"Nice boots," I drawled, leaning casually against the tailgate, unable to resist getting her attention.

She barely spared me a glance, her long blonde hair swaying with every step. "Thanks," she called over her shoulder, sharp but teasing. "But not sure they'd fit you."

"Probably not," I shot back, flashing her a dimple with no remorse. "But they do wonders for your legs."

That earned me an unamused look from her. With a can gripped tight in her hand, she turned away, dismissing me. The wrestling match continued as one opponent finally wiggled free from a head-lock. It was then I noticed a sign girl darting between the spectators, making a beeline for Caroline and her entourage.

"Hey!" I heard the girl call out, breathless, her hands gesturing wildly. "So sorry, I have to go, but you got this, girl!"

Caroline reluctantly took the sign into her hands with an eye roll. Shaking her head slightly, as if to clear it of doubts or annoyances, she stepped forward, shoulders held high as she made her way toward all the attention. When she got close to the ring, I saw her pull up her tank top and tie it up to show off more of her slender stomach.

The crowd's anticipation hung thick in the air as the dust settled from the last match. Caroline, sign in hand, made her way to the middle of the makeshift ring, not one trace of nervousness showing on her face.

Bailey and crew shuffled back, reclaiming their spots on my tail-gate. And then Bailey's gaze locked onto Caroline.

"Holy shit, is that Caroline?" he gasped, squinting against the fading light. "I know she's evil, but she's kinda hot."

Crew leaned forward, elbows on knees, and nodded slowly, as if seeing her for the first time. "I guess I never realized she had a body like that."

A grunt escaped me before I even realized it. "Can we not talk about her like that?"

They both turned their heads at me, confusion written all over their faces. Something slowly shifted in Bailey's expression. "Wait a minute," he drawled, "Is Caroline who you were just foaming at the mouth over? Was she the bathroom hookup that Parker was talking about? He said something about you and some witch but I figured Blair had trapped you in a bathroom again."

I reached for my beer, and took a long sip, buying time I didn't have. "I wouldn't say foaming at the mouth... and possibly."

"Are you serious, dude? Are you into Caroline?" Crew asked, incredulous. I wasn't ready to dissect this subject, especially under their scrutiny. "You don't even like blondes."

"Does it matter?" I said quietly, almost to myself. Caroline was fiery, outspoken, complicated, but a challenge I never knew I craved. My gaze lingered on her as she stood poised at the edge of the ring.

Bailey snorted, his disbelief clear. "Wasn't she hooking up with your brother last summer? And—did I forget to mention—she's evil?" He threw his hands up. "But hey, Blair was evil too, so maybe that's just your type, Reese."

A smirk formed at the corner of my mouth, but it lacked any real humor. "And what if every girl judged you based on your past, Bails?" My eyes met his, unflinching. "You'd end up alone."

"Okay, but that's different," he shot back with a dismissive wave of his hand. "My personality makes up for all the bad things."

I let out a low chuckle, knowing full well that his personality was as much a shield as my own sarcasm. Bailey had a tough upbringing, but he covered it up with humor. We were two sides of the same coin —both hiding our scars, both pretending the past wasn't beginning to catch up with us. But tonight, for reasons I couldn't fully articulate, I felt drawn to her, almost like I needed to protect Caroline.

"Maybe there's a side of her you haven't seen yet," I said, before tilting back my drink and finishing it.

"Yeah, alright. Can't wait to see how this plays out," Bailey said sarcastically, but there was a slight hint of curiosity on his face, like he was beginning to piece together where my mind had been lately.

"We all know I think every woman deserves love," Crew added, breaking into our standoff. "Maybe she just needs someone like Reese to make her less... evil." Crew's statement, innocent as it might have seemed, maybe had some truth to it.

As I watched Caroline holding the cardboard sign up, I couldn't help but wonder about all the mysteries she kept hidden beneath her cold, hard surface. In the shifting shadows cast by the trucks' headlights, her presence was a flame, and I was undeniably drawn to it.

Cheering and shouts from the crowd grew louder, but it was the sharp, punctuating whistles at Caroline that got my attention. Each one sent anger coursing through my veins. I popped open another beer and sipped, the liquid barely registering as I watched her work the crowd, making every head turn. She didn't seem bothered. Instead, she was almost uninterested in the attention. But for me, each whistle felt like a personal attack, an unwelcome claim, and I fought the urge to rise and confront the assholes objectifying her.

Bailey and Crew were focused on the match. The circle constricted, headlights bathing the two wrestlers currently knotted like a pretzel in the spotlight. Bear, "the Bulldozer" was announced the winner after the final match. Around me, engines rumbled to life. Some trucks pulled out, eager to leave. Others lingered, caught up in conversation as they packed up.

I glanced back to check on Caroline, who had two shadows trailing after her. My jaw tightened, anger simmering beneath the surface like a storm as I watched these men closing in on her. With a quick motion, I slammed my truck's tailgate shut, and strode toward her.

"Hey, we're just asking what you're doing after this," one of the men said.

"Actually," I drawled, blocking them from her, "she's going home with me."

Their heads snapped up, and recognition flickered on their faces.

"Shit, Reese, we're so sorry, man. We had no idea she was your girl," one stammered, his voice cracking.

I stared him down, letting the silence stretch. "Well, now you do." I finally broke it.

"We didn't know. No disrespect, man." They backpedaled, tripping over their words. I watched them go, feeling the weight of Caroline's gaze on me. I waited until they were out of sight before I turned to her.

"Not this again," she said, almost disappointed. "We're not around my family. You don't have to pretend. I could have handled that."

"I know you can handle it," I admitted, because I knew the wrath she could unleash. "But you shouldn't have to."

We began to navigate through the parked vehicles, taillights flickering all around us.

"Seriously, Reese," Caroline gave me an irritated look. "I can take care of myself, you know. You don't need to act like some... territorial alpha male who is about to pee on me to prove a point. We're not even really dating."

"I was just looking out for you. Those creeps were about to—"

"About to what?" she interrupted, cutting off my sentence. "Reese, I have a knife in my boot and pepper spray in my purse. Always."

I always knew she was strong and fierce, knew about her faithful independence. But despite her preparedness, I couldn't shake the primal urge to protect her. It was infuriating, this need that swelled within me, unwarranted and unasked for.

"Think of it this way—you've got one more weapon. Me."

She didn't respond immediately, instead she drifted over to lean on the side of my truck, resting the back of one boot against my tire. It was a casual move, too casual, as if trying to shake off the intensity that had built up between us.

"I don't need you for that. You use that power, wealth, and even strength of yours to get whatever you want, Reese," Caroline looked away. Her voice was softer now but still held an edge. "But don't use it for me, that's the last thing I want."

I stayed silent just watching her, taking in the gentle rise and fall of her chest, the way the moonlight played on the strands of her hair, turning them silver. She knew who I was, what I could do, but she didn't care. I could buy anything I wanted, command attention with a snap of my fingers, but here, with her, none of that mattered. Here, with her, I was just me—flawed, reckless, and inexplicably drawn to the fire that burned in her eyes.

I leaned closer, the metal of the truck cool against my palm as I rested it above her, caging her in. "You have no idea the things I'd do to give you whatever you want." My voice dropped to a husky whisper.

Her breathing hitched, almost imperceptible, but I caught it—an intimate tell that betrayed her composure.

"We both know you don't really care about what I want," she shot back. "You just care about you."

"Is that what you think?" I asked, but she said nothing, so I continued. "Tell me then, Caroline," I whispered, leaning in so that our breaths mingled, so that our bodies were almost touching. "What do you want?"

"A lot of things," she breathed. The heat of her gaze flickered between my eyes and lips. "But nothing you can give me."

I wasn't entirely certain what she meant by that statement, but all I could hope was that I was somewhere on that list of hers and that she wanted me just as bad as I wanted her.

"You'd be surprised at the things I can make happen," I said, my gaze dropping to the hem of her jean shorts as my fingers traced the edge, brushing lightly, just enough to tease out a shiver that raised goosebumps along her sun-kissed skin.

"Oh, I've noticed what you can make happen," she forced the words out between quick shaky breaths.

"Well, I noticed you tonight," I confessed, my finger tracing a slow, invisible path lower—just short of danger. "In these shorts, in these boots... you had my full attention."

She swallowed hard, but her voice stayed steady and defiant. "Maybe I'm not interested in having your attention."

A slow smirk tugged at my lips as I leaned in closer, my voice dark with desire. "Oh, you are. And you have it. Because all night, all I could think about was peeling this outfit off of you, leaving nothing on but those damn boots."

"Why do you have to say shit like that?" she whispered, like she was genuinely trying to understand.

My hand hovered, barely brushing the curve of her thigh. "Because it's true." I pulled back just enough to meet her eyes, wanting her to feel every word. "You're not just the kind of beautiful that turns heads. You're the kind that lingers—the kind that gets under my skin, stays in my thoughts, and makes forgetting it impossible."

The breeze pushed a strand of hair across her face. Without thought, my fingers reached up, tucking it behind her ear, lingering against the warmth of her skin. I cradled her cheek tenderly, thumb brushing ever so softly. Her eyes fluttered as she began to close the space between us.

"Caroline, are you ready to go?" Sam's voice interrupted.

Painfully, I retracted, stepping back as Caroline shifted away, her body untangling from under me. "Um, no, I'm okay," she stammered, glancing at Sam before her eyes found mine again. "I'll get a ride home."

Sam's scrutinizing gaze slid between us, searching Caroline's expression for any hint of doubt. "Are you sure?"

"Yeah, all good," Caroline assured her, her voice finding its usual firmness.

"Okay," Sam relented with a nod, then added, "You killed it out there tonight." Her praise was genuine, but her attention flipped back to me, a pointed look sharpening her features. "And seriously, text me when you're home safe."

"I will... promise," Caroline tossed back with a smile.

Sam looked suspicious but she seemed to accept the claim, turning back to Caroline with an affectionate squeeze of her arm before disappearing around the corner.

twenty-one

CAROLINE

"No parties tonight?" I asked, leaning against Reese's kitchen counter, arms crossed, as he walked around with his usual cocky swagger.

He flashed that roguish grin. "Girl, I am the party."

I rolled my eyes but couldn't stop a hint of a smile. "You're something, alright."

He rested both palms on the countertop, leaning toward me. "Wanna go for a swim?"

I raised an eyebrow. "Right now?"

"Why not?" He held my gaze, and a spark of electricity jolted between us.

I looked away, trying to act cool. "Is this some plan to get me out of my clothes?"

"Is it working?" he joked, his voice dropping lower. Against my better judgment, my pulse quickened.

I scoffed, hoping he couldn't hear the catch in my throat. "Not one bit."

Reese laughed, a rich sound that sent a shiver down my spine.

Without another word, he turned and slid open the patio door. I sighed, following him into the backyard.

He strode ahead with easy confidence, the moonlight dancing over his broad shoulders. When he reached the pool's edge, he stripped off his T-shirt in one smooth motion. I swallowed hard at the sight of him. His tan skin seemed to glow, the hard planes of his chest interrupted only by the pendant necklace that hung around his neck.

Reese turned, catching me staring. Something dangerous flashed in his eyes. "Get in with your clothes on if you want."

Before I could react, he leapt into the water with a powerful dive. I jumped back as droplets spattered my legs. When he surfaced, he flung his wet hair back and grinned.

"Come on, Chaos. Live a little."

Throwing caution to the wind, I quickly peeled off my top and shorts. The night air raised goosebumps on my bare skin. I caught Reese's gaze lingering on me out of the corner of my eye, almost as if he was devouring every inch of me.

I dove in. The warm water felt amazing, because of course he had a heated pool. When I came up for air, Reese was treading water nearby, his eyes burning into mine. My heart pounded as he drifted closer.

"Knew you couldn't resist taking off your clothes for me," he murmured.

I tossed my hair back defiantly. "Don't flatter yourself. This is basically a swimsuit." My fingers grazed his arm beneath the water. Maybe he was right, though. He was alluring, and hard to resist, but I would put up a fight first. With a flick of my wrist, I sent water hurtling towards Reese. It cut through the air, splattering satisfyingly against his chest.

"Was that really necessary?" he asked, his eyes a stormy green as they met mine.

"Absolutely," I replied, with a small smile.

We splashed back and forth, laughter mixing with him chasing me around the pool. The night was calm, stars were twinkling above. But as I paused, catching my breath, Reese's gaze softened, and he faltered, water dripping from his hair.

"Tell me about that horseshoe tattoo on your hip," Reese said. The low drawl of his voice almost made me nervous. His rough thumb brushed over the inked horseshoe on my hip. A shiver raced across my skin, raising goosebumps. I could feel every single one of them come alive.

"I'd tell you," I began, my lips curving into a smile. "But then, I'd have to kill you."

"That looks good on you," he said, disarmingly earnest.

"What? The tattoo?"

"Yes," he said, his voice husky. "But I was talking about your smile."

"Why do you always have to ruin the moment?" I countered, trying to deflect, to regain some semblance of control over the erratic pace of my heartbeat.

"Why are you always so bad at taking compliments?" he shot back.

I settled onto the lowest step inside the pool. "Because I never get them," I admitted, staring at the ripples expanding outward from where my hands played in the water. "So when I do, it feels... awkward."

"What do you mean you never get them? You're fucking stunning."

I glanced at him. "I mean, my family doesn't compliment me, and the only guys who hit on me are usually drunk. I never even know if they can see straight."

Then, Reese moved closer, his dimple flashed—that perfect indentation that could tilt the world off its axis. "Maybe guys are scared of you because you walk around with all those weapons," he teased.

"Can never be too safe."

"Guess that's true," he replied with a small shrug.

I splashed a bit of water his way, grinning. "So tell me something about you."

He tilted his head, a curious spark in his eyes. "What about me?"

I held his gaze, refusing to back down. "You're not really just a cocky jerk, are you?"

He gave a charming smile. "Oh, I am definitely a cocky jerk. You forgot arrogant and a little possessive, too."

"I'm not so sure. I'm starting to wonder if there's more to you than that," I managed unevenly. "Maybe you're not who you pretend to be."

His eyes searched mine, his expression unreadable. For a moment, I thought I saw a flicker of vulnerability, but he tossed it aside when he flashed that infuriating dimple. "And who do I pretend to be?"

"The big man on campus. The cocky jock who has it all together." I was acutely aware of his stare and his dangerously close proximity. "Maybe that's just what you want everyone to think."

Something dangerous flashed in Reese's eyes. He moved closer, his hips nearly grazing mine. I inhaled sharply, my skin prickling as I watched his every move.

"Maybe... or, maybe you're wrong, and that is who I am," he whispered, his breath hot against my cheek.

My heart hammered as he trailed a finger down my arm. I knew I should move away, but something held me in place. I arched an eyebrow, trying to ignore the way my pulse quickened at his touch. "I'm never wrong."

Reese's eyes darkened. He slowly licked his lips, sending a shiver down my spine. "Why do I get the feeling that even if you are wrong, you'd never admit it?"

I inhaled his scent—that woodsy, uniquely *him* smell as he used one knee to spread my legs slightly and moved into the space between them. His hard body pressed against me. The heat radiating from him was intoxicating. The proximity should have been a warning, but instead of pushing him away, my hands found the firm muscles of his chest, exploring the dips and ridges. "What are you doing?" I managed to say, even as my fingers continued their exploration, faltering just above the waistband of his shorts.

"Nothing," Reese's voice was a husky rasp. He dipped his head until his lips nearly grazed my ear. "Ball is in your court, remember?"

I tried, God knew I'd tried. I'd held him back, brick by stupid brick. Each encounter with him lately had been a battle of trying to keep him at bay. But here we were again, and my defenses were crumbling. It wasn't humanly possible to resist him any longer. Every instance of resistance, every moment I had fought against this —against us—flickered through my mind like a montage of defeat.

"Okay." The word emerged from my lips, almost a sigh. "But if we do this, it's only until the wedding, and then—" My voice trembled, worried about what I was getting myself into. "Then we go back to hating each other. Which means you cannot Reese and Release me until after the wedding."

His gaze dropped to my lips, and his jaw tightened. "What did you just say?"

Oops. Did he not know about that?

"You know," I said, awkwardly, "the thing women say about you? That you sleep with them, then release them and ruin them for anyone else because you're 'so amazing in bed'... or whatever. Could just be speculation though."

Reese's face cracked with that infuriating grin, one corner of his mouth higher than the other in pure, unadulterated mischief. "That rumor may be the best one I've heard yet. Remind me to tell Bailey about that one."

I raised an eyebrow playfully. "Care to confirm or deny?"

"Are you asking if I'm good in bed, Care Bear?"

"No. Asking for a friend, actually."

"Oh yeah? Who?" he asked, narrowing his eyes.

"You don't know her," I said, tilting up my chin.

His gaze held mine before he finally replied. "Well you can tell your friend that I live up to all the hype," he said, simply. "But the 'released' part? I'm not so sure. If she's the one for me, there's no way I'm letting her go."

This man was his own brand of arrogance. For some reason, his admission didn't make me feel any better, but I was past the point of caring. The boundaries of where we stood had already been defined. I could almost hear the countdown, each second ticking away to my sister's wedding—the termination of whatever "this" was. And I would have to accept it for what it was: temporary, evanescent—like a sunset, the beauty only lasting a few moments before the darkness takes over once more.

"Guess that works out perfectly then," I ventured, the words spilling out with a bravery I didn't feel. "I'm granting you the privilege to release me after my sister's wedding."

"If that's what you want, I'll let you go then. But right now?" His hands grabbed my hips, eagerly pulling me closer. "I'm not letting you go anywhere."

The way he drew out those last words sent a spike of heat straight to my core. His confidence and closeness swept away the last of my resistance. He bit down on his lip, and that look of his crushed every ounce of my self-control. Reese's green eyes locked onto mine, searching for my reaction, and I felt the air between us thicken with unspoken desire. Despite my better judgment, I couldn't look away. I wanted whatever he was about to do, and he knew it.

Then, without warning, he lowered his mouth to mine. His lips were soft and demanding as I closed my eyes to the sensation that ignited every nerve ending. I lost myself in the moment, my hands finding their way to his hair, fingers tangling in its dark strands. His muscular chest pressed against mine, and I couldn't help but arch my back to feel more of him. I was desperate to feel how hard he was against me.

Our kiss deepened, and I breathed him in, every inhale even more addicting than the last. It was as if I'd been craving this moment for years, and now that it was here, I couldn't get enough. His hands roamed my body, leaving a trail of fire as they explored, but somehow, it wasn't enough—I wanted more of his touch, more of him.

He pressed his heavy erection against me, rubbing it against my clit through the water. I moaned into his mouth, digging my fingers into his firm ass, my body needing more.

"Spread your legs," he whispered, and I did as he said.

He slid his hand into my panties, and his fingers trailed through my center. I arched into him with a gasp as he plunged two fingers deep inside me. The water added an electrifying sensation to his touch, making every stroke explosive.

"Even in this water," he murmured, his fingers moving in slow, deliberate movements that made my toes curl with pleasure. "You're so fucking wet."

"That feels so good," I gasp, my voice barely above a whisper.

His mouth moved down my neck, nibbling and sucking my sensitive skin. I was lost in a haze of pleasure, my hips grinding against his hand as his long fingers curled deep to reach that delicious spot. Tension was building in my core, my pussy clenching around him as I got closer to the edge. His thumb pressed against my clit, circling faster, and I came with a cry, my body shuddering, my pussy pulsing around his fingers as he carried me through it, drawing out every last wave of pleasure as I threw my head back.

But, oh no, I wasn't done with him. My hand shot out, grabbing his wrist as he tried to pull away. "No," I whispered, my voice raw, my eyes locking with his. "Don't stop."

He smirked, his gaze dark and hungry as he leaned in, his lips brushing against my ear. "You're insatiable," he growled, his fingers slipping back inside me, deeper this time. "Should have known how fucking greedy this pussy would be."

I arched into his touch, biting back a moan. "And I should've known how filthy your mouth is," I shot back, my voice trembling as I trailed my thumb over his bottom lip.

"You have no idea, Chaos."

"Put it to good use then," I dared him.

"Careful what you wish for," he said before lowering himself under the water, kissing my hip then trailing his mouth down until his tongue replaced his thumb on my clit. I moaned, my hands tangling in his hair as he licked and sucked, his fingers fucking me in time with the rhythm of his tongue. The water paired with the pleasure was overwhelming. A wave of heat and need had me arching off the concrete steps, my thighs clamped around his head. But just as I was about to tip over the edge again, he pulled away, leaving me panting and gasping for breath as a deep, powerful voice shattered the moment. "Am I interrupting something?"

My head jerked up in a panic. Reese's father, Mr. Carrington, stood over us. He was rocking a tailored suit, his hands nonchalantly buried in his pockets.

"Just a night swim, Dad." Reese's casual dismissal of the situation didn't match the panic I was feeling. I wanted to hide. I was horrified, hoping he somehow couldn't see me.

He swam towards the pool's edge, his movements fluid as he grabbed a towel. "You know Caroline Matthews, don't you?"

"Matthews," his dad repeated, and his gaze turned to me. "Right, one of the helpers on the committee."

One of the helpers? I just happened to be the president, and the person who helped their entire season run incredibly smoothly, but what did that matter? His voice held so much judgment that, for a moment, I felt transparent under his scrutinizing gaze. An uneasy silence settled, punctuated only by the soft lapping of pool water against my skin. Reese's father remained an immovable fixture, his shadow almost growing darker as the seconds passed by.

"And what are you doing here?" Reese asked him, before handing me the towel. "Didn't expect you back this week."

"I had to meet a client tonight. Figured I'd stop by before heading back to the beach house. My client happened to mention he saw you getting coffee with Cindee." His eyes locked onto Reese, hungry for a response. "Did you meet with her?"

A muscle twitched in Reese's jaw. "Fuck, not this again," he muttered, tilting his head back—his words carried the weight of a history I could feel but not understand.

"Watch your mouth," his father snapped. "Were you there or not?"

Reese pushed himself up from the pool, water racing down his muscles that glinted in the moonlight. He sat on the edge of the pool, and his presence seemed to command the very water to hush its gentle noises. "Yes, Dad," he said. "What are you gonna do? Ground me?"

His father remained cold and unflinching at his sarcastic words. "Damnit, Reese," he responded, words sharp and final. "You will not go see her again, do you hear me? You don't give that psychotic woman the time of day."

My heart hammered in my chest, an erratic beat echoing the turmoil happening around me. I had always been a little outspoken, defiant, sassy even. And right now I felt the strong urge to defend Reese. And considering the weight of the situation, it seemed wrong not to say anything. I had to speak up.

"Shouldn't that be his choice?" I asked, gently. "I mean, she did a bad thing, but at the end of the day, he should decide if he wants to talk to her, right? It should be his decision."

Mr. Carrington's gaze snapped to me, piercing through the darkness. There was a stillness to him, an eerie calm. But then, out of the corner of my eye, I caught it—the faintest hint of a smirk on Reese's lips.

Mr. Carrington didn't acknowledge my words. "I'm making this clear right now—stay away. I'm not telling you again." He paused, his eyes flicking to me with a glint of disapproval before returning to his son. "And for fuck's sake, wear a condom tonight." With that final, biting command, he adjusted his tie—a meticulous, calculated movement—and strode out without another word.

I exhaled slowly, the tension seeping from my shoulders. Reese's laughter broke the heavy stillness as he leaned back against the edge of the pool.

"He's kind of scary," I admitted.

"I think you gave him a run for his money, talking back like that," he said, amused. "I'm usually the only one who gets away with that, but I'd pay to see you do that again."

"Why does he not want you to talk to your mom?" The words came out more bluntly than I intended. "I mean, if you don't want to talk to her, that's fine, but it should be your choice."

I'd always thought Reese had the picture-perfect life: the successful, handsome father, the beautiful stepmother who'd swept in like some kind of modern-day fairy godmother. But after seeing that interaction, I realized maybe the image I had of him wasn't all accurate.

"I can't figure it out. I know what she did was wrong, and he hates her for it..." Reese trailed off, staring into the water before him. "But he always gets defensive about it. Like I'd be betraying him if I hear her out. She doesn't seem psychotic like he says."

Reese stopped, his fingers grazing the small chain around his neck before he adjusted the pendant on it to lay flat.

"Is that from your dad?" I asked, curiously. I'd noticed that he always wore it. I could always see the chain under his shirts, even when the pendant wasn't out.

"No," he said, running a hand through his damp hair. "It belonged to my mom. It's one of the only things she left behind."

I floated there, the ripples from my movements caressing my skin while I thought about his words. I remembered the countless games where he stood on the mound, the necklace was always visible, even from the stands. For years, I'd watched him walk around this town like he owned it—reckless and untouchable. That cocky swagger of his made it clear he didn't need or want anyone's pity. But now, I could see what he carried—not just her necklace, but some sort of hope or connection to her that he was missing. Was he more hurt than he seemed deep down? Maybe baseball and the image he portrayed to everyone was what held him together—the power, the sarcasm, all a way to hide the scars of abandonment.

twenty-two

"Well, boys," Crew grunted between strained breaths, arms shaking as he held the barbell above his head, "I ended things with the twins."

Across from me, Bailey was changing the weight on the bicep machine. "Doesn't count," he said without missing a beat. "You can't date twins."

Crew was already brushing off Bailey's comment with a grin. "You can date twins, trust me," he said. "But now, I'm dating a woman who's like dating triplets."

"Does that mean she has multiple personalities?" I asked, curiously. "I think my neighbor has that."

"Nah, she's not like that," he panted, his chest heaving. "She's like the whole damn package I never knew I needed."

"Everything you need in one woman, huh?" Parker yelled, his feet pounding against the treadmill. "We'll believe it when we see it, Crew!"

"Yeah, you once told me you'd rather stick a fork in your eye than have to be stuck dating one woman," Boston yelled from the treadmill next to Parker.

"Listen up, gentlemen," Crew began, dropping the barbell on the rack. "I've been changed, snatched off the market before my very own eyes," he declared.

Disbelieving laughter rippled through the room and eventually silenced as Boston brought his treadmill to a halt. We hadn't spoken much since that day—the moment he and Chandler walked in on Caroline and me in the bathroom.

Forcing myself to follow him, I grabbed my water bottle and took a deep breath.

"Hey, Boston," I called out, and turned into the locker room.

He didn't turn right away, and I watched the tension in his shoulders. Conversations between us either went kind of okay or ended terribly.

"About the other day—" I began, treading lightly.

Boston faced me, "Reese," he sighed, the name a surrender of sorts, "let's just leave it."

"Hey," I began, unsure of how to start this conversation. "I'm meeting Cindee for dinner soon. You gonna be there?"

He grunted, rifling through his locker without looking at me. "Yeah, probably."

"Cool." I said, casually. I leaned against the cool metal of the lockers. Then, in the most unsubtle way possible, I added, "Oh, and about Caroline..."

"You don't have to explain," he said, cutting me off before I could finish.

I nodded, relief washing over me. Thank fuck, because truth be told, I didn't even know what I was going to say. He closed his locker with a decisive click, and then, as if he was forcing out the words, he continued. "Caroline is a good person deep down. I know she's not everyone's favorite person, but there's this side to her that not everyone gets to see."

"Yeah, I'm picking up on that," I said, rubbing the back of my neck.

"And I don't know if you two are actually together," he continued, "but if you are, then I support it... even though you don't need my approval."

"Are you two actually getting along?" Parker asked with amusement. He stood at the doorway, towel slung over his shoulder, his hair damp.

"For now," I replied, giving Boston a smirk. "Might be a different story tomorrow."

Bailey strode in and his gaze flickered over us. "True. Reese can go from chill to not chill in no time flat. I've seen Reese smile right before throwing a punch. Sometimes when Reese knocks people out, he acts so chill it's scary." He paused, a smirk playing across his lips. "So even if he acts cool now, I'd be prepared."

I tilted my head toward Bailey. "Shut up," I muttered.

"Anyway," Parker said, almost bored. "Some of us don't have too many nights left in town and need to make the best of it. Are you guys going to Gin & Jerry's tonight?"

"Come on," Bailey responded, "you know we'll be there."

I tapped on my phone screen and pulled up my text conversation with Caroline because, for some reason, I hadn't been able to stop thinking about her since we hung out in my pool. I should probably wait. Play it cool and hope that she shows up tonight so I get to see her... but fuck that.

ME

What are you doing tonight?

I hit send before I could stop myself. Within seconds, the typing bubble appeared.

CAROLINE

I'm busy

ME

Doing what?

CAROLINE

Tonight's my other fake boyfriend's night.
Check back tomorrow.

Other fake boyfriend? I knew she was joking, but why did the idea of her with someone else—even as a joke—piss me off?

ME

Your other fake boyfriend? Should I be jealous?

CAROLINE

I mean he does have a fake yacht

ME

And what if I have a fake private jet?

CAROLINE

Sounds promising. Does it come with a fake private chef?

ME

You're pushing it, but I can make that happen if you tell me what you're really doing tonight

CAROLINE

Going to G&J with Sam

ME

I was hoping you'd say that

CAROLINE

See you there if I'm still alive

ME

Alive?

CAROLINE

On a ladder right now

ME

On a ladder and texting me?

CAROLINE

Taking down some decorations in my committee office

ME

Need me to come spot you?

CAROLINE

Doing just fine thank you

ME

Fair. If you weren't so short you wouldn't need the ladder.

CAROLINE

And if you weren't so tall, you could fit in my car like a normal person.

CAROLINE

What are you, anyway? 5'8?

ME

Try 6'4

CAROLINE

Now you're just showing off

ME

Just happens naturally

I knew this was supposed to be fake, but nothing about the way I felt when she was around felt fake. I wasn't even trying to deny it at this point. I wanted her—not just to help my sister, not for anyone else. Just for me. Now I just had to hope she'd start to see it too.

twenty-three

CAROLINE

"She's the worst," Sam murmured, throwing her purse over her shoulder. "Your sister changes her mind every day about the wedding. She can't make up her mind about anything."

"Told you she'd be a bridezilla," I said, knowing damn well there is no way to please that woman.

"She's the worst kind," she added. "The wedding is almost here, she can't keep making changes."

"Then you're just going to have to tell her no."

"Tell her no," she repeated, and then a smile stretched across her face, and we both let out a loud snick. We knew—oh, how well we knew—that telling my sister "no" was never a word she'd ever accept.

"By the way, you forgot to text me back," she said, narrowing her eyes. "How is your concussion?"

"What concussion?" I replied, thoroughly confused.

"The one you must have to make you so confused that you were caught in a bathroom hooking up with Reese Carrington? Have you lost your mind?" She leaned in closer, her voice dropping to an angry whisper. "I thought it was strange he was taking you home from Taillight Tapout, and Kim just told me the rumor going around that you two were... in Willow's bathroom. Was that the night I left with Crew?"

The truth was clawing at the edges of my conscience. Losing my mind was a definite possibility.

"It's not what you think it is," I murmured, almost pleading with her to understand—except I didn't even understand what was going on.

"So you weren't hooking up with him?" she pressed, hand on her hip.

"Well," I began, the word slipping out as a half-sigh, "I kind of was."

I continued to walk in front of Sam, toward the front entrance of the bar. "Kind of?" she echoed behind me. "You do remember that he was the sole reason for the most humiliating day of your childhood, right?"

I could feel the weight of that memory, the painful beat of my heart when I thought about it. The shame I felt, the sting of betrayal sharp as ever when I thought of Reese's role in it all.

"Trust me, I know," I admitted. "But we were just kids back then, and it's complicated. He's a lot different than I always thought he was."

I knew she didn't believe the diminishment of my pain. It was the kind of moment that carved itself into your memories, no matter how badly you wanted to forget it. Now wasn't the time, though, and I knew I had to downplay it even though that moment still hurt when I thought back on it.

Sam leaned in, her voice rising over the tinkling glasses and chatter. "I can imagine," she whispered, her eyes scanning mine as she tried to understand. "Just be careful. We both know who he is."

As I pulled the door open, I thought about the undeniable force that Reese exerted—the magnetic feeling I had around him, the electricity between us that both thrilled and terrified me. I knew this was the same man who, as a little boy, played a role in my downfall. That moment changed me forever, and I learned how cruel the world could be. It forced me to toughen up in order to protect myself. In the end, it didn't really matter. Reese Carrington was basically dissolving before my very eyes, leaving this place—and me with it—behind soon.

"Oh, trust me, I know."

"Two vodka sodas," Sam told the bartender. As he nodded and turned away, she swiveled back to me, eyes alight with mischief and curiosity.

"Okay, now that we're over the whole 'making sure you're of right mind' thing," she started, then the corners of her mouth twisted into a knowing smirk, "can you tell me now what the heck it's like to hook up with Reese Carrington?"

"Incredible," I breathed out, the word barely more than a sigh. My mind was instantly swept up in the serious and intense expression on his face before he kissed me, the way he smelled so good I'd contemplated finding a way to steal one of his sweatshirts. And then there were his hands—those large, veiny, sexy hands. Sculpted by god knows how many years of gripping baseballs and bats. When had I ever thought hands were sexy? I was definitely losing my ever loving mind.

"His hands," I managed to add, voice trailing off as the memory threatened to swallow me whole. Sam watched me, silently observing the internal tumult her question had unleashed. She offered no words, only a faint nod, understanding immediately.

"Damn," she murmured. "I was hoping the rumors about him were all lies."

"I mean, we haven't hooked up... but we have done a few things, and from what I can tell..."

Sam's gaze shifted past my shoulder to the door, interrupting my trailing words. "Speaking of potential husbands for you," she said with a playful arch of her brow, "look who just walked in."

Wells Clark. The very notion of him as spouse material almost made me spit out my drink.

"I'd rather marry Goldilocks," I declared, flipping my hair like I was in a shampoo commercial.

"Even I can't deny the cuteness of Goldilocks, I'll give you that," she replied with a smirk. "But unfortunately, marrying an animal is outside the scope of legally recognized marriages."

"Typical," I sighed dramatically. "This country's progress is truly disappointing."

I pulled my phone from my back pocket, feeling it vibrate. "Bridezilla's calling," I murmured to Sam, a wry smile tugging at the corner of my lips as I stood up. The phone continued its insistent buzzing, demanding, just like my sister. With a resigned sigh, I slipped out the back door, finding a quiet hidden area outside.

The dim glow from the bar's windows stretched across the gravel, reaching towards the darkness that led to the alleyway.

"Caroline, have you tried on your bridesmaid dress yet?" Her voice crackled through the speaker. I leaned against a brick wall, realizing I should have never picked up her call.

"Not yet," I confessed, tracing my fingers along the rough brick. "But I'm sure it fits."

"Well, you better hope it does because there's no time to get another one. You should have made sure it fit last week," she snapped.

"It'll be fine," I said, brushing it off.

"Caroline, you're so insensitive. Can't you do even one thing right?"

"Insensitive?" I echoed with disbelief. "You're the one inconveniencing everyone by rushing this wedding."

There was silence, but I could feel the weight of her scorn. "Amazing, Caroline. So sorry my wedding is an inconvenience for you," she spat out before the line went dead,

A long exhale escaped me as I tried to shove away my annoyance.

With a flick of my wrist, I slid my phone into the sanctuary of my back pocket.

"That didn't sound good."

Startled, I spun on my heel, the soles of my boots scraping against the pavement as if trying to ground me back to reality.

Wells Clark emerged from the shadowy threshold between two buildings, his figure outlined by the weak light that spilled from an overhead street lamp.

"No, it's never good with my sister," I replied.

"Well, things don't seem too good with us either," he said, inching closer.

I crossed my arms over my chest. "What do you mean?"

"I've heard some rumors," he murmured. "Please tell me they aren't true."

"Well, depends on what those rumors are, Wells."

"Heard you're hooking up with Carrington," he said. I remembered then why I hated this small town.

"Who is saying this?" I asked, trying my best to avoid answering that question.

"It doesn't matter... but I know that can't be true because you've been leading me on for how long now?"

Did he just say leading him on? I never knew what to expect out of his mouth, but certainly not that. I never promised him anything, and didn't owe him any explanation.

"And what if I was?" The words tumbled out from my frustration.

"Then I'd say that's pretty slutty," he spat out. His eyes darkened in a way that made it seem like there was nothing behind them at all. "I've been at this for months now, and he comes out of nowhere, and you just give it up to him?"

I swallowed hard against the tightness in my throat.

"That's uncalled for. I wasn't leading you on," I told him.

"You were," Wells declared with entitlement. "I deserve something... and you're not leaving here until I get it."

"Not a chance." The words left my lips without thought, as I tried not to let him see the panic I was feeling.

His hand shot out, closing around my wrist. I winced, pulse hammering against his thumb as he leaned close. "I can make you feel so much better than he can," Wells murmured, his voice dark and twisted. "Let me show you."

I tried to pull away, but his hold only tightened, fingers branding me with his unwanted touch. A cold laugh bubbled up from the pit of my stomach, mingling with the bile of fear. "Let go of me," I demanded, the command roughened by rising fear.

He refused to release me. My free hand clawed at his grip, trying desperately to pry his fingers from my skin, but it was like fighting against iron shackles.

Suddenly, he pivoted, maneuvering me until my back collided with the brick wall. The impact sent a jolt through my body. But even that physical shock couldn't wake me from this nightmare.

"Let me show you," he grunted. "You and I both know you want this."

Desperation clawed inside me, a silent scream struggling to break free. His words slithered over me, igniting an inferno of defiance within my chest.

"Stop," I gasped, the word fractured. Wells's hand slithered up beneath the hem of my shirt. The world narrowed down to his touch, invasive and unwelcome, making me see pure red. His breath was ragged with anticipation, but then he loosened his grip just enough —a fatal mistake.

Seizing the opportunity, I drove my elbow hard into his stomach. A grunt of pain erupted from him. He staggered backwards, and the predatory gleam in his eyes was dimmed by the shock of retaliation. I spun on my heel, channeling every ounce of fury and fear. My knee connected with his balls, a statement that I refused to be his victim.

I didn't wait for him to recover. With adrenaline moving me, I sprinted back toward the bar, my heart pounding against my ribs. Each step was fueled by my desperation to find somewhere safe. The door burst open under my panicking push, and light and noise flooded over me.

I had tunnel vision as I searched through the bar until—Reese. I ran to him and hurled myself into his arms without hesitation, without thinking. He was the only sanctuary I wanted. His familiar scent enveloped me, the feeling of safety washing over and overwhelming me.

"Reese," I breathed. In his arms I found solace. He was a fierce protector encased in casual defiance. He was the only person I wanted, the only one who could make the trembling cease and give me the strength to pull myself together.

His arms wrapped around me firmly, anchoring me in his warmth. "Caroline, what happened? What's wrong?" His voice was steady and soothing, though his eyes brimmed with unspoken worry that made my chest ache.

My lips were sealed shut because what could I say? I was still in shock.

He pulled back from me, and then I saw the twitch in his clenched jaw. And oh, I knew that twitch. That one that meant he was dead serious right now.

"Caroline, what's going on? Why are you upset?" The anxious voice belonged to Sam, who was seconds away from making a scene. She approached us, her eyes wide, searching for answers.

Reese's gaze snapped to her, "You, sit," he said, glancing from her to the chair behind her. Obediently, and with surprising quickness, Sam did exactly as he said. There was something about Reese in that moment—the raw intensity, the barely contained anger—that made my heart flutter. Fuck, he was incredibly sexy when he took control.

Reese's hand clasped my shoulder, his body shielding me from prying eyes. "Talk to me," he commanded, his voice a low growl. "And don't even think about lying to me or saying you're fine."

My resolve was melting under his steady gaze. I sucked in a deep breath, an attempt to gather my scattered thoughts. But the air hitched in my lungs as the back door creaked open, and I knew exactly who it was. Wells stumbled through, his face pale. The sight of him made me feel sick again.

I glanced at him, then back at Reese, whose jaw remained locked in a hard line. His eyes briefly flicked to Wells, tracking the direction of my gaze. Then, I saw it—the question he didn't want to ask but had to.

"Was it Wells?"

I nodded, feeling the affirmation catch in my throat. The acknowledgment felt like a betrayal, to myself, to the strength I thought I possessed to always take care of myself.

His hands balled into fists at his side. "What did he do? Caroline, if he even touched one hair on your head..."

My pulse throbbed in my ears. "It's okay," I murmured, the words brittle. "I fought back. I—I stopped him."

His broad shoulders tensed briefly before he let out a slow, heavy breath, the sound laced with the weight of his restrained anger. "What do you mean you fought back?" he asked, his voice low and deliberate.

"He said he heard we were together, and he said—" my words faltered.

"He said what?" he growled, another twitch in his jaw.

"He said that he could make me feel better than you can... he held me against the wall," I confessed as quietly as I could. "I told him to stop."

"He did what?" he asked, eyes narrowing.

The green of his eyes were now dark and stormy. The floor seemed to sway slightly under me as I continued. "Then he tried to touch me," I said, closing my eyes for a moment, "but I stopped him."

Reese's reaction was silence, a nod so subtle it could have been missed by anyone not looking for it. But I saw it, a silent understanding of everything that happened.

His voice when he finally spoke was calm laced with something darker. "Can you sit with Sam for a minute?" he asked, his eyes never leaving mine.

"What are you going to do?"

He didn't answer immediately, the muscles along his jaw continued clenching and unclenching. I was seeing a new side of him. The embodiment of the night itself—mysterious, protective, and undeniably magnetic.

"I'll handle it," he promised, the quiet intensity in his words sending a shiver through me.

I reached out, my fingers grazing his arm, his sweatshirt doing little to mask the raw power that was beneath. "Don't—don't do anything," I stammered. "It was my fault. I flirted with him in the past... I gave him the wrong impression."

"Listen to me," he said, his voice firm but gentle. "This was not your fault. This is on me—he came after you because of something between him and I. You did nothing wrong, and you sure as hell didn't deserve this. Do you hear me?"

"Yes," I whispered, barely trusting my voice.

"Wait here for me," Reese said then, his hands gentle as they guided me down into the stool next to Sam.

I couldn't help but notice his stillness. It was the deceptive calmness that was almost scary, a dangerous undercurrent that ran beneath the surface of his collected exterior. But those eyes of his said it all. He was about to obliterate everything and anything in his path.

Sam's concerned gaze flickered to Reese, her lips parting as if to speak but no words came.

Reese's hand rose slowly as he pulled the hood of his sweatshirt up, letting it settle over his dark hair. With the hood casting his face into inscrutable depths, he shot someone a barely perceptible nod. Two of his teammates acknowledged with a slight dip of their heads as they fell into step beside him.

I watched, my breath held in captivity, as they made their way toward Wells. I knew Reese—he was relentless. But it was his stillness that spoke loudest. It was the calm before the storm; a chilling prelude to the damage he could do.

Wells, still pale from our earlier encounter, seemed to shrink back as they approached, his features contorting in dawning realization. He was about to face the consequences of his actions, at the wrath of a man whose protective instincts were as fierce as they were unforgiving.

Reese said something to Wells before they walked out the back door, and his teammates stood at the back entrance after them, protecting the scene like armed guards.

twenty-four

REESE

The vulnerability in her blue eyes, her flushed cheeks, her panic struck at me harder than any curveball ever could. Someone had hurt her, put tears in her eyes—by the fire that had begun to simmer in my blood, they would pay for that.

"What do you want, man?" Wells asked, shrugging like I had no reason to drag him out here.

The anger was definitely there, almost like it was living and breathing inside me. But I held it in check, my jaw so tight I could feel the throb of my pulse in my teeth.

"Round two, I guess," I said, my steps measured as I closed the distance.

Wells' eyes narrowed, uncertainty passing over his face as I moved closer. The dim light from the back door flickered across his face as the moment of realization and fear crossed him, making me grin.

"What are you doing?" he asked as I dropped the amusement in my smile and reached out, pressing him up against the back wall. My hand found his neck, fingers pressing just enough to remind him of who I was.

I could only assume one would not like this. The same way Caroline had felt when he'd done this to her. I could almost taste the rage surging forward at the thought of her—blue eyes wide and defiant but terrified. That image played in my mind.

"Easy," I whispered through gritted teeth. "Do you understand what 'no' means, Clark?"

He squirmed under the grip of my hand, his fingers clawing at my wrist in desperation as he forced out his words. "Are you talking about that bitch, Caroline?"

"Do you have a death wish? Is that what this is?" I said, trying to understand the unfathomable stupidity going on in his mind.

"If that's your girl and you let her out of the house dressed like a slut, then something is wrong with you." His eyes darted toward the bar's exit, perhaps hoping for an escape or someone to save him.

"You want to know why I'd never tell Caroline how to dress?" I grinned, slow and patient.

His breath was ragged, his eyes searching mine for mercy that he wasn't going to get. "Because," he gasped, "you have no control over her."

Control? No, this wasn't about control. It was about respecting her and whatever the fuck she wanted to wear—something Clark clearly knew nothing about. Tonight she was wearing jean shorts and a crop top. But even if she was walking around in lingerie because thats what she wanted to do, then so fucking be it.

"No," I shot back. "Because I'm not afraid to fight anyone who has something to say about it."

Wells Clark was missing brain cells, so I understood he may not get it. I shouldn't have to defend her for wearing whatever the fuck she wanted to wear, but the reality of the situation is that I do. From idiots like him.

I dropped at the last second, his fist flying through the air so close I felt the rush of wind graze my skin.

"She's just a dumb girl," he sneered. "You really wanna risk throwing away your precious baseball career over some whore you'll be over next week?"

My pulse pounded, adrenaline roaring in my veins. He had no idea—I was past the point of having a choice, and baseball was the last thing on my mind. When it came to her, I'd take on anyone. No hesitation. No second thoughts.

"You of all people..." I drawled, the back alley's dim light flickering above us, "should never call anyone else dumb... and I've been waiting for any chance to do this again—"

Before he could react, my fist connected with his jaw, a satisfying crunch that felt just as good as I thought it would. A guttural groan escaped him as he hunched over. That blow was for Caroline, for this piece of shit thinking he could just take what he wanted. His head snapped sideways, shock flaring in his eyes.

Clark's head tilted back, a scornful laugh escaping him. "Alright, Reese... I'll give you that one. But that's the only one you're getting."

Just as the words left his mouth, his fist came at me again. This time, it slammed into my ribs with a force that knocked the breath from my lungs. Pain flared, but adrenaline quickly took over.

"And after hearing what you said to her, it's going to be so much more satisfying when I beat your ass again... with the same hand that made her come last night."

A flicker of rage ignited behind his eyes, the veins in his neck popping out. He launched at me. We collided and went down hard, tangled together on impact. His fist found my cheek, a sting of pain radiating from the hit. I shoved him off as I wrestled my way back on top.

"Get off me!" he spat, voice frantic, high-pitched with rising panic.

And then, my fist connected with his nose, once, then twice. His howl tore through the night, like a wounded animal's cry. Blood splattered against my knuckles.

"That last one was for your little sister being a fuck, too."

"Fuck you," he gasped, the words barely a hiss as they slipped through his gritted teeth.

The world seemed to shrink down to just the dark back patio and the pathetic form of Wells Clark whimpering. I leaned in, a grin on my lips. "You made this way too easy, Clark," I murmured. "I expected you to fight back harder. It's just not as fun when you don't."

He didn't move, just laid there, groaning as I stood and dusted off my clothes. "And if I ever catch you near her or in that bar again," I said, leaning down so I knew he could hear my words, "you will not walk back out alive. Do you understand me?"

I reached down, my fingers tapping on Wells' jaw with an almost tender touch. "Gonna need you to repeat that back to me," I murmured, my voice low and even, "so I know you understand me."

For a second, there was nothing but the sound of our breathing. Then, the words slithered out of Wells. "Don't... come back..."

"Good boy," I said, feeling a dark satisfaction as I straightened to my full height again.

The back door burst open as Bailey's voice interrupted us, "Bro, the quarterback's teammates are getting suspicious."

"We're all done here," I sighed.

Bailey and the Crew nodded and then stepped outside, their laughter rising over Wells' pitiful groans.

Bailey snickered as he rubbed his chin. "This is even better the second time."

The back door flew open again and Wells' friends emerged, one by one. "Clark, there you are!" one called out. "Why are you lying on the ground?"

I watched their expressions shift from confusion to realization as they pieced together what had gone down.

"Are we going to have to fight tonight, too?" Crew asked, letting out a long sigh. "Do I need to finish my beer?"

"You should probably get him out of here," I said to Wells' friends. "He's not welcome back."

"This... this is the only bar in town," one of them said back.

"Find another town," I said with a shrug.

They surged forward, their movements desperate as they scrambled to lift Wells, who was still groaning. "Hey, do you want us to take them?"

Nothing could stop the snicker that escaped me from that question. They'd never be able to take us, but it might be fun to watch them try.

"No. No more fighting. Let's go," Wells gasped out, his voice barely more than a croak.

They nodded and then stumbled away, holding Wells up by his arms. "Man, what the hell happened?" they asked him, before they disappeared into the darkness.

twenty-five

CAROLINE

I traced the rim of the shot glass Sam handed me. "I can't take this anymore," I said, glancing at the back door, anxiety knotting my stomach. "It's been way too long now. What are they doing back there?"

Sam snickered and shook her head. "Wells is definitely getting his ass kicked," she said with certainty. "I would not want to be him right now."

We looked at each other, then we reached for our shots in unison. Together, we tilted our heads back, the burn carving a path down our throats as we continued to wait for that back door to open.

"Should I just go out there?" I questioned, knowing I couldn't stay seated much longer.

"They're walking in now," she said, her voice barely above a breath. "There's one, two, three..." She paused, her count trailing off into uncertainty, her eyes narrowing. "And no Wells."

"Let's go," I said, rising out of my seat.

We pushed past elbows and shoulders to get to the back of the bar. Except once I got there, it was only Crew and Bailey.

"Where's Reese?" I asked Bailey, looking around.

"Bathroom," Bailey shot back, his gaze skimming past me with disinterest.

Unease took over as I turned away to find him. The laughter faded behind me until I stopped at the men's bathroom door, hesitating for a moment before my impatience made the decision for me.

The door swung open, revealing Reese hovering over the sink, hands braced on both sides. His shoulders were hard set. A deep purple bruise was already blooming on his cheek.

"What are you doing in here?" he asked, not turning back but glancing at me in the mirror. The silence stretched between us until I stepped further into his space, the door clicking shut behind me.

I leaned against the dark wall, my gaze never leaving him. "What happened outside?" I asked, already knowing the answer, but it was the only question I could think of.

He watched himself in the mirror as shadows played across the contours of his face, making him look even more intense. "It's taken care of," he snapped.

His shoulders rose and fell with each measured breath. The room seemed to contract around us, the walls closing in, the air heavy.

"Reese," I started, my voice barely above a whisper, "you're shaking."

His hands gripped the sink tighter, knuckles whitening. "I'm good," he said, his voice rough like gravel. "I just need a second."

"Are you hurt?" I asked quietly as I stepped behind him.

He lifted his head slightly, his eyes locking onto mine in the mirror. I glimpsed a storm in them, rage contained but nowhere near completely settled. His jaw worked silently, muscles clenching and unclenching as if trying to calm his thoughts.

"No," he finally said, though it was more a dismissal of my concern than any real assurance. "He tried to fucking touch you... and do whatever else he wanted because of me. What happened to you was my fault."

Without thinking, I reached for him, my hand finding his. "Look at me," I urged as he turned toward me. "I'm fine. And you're not the reason Wells is a dick."

As I drew his hand up, guiding his palm to rest against the curve of my cheek, the roughness of his hand melted into the softness there.

"I should've been there," he said, voice low. "I should've protected you."

"I stopped him, but you... you stood up for me." I said, my heart sort of exploding. I wasn't used to anyone having my back, but for some reason, he kept doing it—over and over. Like it was the most natural thing in the world. But this time, it hit me harder than any time before.

"I'll always stand up for you," he said, stepping closer. "But knowing he tried to... do that to you? I could've killed him for thinking he had the right to touch what's mine."

"But I'm not actually yours," I stuttered, the words tumbling out with confusion. For a second, I forgot about what this was, because the feeling of being his almost felt real. A part of me wanted to believe it could be—wanted to believe happiness for me was possible. But deep down, I knew it wasn't.

"He doesn't know that," he shrugged. "But I promise you, Caroline, nothing like that will ever happen again. I feel sorry for anyone else who tries to fucking test me."

I could see the turmoil on his face, his vulnerability. It was so much different than the image of him that others saw: the confident pitcher, the untouchable bad boy. There was intimacy in his admission, like a secret, one that I wanted to keep close to my chest.

"What you did out there for me... I'm so grateful, but honestly, I don't deserve it." My voice wavered, betraying the emotions I was barely keeping in check. "Reese, you're going to do big things. You have so much ahead of you. You shouldn't be fighting anyone—not for me. No one's worth risking your future."

"Rule number one of being a fake boyfriend is always defending his girlfriend," he said, barely holding back a smirk.

"I didn't know there were rules," I replied, the corners of my mouth twitching. "I like that one... but maybe just use your words next time."

"No promises," he said. Then, the blood on Reese's knuckle drew my focus.

My own fingers trembled as they traced around the injury in the center. "Your hand," I whispered.

Reese glanced down at his hand between mine. "It's barely a cut."

Turning on the faucet, I coaxed his hand under the cold stream. The water cascaded over his knuckles, washing off some of the blood. Beneath my fingertips, I could feel the thrumming of his pulse starting to slow, the silent aftershocks of adrenaline that had been pumping through him beginning to steady.

"Really," Reese said, over the sound of running water, "it's not a big deal."

Reese's shoulders finally started to relax. The comforting smell of his cologne was wrapping around me as I sought his eyes through the reflection in the mirror. "Will you take me home?"

He turned, tucking a stray strand of hair behind my ear before draping an arm around my shoulders—his touch giving me the energy to breathe again. "Yeah, let's get outta here," he nodded.

"Call me later," I shouted to Sam as we passed by her, who was in Crew's arms.

She nodded before Reese and I made our way outside. The night air swirled around us as we stepped out into the dimly lit parking lot, leaving the distant laughter fading behind us.

"Did you beat him up badly?" I asked, breaking the silence. I hated the idea of them fighting over something that had to do with me, but still, I couldn't help but be curious about it. I was only human.

Reese paused next to the passenger side of his truck, his hand finding the door handle before he turned to face me. "Stop worrying about it. He'll be fine in a few days."

I watched as his long arm extended toward me, his calloused fingers gently guiding me inside his truck. Reese closed the door with a soft thud, and then strode around to the driver's side.

As he slid inside, I fastened my seatbelt. "Are you okay to drive?" I asked softly.

Reese shot me a sidelong glance, his green eyes glinting in the dim light of the dash. "Yeah," he said with a half-smile. "You pulled me outta there before I even had a drink."

"Couldn't let you walk around there all hurt and wounded," I teased.

"Wounded?" He chuckled, turning the key and plunging us into the night. "I've had much worse from baseball... and you should see the other guy."

I could only imagine the damage he could do, the secrets he kept tucked away. I turned my head to look at him. His confident lines were softened by the darkness. As Reese's truck turned onto my street, the familiar surroundings welcomed me. I had driven down this street countless times, but doing it with him felt different, as if even the ordinary roads in this average subdivision knew Reese belonged to another world.

As the engine died, the silence grew heavy. The only light coming from my house was the soft glow from the porch.

"Are your parents home?"

"No," I murmured, opening my door. "My sister had a dress fitting a few hours away, which apparently is so important that my mom and dad went with her."

He nodded once, a barely noticeable dip of his head before he opened his door and slid out. We walked quietly before I turned the key in the lock and pushed open my front door. Reese followed me inside and shut the door behind us.

"Wait here," I said, pressing my palm against his hard chest. "I'll be right back."

I slipped down the dark hallway that led to the main bathroom.

Rifling through the medicine cabinet and closet, I gathered some items.

I returned, finding Reese's shadow leaning against the entryway wall, staring at family photos.

"Come with me," I said, entwining our fingers as I led him up the stairs and inside my room. The door clicked shut behind us.

"Let's see that hand," I whispered. My fingers brushed his, tentative at first, then firm as I cradled his injured knuckle in my palm.

"I told you I'm fine," he said, watching me tend to the wound.

"Fine or not, I'm taking care of you."

Reese shifted, the floor creaking under his weight as I finished up. "I don't need anyone to take care of me," he said, looking around my room. "Been doing well on my own."

Everyone knew he was physically strong, and a force as an athlete. But it was in my dark, quiet bedroom that I saw his true depths. He had lost his mother at such a young age, and it forced him to toughen up. As I gazed into his troubled eyes, I couldn't help but feel a deep sense of compassion for the little boy who never got the chance to be nurtured and cared for by the one person he needed most in life.

"That may be the case, but I'm taking care of you tonight," I declared, putting my hand on my hip. "And don't even try to argue with me. You won't win."

He grinned slowly, and it did strange things to my pulse as I cleaned his wound and covered it with a band-aid. "Why are you the way that you are?"

"Because I'm a Leo," I said, playfully.

"Well that explains everything," he said sarcastically as he made himself comfortable on my bed. His eyes never wavered from mine.

"It's written in the stars, and out of my control," I murmured, closing the distance and climbing onto his lap.

His hands found their way to my thighs, staying below the hem of my shorts. Reese's gaze intensified, deepening somehow. "Remind me to call you Caro-lion instead of Care Bear from now on," he said, the quiet rasp in his voice teasing out goosebumps on my entire body.

"You can call me whatever you want," I murmured, breath brushing over his ear. "But that's all you get to do because I'm still taking care of you tonight."

Reese's expression shifted, the corner of his mouth curving up in that charmingly arrogant way. "I've never played this game before," he said, in a husky whisper. "But I'm intrigued."

"The rules are simple," I said, matching his energy with a sly grin. "I'm in control tonight. Your job is to lie back and enjoy it."

The tension between us was electric, his darkened eyes locking onto mine with an intensity that made my pulse race. "Is that what you want, baby?" he murmured, his voice a velvety growl that sent a shiver down my spine. "To be in control?"

I could barely breathe as I nodded, my voice trembling with anticipation. "Uh huh."

"Are you sure you want to do this tonight?" he asked, dragging his words out slowly.

"Uh huh," I repeated. "This is just sex. We don't need to over-think it. No feelings, nothing more."

"Uh huh," he said this time with a wicked grin. He leaned in, his lips brushing my ear as he added, "show me what you got."

My lips found Reese's in a kiss that detonated like fireworks in the quiet of my room. The familiar taste of his mint gum, how soft and tender his lips were, but still somehow so possessive. I was entranced. The way his mouth moved against mine—he was claiming me. It was addictive.

Reluctantly, I drew back, our breaths mingling, foreheads resting together. My voice, a shaky whisper, ured him in the darkness. "Lay back."

He did as he was told. This powerful man was following my directions.

A spark of desire ignited down my spine as my eyes traced over him—his athletic frame sprawled across my bed, the steady rise and fall of his chest. It was mesmerizing. In this moment, I wanted to etch everything into memory: the way Reese Carrington, the most important person on the field, the alpha everyone respected, was willingly surrendering to me. This man, who commanded attention without lifting a finger, was letting me take the lead. I had been drowning in fear earlier, but now, I felt something else entirely—power. Wells tried to take that from me, but this man here, in front of me, was handing it back. He fought for me. Not because he had to. Not because I asked. But because he couldn't stand the thought of someone hurting me. I was reveling in the delicious power I held over him—even if it would never happen again. It wasn't just his surrender; it was the way he gave it over, making me feel like I was the only one in the world who could unseat this king.

My lips found his once more, and the kiss deepened, growing bolder. My fingers traced the outline of his jaw, feeling the stubble that grazed my fingertips. Reese's hands hovered just above where my waist dipped inwards, as though he was asking for permission to break the rules already. I gently guided his hands up and above his head, silently reminding him of the rules. Our agreement.

My lips wandered, leaving a trail of fevered kisses along the line of his throat. Every shudder was a victory, every small moan a testament to what this had become—me unraveling Reese Carrington, piece by piece.

twenty-six

REESE

Normally, I preferred being the one in charge. But for once, I didn't mind lying back and letting this woman do whatever she wanted to me. Could she handle me, though, once she saw what I was working with? I had no idea.

I bit my lip slightly. "You might be biting off more than you can chew."

She grinned and leaned in just a little, "Oh, I can handle it. The real question is, can you?"

Her eyes were heavy-lidded with desire as she looked at me from beneath her lashes. Her soft lips pressed against my throat, nipping and sucking at my skin, sending a jolt of electricity straight to my cock.

She lifted the hem of my shirt, her fingers skimmed over my abs. The fabric bunched up near my chest, and then she froze—her fingers pausing just before the soreness in my ribs. Wells must've landed a solid hit earlier. She didn't say anything, but she didn't have to. Her gaze did all the talking. She bent down, her blonde hair tickling my skin as her lips grazed the softest kisses on the fresh bruises.

Each one sent an ache through me—not just from the pain, but from the reminder that some piece of shit had tried to hurt *her*.

As she pulled my shirt off, I took a moment to take in the sight of her—her tits heaving with each breath, her nipples hard and pink beneath the thin fabric of her top. She began shedding her clothes at a slow, agonizing pace. I watched, entranced, as she revealed more piece by piece. My cock throbbed in my pants, aching for some kind of attention, resistance, anything.

She leaned down, bringing her lips to mine again as she grinded her hips against me, her movements desperate with need. She lowered herself down as she began to undo my pants, and once I sprang free, she gasped. "Damn, the group chat wasn't lying."

"Because nothing turns me on more than my dick being discussed in a group chat," I said sarcastically.

"You seemed pretty turned on to me," she said softly, running her hand along my length.

"I'm always fucking turned on around you." I sucked in a breath, "But what's your next move? Are you just going to stare, or are you going to let me taste you?"

"Not tonight," she said, her voice firm. "I need you inside me. I don't want to wait anymore."

"Tell me how much you want it, baby."

"I want it so bad," she said. She took my hand and guided it inside her panties, and I moaned at the feeling of her wet pussy against my fingers.

"Fuck," I breathed, biting my lip, not being able to resist rubbing her clit in slow circles with my palm, watching as her hips grinded against me, urging me to dive deeper. I slid my fingers beneath the damp fabric, plunging my fingers inside her, feeling her muscles clench around me. She was hot, so fucking hot, like a volcano about to explode.

"Oh god," she moaned, closing her eyes.

I was on the verge of taking control completely, flipping her on the bed right now and fucking her, but I held back, letting her wetness coat my fingers as I curled them slowly, steadily.

I pulled my fingers out, watching in awe as her pussy clung to me, unwilling to let me go. I brought my fingers to my mouth, tasting her sweetness on my tongue. I groaned, not realizing how hard it was actually going to be to wait, to let her be in charge.

Her fingers trembled as she reached into the drawer and pulled out a condom. The wrapper crinkled in her hand, and I could already feel my cock twitching in anticipation, hard and aching, like it had been begging for this all fucking night. I watched, fucking mesmerized, as she rolled it down my length. Her touch was electric, her fingertips grazing my shaft, and I hissed through my teeth, already on the edge.

She climbed on top, her body a fucking masterpiece of perfection, all smooth skin and perfect curves. Her eyes—those goddamn eyes that were their own shade of blue—dangerously locked on mine. She straddled me, her thighs slick against mine, heat radiating from her core. She shifted her hips, her pussy hovering just above my cock, so close I could feel the wetness of her against the tip. With an agonizingly slow motion, she lowered herself onto me, inch by torturous inch. Her breath hitched, her lips parting in a silent gasp, and I could feel her body stretching to take me in, her tightness gripping my cock until it disappeared. A growl caught in my throat, my hands gripping her hips hard enough to leave marks. She was so fucking wet, so fucking hot, and every inch of her felt like warm silk wrapped around me—it was fucking heaven.

"Tell me all about how much you hate me now," I dared, my hands still gripping her hips. She cried out, beginning to move as she threw her head back. A flush spreads across her chest, up her neck, and to her cheeks. I couldn't help but smirk at the sight of her—a dream.

"You're still the worst," she panted, gripping onto me. "But you feel so good."

I growled in approval, feeling myself get close. But I wasn't ready to let go yet. I wanted more. I wanted to make her scream my name until she was hoarse. I wanted to feel her body shaking as she came apart on top of me. Her cries grew louder, her hips grinded harder against me. I reached up to tweak one of her nipples, earning a sharp cry from her. She was close, so fucking close. I could feel her walls clenching around me, her movements becoming erratic. She cried out, lowering her head, and I couldn't resist pulling it up by her chin, forcing her to look at me as she fell apart.

"You're so beautiful when you come," I told her, barely able to get the words out because she was so goddamn tight, her pussy gripping me like I belonged inside her.

I let out a groan as I felt my own release approaching, my balls tightening with the sensation. But I held off, wanting to savor every fucking second of this. I could feel her body still trembling with aftershocks as she continued moving, panting heavily, sweat glistening on her skin.

She wasn't finished with me... she continued, only changing her pace, moving her hips slower, taking me in long, deep strides.

"You keep moving your hips like that and you're going to make me come," my voice was ragged with pleasure. "You have to give me one more first."

Her breasts bounced with each movement, her hips never stopping their maddening rhythm. "I'm in control. Remember? You have to deal," she breathed, her lips brushing against my ear.

I nodded, my hands gripping the sheets as I let her do exactly what she wanted. Her walls clenched around me again like she was trying to milk every last drop of sanity from my body. She smirked before her lips parted just enough to show the tip of her tongue as she licked them slowly. "Good boy," she purred, and the words hit me like a fucking wrecking ball.

"Definitely don't fucking say that," I warned, about to lose it at her praise. She let out a low, throaty laugh that made my cock twitch inside her.

She pulled me up until I was sitting straight, bringing me closer to her as her arms slipped around my shoulders. Her breasts pressed against my chest, her nipples hard and teasing. She moved slower, the rhythm more intimate. It was almost too much to bear.

"You feel so fucking good, baby," I rasped as her nails dug into my skin.

"Don't stop yet," she breathed, holding on tight.

She rode me harder, and I could feel myself getting closer to the edge, my balls tightening with each movement. But I didn't want to come yet—I needed to make this last. I thought about baseball, anything to distract myself from the overwhelming pleasure. Parker's fucking glove. Coach Levy's suicide drills. Boston's terrible swing.

"Come again for me," I demanded, because I was about to break. "And scream my name when you do it." And with her last movements, she did as she was told.

"Reese, right there... I-I'm coming."

She yelled my name as her orgasm tore through her, leaving her gasping for breath and limp in my arms. I followed shortly after, letting go as I held her. I rolled us to the side, and we lay there, panting and spent, our bodies glistening with sweat.

"Holy fuck," she murmured, her eyes half-lidded with pleasure.

"My thoughts exactly," I said, running my fingers through my hair.

"Why couldn't that have been horrible?" she said, her breath still shaky. "Or better yet, why couldn't you have a micro-penis?"

"How could I ruin you for anyone else if I had a micro-penis? I have that reputation to uphold, remember?" I said, grabbing her and pulling her into me.

"There's that ego of yours I know and love." She laughed, then. It was the most beautiful fucking sound.

twenty-seven

CAROLINE

"I can't believe Wells did that last night," Sam said, her eyes wide as she scanned the room, taking in the handmade bridal signs. The plates were covered with cursive written notes.

"I know," I whispered back. "I've never seen someone's eyes look like that, like there was nothing behind them."

Around us, Charlotte's bridal shower buzzed with excitement, and the champagne flutes were being poured. Everything was how I'd imagined it'd be.

"And then you left with Reese," she said, giving me a teasing smile.

"I know," I sighed, tilting my head. "And I am so stupid because... *it* happened."

I had no regrets about what happened. In fact, it was so hot that I had found myself on several occasions biting my lip just at the thought of it. But I was fully aware that I couldn't allow myself to get too attached to him. I was aware of the damage he could do.

"It happened?" she questioned, searching my face.

"Yes," I admitted, forcing out the words. "And it was so bad."

"It was bad?" she whispered, taking a step back.

"No.. I mean he was amazing," I paused, the memory taking me back. "I almost had a mini orgasm just looking at his body." My eyes drifted closed for a moment, thinking about how annoyingly delicious he is, and how I could almost still smell his cologne.

I looked up to find her biting her nails in anticipation. "Tell me more."

"I know what you want to know," I said quietly enough so no one else could hear. "And it happened twice... I had two of them."

She threw her hands up in the air, a dramatic gesture that made a nearby cluster of women glance over before quickly returning to their own conversation. "You had two of them?" she asked, clearly in shock. "Oh, you're fucked."

I pulled back a chair and took a seat at one of the back tables. "Yep. It's official. I'm next in line. I have a first-class seat to be 'Reese'd and released.'" The worst part was that I had no one to blame for this but me. "I knowingly allowed it to happen."

"Hey," she said, softly. "It's not the end of the world." She reached for my wrist. "There's a high chance that might happen, yes, but Care," her grip tightened, "the way he was looking at you, it was like he was ready to burn down the whole damn bar. And I've never seen him look at anyone like that."

The possibility that someone like Reese could see something in me that was worth burning down the bar sent a rush through my body, igniting a small, barely there-flicker of hope. Was he really looking at me like that? Was it even possible for someone like him to actually have feelings for someone like me? Or, was last night more about Wells than anything else?

"Be cautious, because you know you've already been burned by him," she continued, "but I think... I think you need to see where it goes."The clinking of silverware and the rustle of tissue paper filled the air as the room began to settle, each guest finding their way to tables adorned with white linens and delicate floral centerpieces.

"He's going to be my date to the wedding," I said quietly, reaching for my glass of water, "but after that, he's leaving this town and everything in it behind." The draft wasn't far off, and everyone knew he'd be chosen early. He was literally out of here. I was admitting as much as I could without revealing the whole truth—that Reese and I were nothing more than a beautifully crafted lie.

"Whatever you say," she said, her voice a sultry whisper. "But I know that look. And if he looked at me like that, I would do anything that man said."

Voices settled into a gentle hush as my sister, the bride-to-be, stood at the center

of the room, her hands poised to unwrap the mountain of gifts piled around her. She flashed a radiant smile as she looked around the room.

"Thank you all for being here," she said, her voice a pitch I only ever heard when she was trying to impress someone. With each present she unwrapped—a gleaming new toaster, a set of plush slippers, fancy new lingerie—I found myself smiling at her excitement, hoping I'd get to experience this one day, too.

"Caroline," my mother leaned closer to our table, "you and Reese need to be at the reception tomorrow at five. The rehearsal dinner is directly after, so don't be late."

"You got it," I replied, giving her a small smile.

My mother's eyes lingered on mine for a moment longer before shifting to Sam. "And Sam," she added, "the next two days, you'll be running the show. Don't disappoint us." She laughed an almost evil laugh.

"Wouldn't dream of it," Sam shot back with a forced smile.

As the guests began to disperse, I packed a box full of gifts to load into my sister's car. I walked past the ballroom—the next room over from Charlotte's bridal shower. Through the open doorway I saw men in suits and ties, and women dressed in business attire.

But there were two men who caught my eye. I could tell them apart from anyone, even with their backs to me—Reese and his dad. And that's when *she* appeared, one of the most stunning women I had ever seen. Even her laugh was gracious and sweet as she pulled

Reese into an embrace that lasted a few moments too long, her hand lingering on his arm. Even Reese's dad offered her a smirk of approval, which was a huge upgrade from the stink-eye he'd been handing out to me like party favors.

I had no claim over Reese, and she was definitely his type. It was insane to feel the hollow twist of jealousy, so I looked away and continued on my path. I held the box I was holding tighter, its weight grounding me back on track. Each step was an effort to shake off the image of Reese and that brunette.

I slid the box into the trunk and shut it. Then, I took a deep breath before making my way back inside to grab more. Walking through the entrance, a voice pricked at my ears.

"Reese agreed," she was saying to another woman in a navy business suit. "We have a date set for next Thursday. His father was excited about it."

I swallowed hard, trying to push away the anger. Why was this bothering me? Reese and I, we were destined to be enemies. But, the thought of him with her made my stomach turn.

It was irrational, this burning resentment toward someone who simply existed, unfairly beautiful and probably just as kind.

Gathering the last of the bridal shower gifts, I shoved them in the car, packing my sister's trunk full.

"Caroline, that's a toaster," my sister adjusted a box. "If you broke it, then you're giving me yours."

"Don't have one," I said, wiping sweat off my brow.

"Don't be late tomorrow," she said, before shutting the truck.

twenty-eight

REESE

I turned on my headphones before starting my workout. I dropped my bag into my locker, the sound drowned out by my music blaring in my ears. Stepping into the weight room, I approached the machine I usually started on and set the weight. But just as I gripped the handles, something pulled at the corner of my vision.

Through the large glass windows, her car caught my eye. It was Caroline pulling up out front. It was a fiery red, compact little thing that seemed almost like an extension of her indomitable spirit.

Even from this distance, I could see the concentrated look on her face as she attempted to parallel park, though "attempted" might be too generous a term. I couldn't help but grin, captivated by just how spectacularly bad she was at it. It was as if she'd skipped the entire parallel park chapter in driver's ed. She inched backward and forward in a scattered shuffle. Each try brought her no closer to the curb. Honestly, it was kind of cute and oddly endearing. I watched, amused, as her petite frame hunched over the wheel, her blonde hair falling around her shoulders in frustration.

After a few more minutes of this nonsense, I left my machine and pushed open the door as I stepped outside. It was time for this embarrassing spectacle to end. The glare of the sun did little to prepare me for the intensity of her gaze as it found mine through the windshield. With a casual gesture, I motioned for her to roll down the window.

The window slid down slowly, and she slid her sunglasses from over her eyes to the top of her head.

"Yes?" she asked innocently, and I leaned closer, resting my hand on the top of her car.

"What exactly are you doing?" I questioned, doing my best not to laugh.

"Oh, nothing much," she said, like I was interrupting her. "The space just seems to be a little tight."

"Oh yeah?" I grinned, glancing over at the oversized spot that could easily fit two of her cars. "Your car's so small it's practically a Hot Wheels. How can you be so bad at this?"

"You've been watching me?" she asked, glaring now.

"I was in the weight room," I said, nodding towards the gym. "You know, the one right in there with the large windows and unobstructed view of the parking lot."

"Well, you can go back in," she said, stubbornly. "I've got it."

"Step out of the car, Caroline. It has been painful to watch you do this."

Her gaze lingered on the rearview mirror, before she shifted the gear into park. "If you insist," she said. With a resigned sigh, she stepped out of the car, surrendering the driver's seat to me.

Slipping behind the wheel, I crammed myself in the tiny car. Effortlessly, I backed the car into the spot and within moments, it was nestled perfectly near the curb.

"How did you even pass driver's ed?" I asked, handing her the keys with a smirk.

"Who said I passed?" she shot back, tossing a grin over her shoulder as she headed for the entrance.

"Wait, you're joking... right?"

She rolled those ridiculously striking blue eyes, the keys jingling in her hand like she couldn't be bothered by my existence. "Obviously," she drawled. Then, with a sly smile, she added, "But I didn't expect to run into you here. Squeezing in a quick workout before you're stuck as my date all weekend?"

"Gotta look swoll in that tux because my date is gonna be a knockout. Some might even say she's way hotter than the bride."

"No one has ever said I'm prettier than Charlotte," she laughed.

"I find that hard to believe," I said, flashing her a dimple.

"Reese," she began, shaking her head, "don't you like brunettes anyway? Me and Charlotte are probably the complete opposite of what you'd normally go for."

It was true, I usually always went for brunettes, but honestly, none of that really mattered. Sometimes you meet someone and you just connect with them. For me, that usually just happened to be with brunettes.

"Things change," I said with a shrug.

"It doesn't seem like it. And speaking of which, you should really let your 'fake' girlfriend know if you're going on real dates with these brunettes," she tossed over her shoulder. "Word gets around fast in this town, and you could have messed up the entire plan." Her voice trailed off as she scanned her key card, and the door shut behind her.

"Damnit," I whispered to myself, patting down my pockets, realizing my keycard was inside. My knuckles tapped on the door as I peered through the glass, catching sight of Caroline pausing mid-stride, and slowly turning back around.

"What are you talking about?" I asked, as the door swung open.

"I know about your date on Thursday," she said, crossing her hands over her chest.

I rubbed the back of my neck, racking my brain to figure out what the hell she was talking about. Then it hit me that there was only one thing on Thursday. She began to turn on her heel to continue on her path.

"Are you talking about the meeting I have with my PR consultant?" I reached out, my fingers wrapping around her wrist. "I just got introduced to her at my draft strategy meeting my dad set up today."

Caroline's cheeks turned some shade of pink as I let go of her wrist, her wide eyes blinking as if she needed a moment to process. "Your PR consultant?" she repeated, her voice a touch softer, the surprise clear in her tone.

"Exactly," I drawed, gripping her chin to make her look at me. "And, you know, I could be wrong, but you seem pretty jealous for someone in a fake relationship."

Her breath hitched, the tiniest pause that gave her away, even if her words tried not to. "I'm not," she whispered, her voice barely holding together the lie.

"Well, you should know, I would never let you be insecure. I will open mouth kiss you, or do anything else you want me to in front of the whole damn world, without hesitation, because when you're mine"—I stepped even closer, my tone edged with a possessiveness that made her heart flutter—"I don't care who knows it."

The effect I had on her was obvious, even if she'd never admit it. She swallowed and shot back, "I am not insecure or jealous."

At this point, I knew how I felt about her and that I wanted her in whatever capacity that meant, but I understood it would take her longer to accept how she really felt about me. There was something still holding her back from opening up to me, but I'd figure it out, whether she wanted me to or not.

I leaned in closer, matching the gravity of her gaze. "Is that so? I think you're lying, and it's about time I show you exactly what happens when you're dating me and you lie to me."

Caroline's teeth caught the plushness of her lower lip. "What happens?"

I didn't break eye contact, holding her stare as I stepped past her. My jaw tightened as I tipped my head toward the Blue Devils' locker room. "Come."

She didn't move, stuck to the spot she was standing, either from defiance or desire, couldn't tell which. "Make me wait, and it'll be worse for you," I warned, as I adjusted my watch.

twenty-nine

CAROLINE

Reese disappeared into the locker room. That man made me feel every emotion known to humankind. Anger at his audacity, excitement, nerves, and heat—oh, an unbearable heat that flushed my skin and ran through my blood with anticipation.

In any rational state, my mind would talk me out of following after him, but any trace of rationality had packed its bags and hopped the last train out of town ages ago. My heart was pounding at the thought of what he wanted to do in there. God only knew. But my feet? Oh, they'd already made the decision for me, dragging me straight ahead.

I paused at the locker room entrance as the heavy door closed behind me. Fidgeting with the delicate necklace around my neck, I stepped into the dimly lit space. Reese leaned against the wall, his hypnotic eyes locked onto mine. "Take your pants off," he commanded.

"What?" The word slipped out as I took in the large locker room that surrounded me. Reese didn't move, his athletic build casually waiting with expectation.

"Last time," he began, his voice low and steady, "I let you call the shots." His hand lifted, as he drew a circle in the air. "But here, I run the show." The corner of his mouth tugged into a dangerous grin. "So, I'm going to repeat myself one more time. Take off your pants."

Before I could fully process it, I was slipping my shoes off, guided by an impulse that was both rebellious and out of my control. I tugged off my leggings, and they pooled at my feet. I stood there in my dark green panties, suddenly exposed, but Reese's gaze—it memorized, it praised, it undressed every layer of my soul. The way he looked: eyes dark, lips caught between his teeth, raw hunger in every inch of him... I knew then that my resistance was long gone, just like my self-control at a pizza buffet.

"Good girl," he finally said as he closed the distance between us. His lips found the line of my jaw, blazing a gentle trail of kisses down to my neck.

"Sit," he ordered, his voice a low growl between kisses. His finger pointed firmly at the wooden bench in the center of the room.

"What if someone comes in?"

"I come in this time every day, no one usually comes in for a while," he said.

He pulled off his black hoodie, giving me a brief glimpse of his rippling abs, which glistened as his shirt rode up. Then, with casual ease, he tossed the hoodie near his locker. He closed the space between us, then leaned over me, his mouth crashing down on mine. He bit my lower lip, then soothed it with his tongue before he continued. The confidence in everything he did was just as much a part of him as the sharpness of his jaw or the green of his eyes.

He dropped to his knees, his face mere inches from my waist. His warm breath tickled my skin as he dragged soft kisses along my stomach, making me shiver in anticipation. He traced the outline of the tattoo on my hip with his tongue, following it down to my thighs with agonizing slowness. I bit back a whimper as I felt his fingers graze the waistband of my panties, before he slid them off, making me more impatient by the second. His hands were rough and posses-sive as he yanked my thighs apart, exposing everything.

"I've been waiting too damn long to taste you again, and I'm fucking starving," he said. His eyes met mine for a brief second before he lowered himself between my thighs and lifted my legs over his shoulders.

He didn't hesitate, didn't tease—just went in, relentless and unstoppable. His mouth was hot and wet against my pussy, his tongue lapping at me like he'd only come here today for this—like he had been starved on the street for years. Every flick, every suck, every sinful swirl drove me deeper as he worked me over, his stubble scraping against my sensitive skin. Every flick of his tongue sent a lightning bolt of pleasure coursing through my body.

"Oh, god,' I said, arching my back, moaning as he slipped two fingers inside me, curling them in a way that made me see stars.

"You like that, baby?" he whispered against my skin before continuing.

"Yes." I moaned, "God, yes."

I was already close, so fucking close. My hips grinded against his face, my fingers gripping the bench. I knew he could feel my body tensing, but just as I was about to tip over the edge, he pulled back. "Hold up. I need you to start being honest with me."

I whimpered when he pulled his fingers out of me, denying me the release that was so tantalizingly close. I sighed in frustration, still reeling. "Yes," I gasped, "I'll tell you whatever you want to know."

He chuckled darkly. "That's a good start. Now tell me what you want."

"You," I breathed out, barely able to speak. I wanted him more than anything—his touch, his taste, his body against mine. "I want you. I'm on the pill, and I know we're both clean, so just do it without a condom. I want to feel you."

"How do you know I'm clean?" he asked, narrowing his eyes.

"I may have snooped on your paperwork in the office," I tried to say as innocently as I could.

He didn't waste a second. He grabbed me, lifting me off the bench like I weighed nothing, and flipping me onto my knees. My ass was up in the air, my pussy dripping as I heard the sound of him pulling down his pants, then freeing his cock as he said, "You're more naughty than I thought you were."

I moaned, burying my face in the crook of my arm as he teased my entrance with his cock before sliding inside me with one relentless thrust. He felt so good—so hard and thick and perfect.

"Fuck, I missed you," I cried out. The stretch of him was almost too much, but he didn't stop.

"Good girl," he growled, his voice sending tremors down my spine. "That's exactly what I want to hear when I slide inside you."

He started rolling his hips, thrusting into me with the most delicious and relentless rhythm. He fucked me hard and fast, his hands gripping my hips so tight I knew there'd be bruises tomorrow. I was already on the verge again, my walls clenching around him.

"I'm about to—" I started, just as he cut me off.

"Not yet," he growled, stopping his movements completely and holding me back for the second time, making me angrier by the second.

"Reese, what the fuck?" I breathed, my frustration at an all time high. "This is torture."

I gasped as he shifted me, lifting my body until my back was pressed flush against his chest. His breath was hot on my ear as he bit down lightly. One hand slid around my waist, his fingers finding my swollen clit and rubbing it in slow, tantalizing circles. The other hand gripped my throat, holding me in place. I whimpered, so desperate for release I could hardly think straight. I tried to press my hips back against him, desperate for relief, but he held me still.

"You want me to make you scream? Fuck you until you can't walk, Chaos? Tell me if you were jealous," he demanded, his fingers teasing me mercilessly.

"Fine. Yes," I admitted, my voice unsteady. "I thought you were taking her on a date." I swallowed hard, my heart pounding. "But it wasn't just jealousy... I thought you were going to humiliate me again."

Reese stilled. His fingers stopped, tension snapping into the space between us.

"Again?" he echoed, his voice suddenly sharp and unreadable.

Just then, we both heard the door to the locker room open. I held my breath, my body tensing. "This can not be happening," I said under my breath.

The unmistakable echo of footsteps reverberated through the locker room. Reese's reflexes kicked in quickly. He scooped me up with ease. He swept up our discarded clothes and tossed them into his open locker.

"Shhh," he breathed as he carried me toward the showers, my legs wrapped around him. The curtain shut behind us as Reese closed us inside.

"No one can see you in here," he whispered. Reese they'd be able to see, he towered above the shower wall. But I was safely out of view, the first time being short has come in handy.

"You said no one would be in here," I said, shooting him a glare.

He grinned, obviously liking the danger of this moment. "Guess I was wrong," Reese murmured, showing no signs of regret.

"Reese?" Bailey shouted from across the locker room.

"Take the rest of your clothes off," Reese commanded, his voice low and urgent.

He slid off his clothes and held them in one hand, exposing every glorious inch of him. As he moved towards me, his fingers brushed against my skin, electric and burning, as they trailed up to grasp my shirt, tugging it over my head. My bra followed, and then we were both completely exposed. Reese took our clothes and hung them on a hook just outside the shower.

The sound of running water began to fill the space, drowning out Bailey's voice that was inching closer.

I stepped closer to Reese, my fingers running across the cool metal of the pendant necklace that he always wore. The droplets from the shower made it gleam against his tanned skin. "You really never take this off, do you?" I whispered, not being able to imagine him without it.

Reese shook his head, a motion that sent water trailing from his dark hair. "Never," he responded.

"Saw your truck out front." Bailey called out, the voice getting closer.

"What's up man?" Reese yelled back, trying to play it cool.

The steam was thick, covering us like a dirty secret, clinging to the tiles and fogging up the shower. I knew we weren't the only two people in here, but I didn't care right now. Not when he was here, his body towering over me, his tanned skin slick and steaming under the scalding water.

"Just wanted to see if you were almost done with your workout," Bailey responded, like he was right next to us now. "Thought we could grab some food."

His muscles were taut, water dripping down his chest. I smirked to myself, thinking about how he was torturing me a few minutes ago, and now it was my turn to return the favor—two could play this game.

My lips brushed his collarbone first, feather-light before I trailed kisses lower, my tongue darting out to taste the water on his abs.

He barely got the words out to Bailey, who was waiting for his response as he said, "Nah, man, not hungry. I'll catch you later."

When my mouth grazed along the v-line of his waist, I felt his body tense, he knew exactly what I was about to do. His fingers traced my jaw, tilting my face up to look at him, "bad girl," he mouthed, before swiping his thumb over my lower lip.

Bailey was probably just a few feet away, oblivious—or pretending to be. The thought of getting caught was nerve-racking but also thrilling. His jaw clenched, his Adam's apple bobbing as he swallowed hard. I wasn't going to stop, not now. I sank to my knees, the water trickling over me as I wrapped my hand around the base of his cock. It was hard, thick, and already leaking pre-cum. My lips parted, and I took him into my mouth, every inch, savoring the way hips jerked forward involuntarily, the way I had just started and he was already losing control.

"Fucking hell," he bit the knuckle of his index finger to stifle a moan.

I pulled back slowly, my tongue dragging all around his shaft before swirling around the tip. His breath was ragged now, and when I looked up at him, his eyes were dark, pupils blown wide with lust.

Bailey chose that moment to speak again. "Did you do legs today?"

He was almost suffering now—his voice strained as he managed, "Ch-chest day."

"Ah! That's right," Bailey shot back.

I smirked around his cock, taking him deeper this time, my throat constricting as I swallowed him whole. A hand gripped the back of my head, fingers tightened in my hair, tugging just enough to make me moan. I could feel him fighting it, trying to stay quiet, but I wasn't going to let him off that easily. I bobbed my head faster, sucking harder, my tongue working him in ways that had his knees buckling.

"You're going to kill me," he said, pressing a palm against the shower wall to steady himself, like it was the only thing keeping him upright.

I loved it—every fucking second of it. The way his breath hitched, the way his abs tensed, the way he bit down on his lip to hold back his moans. I could feel the tension coiling tight in his body as I brought him closer and closer to the edge. Just when I felt like he was almost there, I pulled away.

Reese closed his eyes and shook his head, giving me all the satisfaction I needed.

"You sure you aren't hungry?" Bailey asked, apparently not getting the message.

He pulled me to him, his chest pressed against mine. His cock was thick, hard, and wedged against my stomach, and the heat of it made my clit throb like a second fucking pulse. I slid my hand between us, fingers wrapping around his shaft, and the way he rolled his eyes, and tilted his head back sent a jolt of pure electricity straight to my core.

"Finish what you started," I whispered as I felt him twitch in my hand, his hips jerking forward like he couldn't help himself. The water pounded down on us, hot and relentless, but it was nothing compared to the heat between us.

One of his hands slid down my back, fingers digging into the curve of my ass as he lifted me effortlessly, my legs instinctively wrapping around his waist. He was strong—so fucking strong—and the way he handled me like I weighed nothing only made me more wet. I kept my head low enough not to be seen as I kissed his neck, my mouth hot on his skin. His other hand found my breast, thumb flicking over my nipple until it was hard and aching.

"Reese?" Bailey asked again, getting impatient.

"Y-yeah, all good," Reese responded as he positioned himself at my entrance, the head of his cock brushing against my clit, teasing me, driving me insane. He had a crooked grin on his face, but me, I wanted to scream, to beg him to shove himself inside me already, but I couldn't. Not here. Not with Bailey on the other side. So I settled for grinding against him, my hips rocking in small, desperate circles as I tried to tempt him into moving further.

"Patience, Chaos," he rasped, and I hated him for it. Hated how he could be so calm when I was a fucking mess. But then he finally—finally—pushed inside me, and all coherent thought left my brain in a rush of white-hot pleasure.

"Alright, guess I'll have the pizza all to myself," Bailey complained, then said a few muffled words I couldn't focus on.

Reese whispered, "Fuck you feel good," under his breath. Then, louder, "Bails, unless you wanna see my dick, get out of here."

My nails dug into his shoulders as he filled me completely. And then he started to move. Slow at first, then each delicious thrust was a torturous drag that had me biting down on my own hand to keep quiet. He picked up the pace, his hips rolling and slamming into mine with a force that had me seeing stars.

"You know your dick is pretty impressive." Bailey laughed to himself.

Before Reese could respond, I whispered in his ear, "Don't you dare stop this time."

The sound of skin slapping against skin was drowned out by the shower, the steam swallowing us whole as he fucked me so hard I thought I might break. Each time he bottomed out, I could feel his cock hitting that spot inside me that made my whole body tremble, my orgasm building, ready to fucking explode.

"You could have mentioned mine was impressive too, you know," Bailey added, annoyingly. "Maybe we've been changing around each other for too many years in locker rooms. It's tragic, honestly."

Oh my god, this was now insane. I was resisting the urge to throw something at him.

"Bye, Bailey," Reese snapped, dismissing him.

Bailey didn't faze him, though. Reese placed a hand on the shower wall, his other hand still held me up with ease as he continued to thrust in and out of me. It took everything in me not to scream. The hot water trailed down our entwined bodies, and Reese kissed away the water drops on my collarbone.

I gave him a pleading look, my eyes wide and begging him to keep going. "Don't stop," I whispered, my voice hoarse with desire. "I need to—"

He leaned in close, his lips brushing against my ear as he whispered, "I know, baby. I know."

"Alright, I'll hit you up later... and don't forget you dropped your pink bra on the floor before you go, Coach will kill you if he finds that." Bailey was now officially talking to himself, and I hoped he was finally letting himself out.

"Right there," I whimpered, my voice barely more than a whimper, and he growled in response, his grip on my ass tightening as he pounded into me harder, faster. I could feel his control slipping, his thrusts becoming erratic, and I knew he was close too. He covered my mouth to muffle my cries as I finally came hard, my body shuddering with pleasure.

"Thank you," I breathed in relief, my lips brushing against the hollow of his throat. And just like that, he let go, his cock pulsing inside me as he came, his hips stuttering as he buried himself deep. The feel of him spilling inside me for the first time and letting himself go was intoxicating.

We stayed like that for a moment, both of us trembling and breathless, the water washing away the evidence of what we'd done. But I knew one thing for sure—whatever this was between us, it was far from over. Not even close. And the worst part? I had actually admitted I was jealous.

Later that day, I lounged on the ratty couch in the lounge room of the dance studio, a place where I often collapsed between classes.

Sam held out a paper bag. "Brought you sustenance," she said. Being the saint that she was, she occasionally stopped by on my breaks when she was running around.

"Thanks," I said, taking the bag and laying it on my chest.

"Are you doing okay?" Her tone was playful yet probing. "You never hesitate to rip open a sandwich."

Sam had an uncanny ability to pick up on anything going on with me—sometimes she'd even know things before I did.

"Doing just great," I lied, the words muffled as I finally opened the bag and took a reluctant bite of the sandwich. The flavors mingled in my mouth—savory turkey and provolone cheese. I chewed mechanically, feeling Sam's gaze, doing my best not to look at her.

She leaned back against the cushions. "Well... I am so glad this wedding is almost over," she sighed, a flicker of exasperation softening as she turned to me. "I love you and your family, but I think I've had my tolerance of Charlotte."

"Yeah, the big day is almost here," I said, swallowing hard. Sam watched me, her brow furrowing slightly as she tried to decipher my expression. The closer we got to the wedding day, the more I felt the ticking clock on whatever this was with Reese. It was a countdown to an ending I wasn't prepared for, no matter how badly I tried to protect myself.

"Hey," Sam said, breaking into my thoughts with a gentle nudge. "No offense to Charlotte and Dan, but you and Reese are going to be the most gorgeous couple there."

Her words should have comforted me, should have made me excited, but instead, it was depressing. It made me feel worse. This was all supposed to be fake, just for show. But it felt less like an act every time I was around Reese.

"Ever since I was little," I confessed, putting the sandwich down on the table next to me, "I've been dreaming about what it would be like to impress my cousins, to see that look of awe on my grandparents' faces when I show up to a family event with someone they'd all be proud of. To be with someone like Reese."

"Then why don't you look excited?"

"I've been keeping something from you," I murmured, about to rip this bandaid. I had to tell someone, and she's the only person I could trust.

"Which is?"

"Reese and I... we're not what everyone thinks," I began, the words tumbling out before I could talk myself out of it. "We've been pretending. Everything has been a lie, an act, until—it sort of wasn't. One moment led to another, and suddenly, we were really hooking up. But it all ends after Charlotte's wedding."

I'd known our arrangement would be coming to an end this entire time. I told myself I wouldn't fall for him. That I couldn't. But no matter how much I was fighting it, my heart wasn't getting the memo. I couldn't keep going down this dangerous path, I couldn't keep heading in a direction that could only end in destruction. And even if somehow Reese and I did become something real, he still had the MLB draft just days after the wedding. He'd still move far away and be in a world that I'd have no place in.

Sam's expression didn't change as I continued. "I wanted so badly to just impress my family and to finally belong. I wanted to walk in with Reese on my arm and bask in a moment of my own. So, I struck a deal with him—even knowing what he did to me in sixth grade. But now, nothing feels right anymore. Reese... he doesn't seem like the same person who did that to me. Or, maybe it's me who's changed. I'm just so lost, Sam."

"I knew something was off," she whispered. "I knew how badly he hurt you. There's no way you'd just get over that... but if he's doing all this for you," Sam continued, "what are you doing for him? What's your part of the deal?"

"I told him... I'd make sure his sister made the cheer team."

The sharp clatter of a water bottle falling on the floor hit me like a sharp slap to the face. A chill crept up my spine as I turned toward the sound, only to find Lola, eyes wide and accusing. Her gaze locked onto mine, and then I saw the hurt take over her expression.

"So you weren't doing this because you wanted to help me? You used me to make my brother be your date to a wedding?"

"Lola, wait!" I blurted, the word tumbling out in a breathless rush as I shot to my feet. "Let me explain."

Lola reached for her water bottle, her movements quick with wounded pride. "No," she snapped. "I heard everything I need to know." She clutched the bottle closer. "I don't need any more of your 'help.'"

Her words were a gut punch. The dance studio had always been a place of escape, but right now, I felt ashamed, the mirrors reflecting back an image of myself I hardly recognized anymore.

thirty

REESE

Caroline stood toe-to-toe with her sister, that irritated look of hers I knew too well by now written all over her face. "You had to wear black to my reception like it's a funeral?" her sister spat out, looking Caroline up and down.

"I'm sorry, your itinerary was seventy-eight pages long. Did I miss the approved list of colors?" Caroline shot back. They continued to bicker back and forth until I decided to make my presence known.

I stepped out from the shadows, the dim light catching on my tie as I adjusted it. "I think you look damn good in that dress," I said, making them both turn toward me.

Her sister crossed her arms tightly across her chest, narrowing her eyes on me.

"Shall we?" I offered, extending my hand toward Caroline.

Her fingers slid into mine, and together, we wandered inside the venue. The main room itself was glowing with soft lights and neatly arranged chairs already set up for the wedding tomorrow. Flowers were everywhere—on the floor, on the tables.

"Excited for tomorrow?" I asked, taking it all in—the romantic setup around us, to the most gorgeous girl standing beside me. I knew that we had planned for tomorrow to be the end of this, and I'd agreed to that, but I was not the same man who made that deal. Not anymore.

"Yes, only one more day you have to put up with me, then things can go back to normal," Caroline replied with a weak smile on her face.

Normal? Being with her lately was the first time I'd felt normal for I don't know how long. I craved her presence—and it didn't just feel normal; it felt like breathing. I didn't want any of this to end. I never meant for it to happen, but somewhere along the way, I fell for her. Hard. And now, there was no turning back. Even if this ended with me getting hurt in the process, being wrecked, I'd take the hit. Because having her, even for a little while, was worth it. She was worth it. I'd risk any amount of pain or heartbreak just to be hers, even if she never really ended up being mine.

We reached the altar, standing before the tall glass wall that overlooked the lake. I stood beside her, and we lingered there for a moment, taking in the view. "Is that what you really want? Things to go back to normal?"

Her eyes drifted past me, like she was looking for answers in the glass window's reflection. Outside, the dark lake mirrored the sky—it all blurred together just like my racing thoughts. She barely nodded, and I could almost hear her silent thoughts caught between wanting to be honest and the fear of what would happen if she was.

My hand found its way around her slender waist. "I think you've been enjoying this just as much as I have," I whispered into her ear.

She was still lost in the backdrop of the dark lake. "I have," she admitted. "I was wrong about you. I thought being with you would be worse than a hundred tiny cats mauling me to death."

I chuckled, now having that mental image in my mind. "Why are the cats tiny? Are they kittens?"

Caroline turned to face me, her blue eyes reflecting the moonlight that streamed through the glass walls.

"Reese, I'm serious. Thank you—for everything. For being there when I didn't know how to ask for help. For showing me that there's more to you than I ever let myself see. And for making me feel like I was enough... even when I wasn't sure I ever could be."

I reached out, fingers hesitant as they brushed her cheekbone, tucking a loose strand of hair behind her ear. "I'd do anything for you," I said honestly, meaning every word.

Her mouth opened, then closed as the sound of a sweet elderly woman interrupted us, "There they are."

Caroline opened her arms, inviting her Yaya in for a hug. But Yaya bypassed her completely. Her warm arms wrapped around my waist, her fingers playfully grazing the fabric of my shirt. "Oh, Caroline, can I steal your date tomorrow?" she teased, eyes twinkling with mischief as she made Caroline laugh for the first time tonight.

"Alright, I think everyone is here," Sam's voice boomed, cutting through the laughter. "Bridal party, come with me. Everyone else, please have a seat as you watch the show. Hopefully we can knock this out in just a few practices so we get it perfect for tomorrow."

I watched the bridal party take their places, following Sam's instructions. As they found their places, I relaxed back in my seat. Caroline's Yaya was on the other side of me. Her eyes gleamed playfully as she offered me a wink.

I turned just in time to catch the bridesmaids shuffle down the aisle, all attached to a groomsmen doing their best to stay on pace with the music. But it was her—*Caroline*—who stole the breath from my chest, who made every other person in the room disappear just because of her presence.

The black dress her sister didn't approve of clung to her like it was made to show off the curves of her body. She was oblivious to the effect she had on the space around her, to the way the light seemed to bend toward her in the most perfect way.

Yaya's elbow nudged me discreetly. "She is a beauty, isn't she?"

"That she is, Yaya," I agreed as I watched her, flustered because her brother was walking too fast for her to keep up with.

The final run-through came to an end, and the wedding party

began to disperse as Sam gave final words of encouragement. I lingered in my seat for a moment longer, casually sitting back, waiting for Caroline to finish up.

"Can I speak with you for a moment?" Caroline's mom asked, tapping me on the shoulder.

I turned. Mrs. Matthews was pointing toward an empty corner of the room. I walked with her to the secluded area, my hands resting in my pockets. Not a clue what she'd want with me, but I was all ears.

"I know what's really going on here," she said, a tight smile on her face.

"You do?" I asked, suspiciously. How could she possibly know about Caroline and me?

"I do," she said, her voice a blend of disappointment and accusation. "I know this is some sort of pity thing, or maybe even some fun meaningless fling before you move on to your real life in some professional athlete world that the rest of us could never dream of. She's what to you, really? A temporary distraction until you get to finally leave? Because in the end, she's not enough for you. Is she? Not good enough for the world you're destined for, and we all know it."

My jaw involuntarily twitched, blood boiling as her eyes locked onto mine in a way that said she had just figured me out, was seeing right through me.

"But our entire family will be at the wedding tomorrow, and a lot of eyes will be on you," she continued, "So, I suggest that you either take the importance of tomorrow seriously or you do not show up at all."

Caroline was one of the most hardheaded people I had ever met, and I was starting to understand why she didn't trust anyone. Her own mother thought I'd do this out of pity? That I'd use her?

"Mrs. Matthews," I cleared my throat, "respectfully, you're wrong. This isn't pity or some meaningless fling. Caroline is way too good for me. If anything, she deserves better than me, and I know that every damn second I'm lucky enough to be with her. But pity?

No. The only person I feel sorry for is you—because if you can't see how incredible your daughter is, then you don't know her at all."

Mrs. Matthews remained silent, eyes scanning my face, searching for a lie that wasn't there. With nothing left to say, I turned to leave, my voice calm as I added, "If you'll excuse me—she's waiting."

Her expression was one I couldn't quite read—maybe shock and a small sliver of respect. Whatever it was still left me feeling unbalanced and frustrated.

Caroline stood with Sam and a few of the bridesmaids. "Hey," I said softly as I approached, brushing her cheek with a kiss, the brief contact bringing my mind back to ease.

Her eyes, the ones I couldn't stop thinking about lately, flickered up to mine. "Were you just talking to my mom?" she asked, turning to face me.

"It was nothing," I said, dismissing it. Caroline didn't need to know the terrible things her own mother just said—not now, not when I knew how much this weekend meant to her.

"Come on," she said, tilting her head toward the exit. "I have something to show you before the rehearsal dinner."

"Lead the way, Chaos."

She smirked, a playful glint in her eyes as she leaned in close enough for me to catch the faint scent of lavender in her hair. "You, sir," she whispered, "are about to finally find out the secret behind my tattoo."

Dropping my hands in my pockets, I followed her lead as we headed outside.

"Does this mean you're going to have to kill me after?" I asked, only half-joking as the barn door creaked open. "Because I need to make sure anyone but Bailey gets my shoes."

"Why can't he have your shoes?" Caroline questioned, her head tilted while she continued forward, guiding us inside the dark barn. I followed, drawn by the secretive smile on her lips.

"I loaned him a pair once," I murmured as she looked around for a light switch. "He destroyed them in a day. Those shoes weren't just messed up, they were talking."

"Talking?" Her voice drifted back to me, but I could no longer see her.

"You know, when they're so torn they flap open and closed as you walk. Like they're trying to speak their last dying words."

She switched on a light before letting out a laugh. And then she moved again, leading us onward. "Meet Goldilocks," she announced, stepping in front of a stall to reveal a horse.

I watched her approach the horse, a creature almost as beautiful as Caroline herself, with a tan coat and blonde hair. The mare's eyes, sweet and understanding, seemed to recognize her immediately.

"Hi, Goldilocks," I murmured, reaching out with a gentle touch. Caroline continued to pet her as she handed her a treat. "They let us be a part of their world here. My sister and I used to sit right there," she gestured to a hay bale. "We'd help out with the horses, then read and do our homework until our parents picked us up. When she was a baby, we read *Goldilocks and the Three Bears*, and her ears twitched with every 'just right.' They let us name her. I guess she's always been a bit of a sanctuary for me." Her gaze drifted away, lost in the memories. "Life gets busy," Caroline continued, her fingers tracing patterns on Goldilocks' neck. "I don't get to visit her as often as I used to, but she's been there for me through so many rough days."

"That's too bad," I said, watching Caroline with Goldilocks, the way her fingers tenderly brushed through the horse's mane.

"Charlotte always wanted to get married here—having a view of the lake and the horses," she said, her voice softening as she glanced over her shoulder, pointing towards the lake where tables had been arranged and set up for dinner. Candles flickered in the gentle breeze.

I watched her, this woman who could start a fire with her words. And as she stood there in the dying light, conversing with a creature as wild-hearted as herself, I couldn't help but feel my cold heart starting to melt.

"You're beautiful," I whispered, leaning an arm on the weathered wood, watching them together.

Caroline glanced up, misreading my intent, her gaze returning to the horse. "I know," she agreed. "I might be partial, but I think she's the prettiest horse I've ever seen."

Goldilocks seemed to sense the compliment, letting out a contented snort of approval that ruffled the quiet.

"I wasn't talking about her," I said quietly.

Caroline paused and almost looked disappointed at my compliment. She stepped away and took a seat on a haystack. "Don't do that," she breathed.

"Do what?"

"Say things like that," she whispered, delicate but heavy with emotion.

"Why not?" I asked, watching as she stared at Goldilocks, almost like they were having a silent conversation—the horse, in all her wisdom, urging her to be honest.

"First of all... your sister knows about our deal. She overheard me telling Sam. And Reese, she's so hurt. I hate that she found out like that. I really care about her."

I exhaled, running a hand through my hair. "Trust me, she'll be okay. She'll forgive you. Might hold a grudge against me for a while, though."

"I thought I could do this," she continued, not looking at me. "I thought if we were together in front of my family, it would finally impress them." A bitter laugh escaped her. "That I wouldn't be some disappointment for once... but now that it's here, I don't think I can go through with this."

"Why do you need their approval? Why does impressing your family even matter so much?"

She looked down, playing with the bracelets on her arm. "You wouldn't understand what it's like," she whispered painfully. "To always be the disappointment—not perfect like Cooper or Charlotte. Every kid grows up wanting their parents' approval... wanting them to be proud." Her fingers traced the bracelets. "I've never had that. Not once. And I know we've come all this way..." She shook her head, a tear dropping slowly down her face. "But, I can't finally make them proud of me with a lie."

I moved closer, bending down to wipe the tear off her cheek. "Caroline, do you really believe this is a lie?"

Her glossy eyes finally met mine as she whispered, "We both knew what this was. None of it was real."

The denial stung, because I knew she felt what I did. The realness.

"I don't believe that," I said, calm but serious. "It's felt pretty fucking real to me." I stood back up, leaning against the stall. "I care about you. And I know you feel something too."

"Reese," she finally said, her voice breaking in a way that clawed at my chest. "Maybe I got carried away with how good it all felt." She put her head in her hands. "Pretending things could be real... that I could actually be with someone like you... but we both know I'm not the girl who gets the happy ending. You're the guy who ends up with the fashion model, the dream house, you get the perfect life. Yes, maybe I was feeling things, but I'm not going to pretend you would actually end up with someone like me."

I wish everyone would stop saying that, stop telling me who I was destined to end up with, or what my life was supposed to look like. I know what feels right, and when I'm with her, *everything* feels right.

"Caroline, don't do this. I get it now, why you see yourself the way you do, but fuck, you're so much more than you give yourself credit for. You have no idea how amazing you are. If you could see yourself how I see you, you'd never question that."

The gentle rhythm of Goldilocks' breathing filled the quiet space between us, a comforting backdrop to the uncertainty that hung heavily in the air.

"Let's just get through dinner," she said, her tone resolute. But I heard the tremble she couldn't hide. "After tonight, this has to be done. I can take on tomorrow by myself."

Her words stung, and I was doing everything I could to hold back the overwhelming feeling of panic when I thought about the possibility of losing her. I knew I used to have a life without her, where I was okay with her hating me and staying in different lanes, but I didn't want that life anymore.

"If that's what you want." I gave in, not because I thought she actually wanted that, but because sometimes to get what you really want takes knowing when to fall back. And make no mistake, I was getting what I wanted—I had no intention of giving up.

"It's what I want," Caroline said before standing up and leaning her head against the horse's broad forehead and saying goodbye. She closed her eyes for a brief moment, absorbing comfort from Goldilocks.

"You were right about one thing," I murmured, petting Goldilocks one last time—I swear she gave me a look like she felt sorry for me. "You'll never get your happy ending if you keep standing in your own way."

She didn't say a word. She turned off the lights and closed the barn door. As we walked towards the rehearsal dinner, I let my gaze linger on her, taking in every detail—the way her hair fell in soft waves down her back, the subtle lift of her shoulders as she breathed in the night air, the slight quiver of her hands.

"Tell me one more thing," I urged, lifting her chin to look up at me.

"Anything," she said, honestly.

I could see the questions swirling in her mind, those eyes reflecting the same confusion that twisted inside me. There was an expectant pause, our breaths mingling in the stillness of the night.

"Earlier today," I began, thinking about what had been on my mind ever since. "You said you were worried I was going to humiliate you again." My gaze narrowed onto hers, searching. "What did you mean by that?"

"Sixth grade," she answered after a moment, the words falling softly between us, like I knew what that meant.

"Sixth grade?" I echoed, waiting for her to explain.

She looked away, her gaze settling on the tables where guests were now seated. "The dance," she continued, shaking her head. "The one you had Evan ask me to be your date to."

I blinked, my thoughts racing back, but my mind was coming up blank.

"Then you showed up with someone else. That someone else being the girl who poured a drink on me... I was humiliated. Horrified."

I remained motionless, trapped in thought. The dance I'd gone to with Emma King? I never knew Evan asked Caroline to be my date. I hated that kid. Not a clue in the world where he was now, but I was better off. I remembered commotion happening around the punch bowl, but no one ever told me it had anything to do with Caroline. I remembered Emma and I having nothing in common. I don't think we talked again after that dance.

"I know we were just kids, but that day," she said, her voice a hoarse whisper, "it makes me physically ill to think about."

Realization settled thick and heavy around me. Guilt pricked my stomach. What could I possibly say to make it all better? How could anything take away the pain she'd gone through? I was just like everyone else in her life who had failed her. If I had known, if I could have done something that night. Would it have changed everything between us? All those years of animosity over some shitty sixth grade dance. I never even realized there was a reason behind it all.

thirty-one

CAROLINE

"I want a little more curl on this side." My sister instructed her stylist through her reflection in the mirror as she pointed at a lock of hair.

I stood by the window, gaze drifting past my own reflection to the lake I had known my whole life. The sun sparkled off the water's surface, while the tables just outside were decked in flowers and candles, waiting for celebration. Goldilocks was meandering with a few other horses in the fenced pasture. I should have been ecstatic for my sister, but all I felt was an emptiness that gnawed at my insides.

I could deal with the pitying glances, the whispered judgments about my solo presence—I had braced myself for it. But nothing could have prepared me for this hollow ache that was spreading through my chest, knowing Reese wouldn't be here. It wasn't that I needed him to fend off the judgment or save me from the disappointment. It was the startling realization that I just wanted him here with me. For me.

Reese, with his otherworldly eyes that seemed to dive into the depths of my soul, always finding a way to stir up my emotions.

There was something tantalizing in his recklessness, in the small glimpses of complexity that lived beneath his rough exterior. And now, with him not here, I felt how much I was starting to really care about him.

Behind me, the room buzzed with last-minute preparations.

"Caroline, lip gloss," my sister yelled. Her reflection in the mirror was pure perfection, exactly how I had always imagined she'd look on her wedding day.

I reached into my small clutch, pulling out the gloss and extending it towards her with a practiced smile that I knew didn't quite reach my eyes.

"You look perfect," I told her, as she carefully painted her lips. She flashed me a grateful look, her expression softening for a moment.

"Thank you," she nodded just as Sam burst into the room with urgency.

"Five minutes until we need to get started," Sam announced. "I need the bridesmaids first."

The room sprung into action, sounding of rustling dresses and whispers. I took a deep breath as the bridesmaids before me fluttered into formation, each paired with a groomsmen who waited nearby.

"Looks like you need an escort," Cooper said, turning to hand me his arm with a warm smile.

"Cooper! Oh, am I glad to see you," I replied, my voice barely above a whisper as I placed my hand lightly on his arm. He always made me feel safe and loved, even when he didn't say anything.

"It's good to see you, sis. You look beautiful."

"Thank you, Coop," I said, peering through the space between heavy drapes where the crowd was seated, waiting for the ceremony to start. Reese wasn't going to be here; I had made it clear to him that I didn't want him to come. But, I found myself searching for him anyway—scanning for him. He was nowhere to be found.

"Let me guess," Cooper said with a knowing smile. "Looking for the pitcher?" He stood beside me, his posture relaxed but observant.

"I told him not to come today," I confessed as we fell in line waiting for our cue.

"Why?" he asked, his eyes narrowing ever so slightly in that calculating way he always did.

"Because..." I began, struggling to articulate the emotions I was feeling, "I don't need a date just because everyone says I do."

"Fair," he nodded with the slightest tilt of his head. "But you were the only one I just saw searching for him. Maybe you really just want him here for you, not anyone else."

I swallowed hard at the realization that struck me at his words. All this time I wanted him here to impress everyone else, but now... now those prying eyes, all the petty judgments, they blurred into insignificance. I didn't care about anyone else. I just wanted him here for me.

"Ready?" Cooper asked, as the music swelled, signaling our turn.

"Let's do it," I replied, stepping forward with him into the stunning ceremony, feeling every eye on us.

The ceremony went faster than I expected. Charlotte's beauty captivated the room, and I knew it was every bit of perfection that Charlotte had hoped for. The bridal party got to leave the ceremony first, and I knew exactly where I was headed before we needed to get to the social part of the evening. I slipped outside, headed straight to see Goldilocks. The barn was open, and she must have wandered inside.

"Hey there," I whispered, vaulting up onto the gate, my fingers finding her softness. "What's wrong with me, Goldy? Was he right about me ruining my own happiness?"

She tilted her head, those big, beautiful eyes reflecting back my own uncertainty. And then Goldilocks let out a sound—a low, thoughtful mewl. It was as if she understood, as if she agreed.

"You're not supposed to agree with him." I chuckled and stroked her back, smoothing down the fine hairs. "I think I was really liking him, maybe even falling for him, which is absolutely wild."

Goldilocks shifted, giving me a knowing look.

"Don't give me that look. I can't have him—blondes aren't his type. And men like him don't end up with women like me," I added, and yes, there I was, spilling my heart out to a horse—having a full conversation.

A deep, gravelly voice cut through the doubt. "Then he's an idiot... because if he had any sense, he'd know how incredible you are."

The phrase struck me like a lightning bolt, sending a jolt through my entire body. I froze, the hairs on the back of my neck standing on end as the atmosphere thickened with a suffocating intensity.

There, Reese stood in some suit that made the groom's tux look like it was some worn hand-me-down, its dark fabric hugging his athletic body in a way that made my mouth water. My breath hitched, eyes wide as they drank in the sight of him—the way you knew his wealth and masculinity just from the way he carried himself.

"Reese?" It was the only word that came to mind before I forced out, "Why are you here?"

"I know you can do this on your own," he said, approaching slowly. "You don't need me to get through this, but I want to be there for you anyway."

My fingers twitched at my sides with the urge to close the distance between us, to feel the safety of his arms. I imagined his hard chest pressed against me, his warm breath on my neck, his heartbeat steady and reassuring.

But I had to pull myself back. Spending tonight with him, allowing myself to fall back into the habit of pretending we were together, would only leave a deeper wound when he inevitably left me behind. No matter how fiercely I wanted him or how much him standing here right now made my heart do embarrassing, Olympic-level gymnastics, he still had the draft coming up. He'd be leaving. The last thing I needed was to be the distraction that messed with his future, or pretend a long distance relationship would work. Nope. I'd just swallow my feelings like a responsible, emotionally stable adult... or, at the very least, try really hard to keep myself together long enough to do what's right.

"I... I need you to stop saving me. Stop trying to be the hero," I forced out, my voice heavy with emotions I didn't want to unleash.

The moonlight filtered through the cracks in the wooden walls and played across his face, highlighting the chiseled lines of his jaw. He had his hands buried in the pockets of his pants in a casual pose that didn't match the intensity burning in his green eyes.

"Last thing I am is a hero," he said, with a small chuckle. "But I know you well enough to know when you're pushing me away when you want the exact opposite."

I averted my gaze from him, seeking refuge in the familiarity of Goldilocks and her now judgy eyes. "Reese, our deal is over. This is done."

There was no immediate response, just the sound of Goldilocks shifting restlessly on her hooves. Then, a soft huff—a frustrated exhalation from her—as if she didn't even believe what I had just said. Goldilocks turned on her heel, her tail flicking in quiet reprimand before she sauntered out of the barn.

"We're not done, Caroline," Reese said, smooth and dangerous. "We haven't even started yet."

"Don't say that." I turned to him, my voice barely a whisper. "We are not doing this." I pressed my hands against his chest, trying to push him away—but he didn't budge.

"Like fuck we aren't," Reese said, before he kicked the stand propping open the barn door. The heavy wood slammed shut, sealing us inside the barn.

"What's the point?" My words were half-lost in the moment, my defiance struggling to find its footing. "We both know what we signed up for. We both knew this had to come to an end."

"You are a fucking headache. But you... you also push me, challenge me to be a better man, and I need someone who does that. I need you. And you need someone to pull you out of those flames you always seem to be in. You need someone to be your safe place. You need me too."

"You think you see something in me that needs saving, that I'm some helpless damsel trapped in a fire. But maybe these flames are where I belong. I can't be the person you want me to be, and I don't need a safe place."

"You're lying," his voice was low and husky. "Everyone needs a safe place."

"Just let this go, Reese. It's over. You can release me now," I said, the words crushing my own heart along with it.

But he wasn't letting this go. Each slow, deliberate step he took closed the space between us. Heat rolled off him in waves. My back hit the rough wood of the barn, the faint flicker of shadows passing by outside barely registering.

"We're not over," he said. His dangerous and raw tone unraveled me in a way I wasn't ready for. He leaned in, smug and unhurried. "If I pulled your dress up right now, what would I find, Caroline?"

"You'd find nothing but some very dry, pink lace panties."

I did everything I possibly could—kept my face blank, my breathing even, my whole body in check. Anything to make sure he didn't see right through me. Because if he did? Game over.

"That's funny, because I know for damn sure your pussy isn't done with me. I bet it needs me so goddamn bad that it's soaking wet right now, begging for me."

My heart hammered wildly, now betraying my composure. I fought the unrelenting ache between my legs as I clenched them together, smelling his cologne. Being inches away from him but not touching him was killing me—it took everything in me to resist.

"Wrong again," I forced out, but I knew he didn't believe those words either.

Reese leaned in as he whispered against my ear, "Oh yeah?" The words sent a shiver down my spine, my dress already riding up my thighs as his fingers crept beneath the hem. His dragging touch was electric, as if he wanted to savor every inch of me. His rough calluses grazed the tender skin of my inner thigh.

"Yeah," I said as I bit down on my lip to keep myself together.

He clenched his jaw as he said, "You're so goddamn stubborn."

He didn't stop there. Oh no. His hand inched higher, pushing the fabric of my dress up, up, until he reached the edge of my panties. His fingers slid over the lace, and I felt the heat of his palm as it cupped my pussy.

"Hate to break it to you, baby," he growled, his lips brushing my ear as he gently bit down. "You're not just wet, your panties are fucking drenched." I could feel his smirk, the smug asshat. He pulled his hand away, letting the dress fall back into place. "You're mine... you know it just as much as I do."

"I'm not yours," I breathed, the fight in me dying as I ached for him to keep touching me.

His hand trailed up my body, leaving me gasping until he wrapped it around my throat. His thumb pressed against my pulse point, and I could feel the erratic thrum of my heartbeat under his touch.

"Tell me to stop then," he dared, but I couldn't—I wanted him, needed him like oxygen and he knew it.

I looked him in the eyes, my chest heaving as I whispered, "No."

He stared at my lips before crashing against me in a possessive and demanding kiss. He tilted his head, and his tongue slid into my mouth, owning me as I moaned into him. He broke the kiss only to tug my dress down, exposing my tits to him. His mouth was on me in an instant, his tongue swirling around one nipple while his fingers pinched and teased the other. I arched into him, my back pressing against the rough wood of the barn wall.

"Oh god," I moaned embarrassingly loud, realizing that people were now taking their seats for dinner just outside the barn. "What if someone finds us? Hears us?" I gasped, my voice trembling with a mix of fear and desire.

Reese pulled back just enough to look me in the eyes, his gaze dark and hazy. "Ask me if I give a shit right now?"

I didn't. His hand moved back down, slipping between my thighs, and I could feel the slickness there, the undeniable proof of how much I wanted him. His fingers teased my clit, circling, pressing, until I was writhing against him.

Then, without warning, he slid one finger inside me, and I gasped, nails digging into his shoulders. He added a second finger, then a third, his thumb still working my clit as he curled his fingers, and I was lost, my head falling back against the wall as he fucked me with his hand.

"Tell me you want me," he demanded, his voice rough with need.

"I want you so bad," I panted, arching my back into him.

"Do you want proof that you own me? That you make me so fucking hard I can't see straight?"

"Show me," I urged, trailing my fingers over the buttons on his dress shirt.

He pressed his palm flat against the wall above me, the hardness of his body caging me in, his chest rising and falling with the kind of urgency that told me he was barely holding on. I could feel him, the way his breath hitched as his other hand worked the zipper of his pants.

His cock sprang free, and Jesus fucking Christ, I was down bad. Thick, veined, and already glistening with pre-cum, it pulsed in my hand like it had a heartbeat of its own. I wrapped my fingers around him, feeling the ridges, the way he twitched under my touch like he was fighting not to come right then and there. He groaned, low and deep, the sound vibrating through me as he slowly shifted his head back, his Adam's apple bobbing as he fought for control.

"Fuck," he hissed. "You're everything I want."

He straightened up long enough to hook his hands under my thighs, lifting me effortlessly. My legs wrapped around his waist, heels digging into the small of his back as he slid my panties to the side and positioned himself at my entrance. The tip of his cock pressed against me, teasing, and I whimpered, nails scraping down his back as I tried to pull him closer.

"Please," I begged, the word torn from my throat. "Please, just—"

He didn't make me wait any longer. With a delicious thrust, he slid himself inside me, inch by relentless inch, until there was no space left between us. I gasped, my body stretching to accommodate him, every nerve ending on fire with sensation. He was so fucking big, so impossibly thick, and the way he filled me had my entire body feeling it.

"Shit," he growled again, his voice rough. "You feel so goddamn tight wrapped around me. Like you were made for me."

He pulled out slowly, agonizingly so, until only the tip remained, and then he slammed back in with a force that made me cry out. He set a tantalizing rhythm, snapping his hips as each thrust hit that sweet spot deep inside me. My toes were curling, vision blurring. His hands gripped my thighs like he was afraid he'd lose me if he let go, and every time he buried himself inside me, I could feel the way his cock pulsed. He was marking me as his.

I screamed louder and he covered my mouth with his hand, his fingers pressing against my lips as he fucked me. I could see people through the cracks in the wood, walking by, their voices faint but too close for comfort.

He didn't care. He didn't slow down. If anything, he fucked me harder, his hips thrusting hard and heavy against mine, the pleasure building until it was almost too much to bear.

"You like that?" he asked, his breath hot against my ear. "You like how deep I'm fucking you?"

I couldn't answer—words were beyond me at this point—but I didn't need to. My body answered for me, clenching around him as a wave of pleasure crashed over me. He groaned, his rhythm faltering for a moment before he continued, his hips snapping against mine with a desperation that matched my own.

"Reese. Right there. I'm close—"

"That's it, baby. Come for me."

I wanted to feel him come undone with me, to feel his cock twitch and spill inside me as I was falling apart. And when he did, it was with a guttural groan that seemed to come from the very depths of his soul. His hips slowed as he emptied himself into me, his cock pulsing in time with my own orgasm as I came around him, my vision blurring as pleasure consumed me.

"Fuck," he groaned, muffled against my neck as he dropped his shoulders.

"Fuck is right," I drew in a shaky breath, my chest tight with the undeniable truth—this man had me in a chokehold. He was always in my head, wrapped around every thought I tried to suppress. No matter how hard I fought it, I was his.

He pulled back slowly, just enough to look me in the eyes. "This isn't done."

I kissed his jaw, my lips brushing against the stubble there, and whispered, "No, baby. It's not."

Falling for him was never part of the plan. I was supposed to keep him at a distance and guard my heart. But every time I was with him, I slipped a little further. He was going to leave. I knew the reality. The draft was coming. Soon, he'd be somewhere else—with a whole new life far away. I'd tried being logical about this, I'd tried to pull away before it was too late. But it was already too late. I might get hurt. No, I probably would. But for once, I don't care anymore. I couldn't keep fighting this. Not when he looked at me like I'm the most precious thing on this planet.

After getting ourselves together, I followed Reese to the side of the barn hidden away from guests. He slid open the door slowly, the rusty hinges resisting. We walked out into the night, but we weren't alone. Giggles and fragments of a hushed conversation drew our attention.

"You know I can't refuse you anywhere," a man's voice murmured from the darkness.

My eyes adjusted to the shadows, my mind working to figure out what I was seeing—a girl, her back pressed against the rough planks of the barn wall, her head tilted back. A man leaned into her, one hand in her hair. My breath caught in my throat as the man moved to kiss her neck, revealing a glimpse of his face.

In the stillness that followed, the only sound was the soft rustle of fabric and my quickening pulse thundering in my ears. My hand trembled, and without warning, my phone slipped from my grasp, clattering to the ground and shattering the silence.

I looked over at Reese, searching for some reaction in his usually calm demeanor. He stood next to me, frozen, jaw clenched tight. I knew he was seeing exactly what I was seeing.

thirty-two

REESE

"Wh-what the—" The words stumbled from Caroline's lips, stuttering with disbelief and outrage.

It was the groom, Caroline's sister's fiancé, or now her husband. This guy should have been swept up in celebrating his wedding, I don't know... maybe focused on the bride. But here he was, busy marking his territory on Stella, the maid of honor.

In that moment, everything else faded—the music from the reception happening on the other side of the barn, the laughter, the clinking of glasses.

Behind us, a loud gasp made us turn before a voice tumbled out in hurt, "Someone mentioned they heard noises coming from the barn... and I had the worst feeling when you were nowhere to be found... how could you do this to me? And on our wedding day?"

Caroline's grip on my arm tightened, her slender fingers pressing into my flesh as her sister stalked past us. I wasn't sure if that reaction was because of the situation we'd just walked into, or because her sister mentioned noises from the barn. Either way, her sister needed to know what was happening.

"Charlotte, I—I was going to talk to you about this," Dan stammered. There was something pitiful in the way he reached for her, like there was a way to fix what she'd just seen.

Charlotte's death glare shifted, refocusing from the betrayer to his accomplice. "Tell me what? You were hooking up with my best friend? Well, now my ex-best friend."

Stella's lips parted. "Charlotte, we were going to tell you," she said, stepping away from the groom. "We didn't think you'd choose to have the wedding happen so quickly... and there was never a good time to tell you."

"Never a good time?" Charlotte threw back. "Maybe *before* I got married?"

The murmur of voices around us grew as an audience began to gather. Caroline's parents, uncles, aunts, and cousins were now watching this scene unfold. Their presence seemed to amplify the gravity of the moment, each set of eyes reflecting a collective disbelief. The Matthews family had not seen this one coming.

I reached for Caroline's arm, my fingers closing around her slender wrist. "Let's give them some space," I whispered, leading her away.

She nodded, and we walked off together, leaving the chaos behind. The dance floor was practically abandoned, the DJ hanging out nearby with nothing to do. Overhead, fairy lights flickered, casting a soft glow over a party that felt like it had already ended.

"Dance with me?" I asked, doing my best to distract her.

Caroline let out a soft laugh as she took my hand. "Didn't see that coming," she mused, gazing at the abandoned space around us. "I guess we don't have to worry about impressing anyone now."

"You impress me," I confessed, the words spilling out like a secret. Her eyes met mine, reflecting the depth of the night sky, and for a moment, it was like time itself had paused, waiting for her to respond.

She let out that small laugh again, but it was different this time —sadder. Her gaze fell, and she pulled slightly closer. "I don't impress anyone. I made so much of this wedding about me and hoping that I didn't look pathetic, and now, I just feel so bad for Charlotte," she whispered.

"Yeah," I agreed. "But, eventually she'll be okay. And I have a feeling this unnecessary pressure your family puts on you both to get married won't be an issue anymore."

A sharp scream shattered the quiet, yanking us out of our little bubble. Suddenly, Stella came sprinting out from the side of the barn, her face full of panic. "Charlotte!" she cried, her voice cracking with desperation.

I turned just in time to see Charlotte, her wedding dress swishing behind her as she ran after her ex-best friend. Their parents trailed in a flurry after them, outstretched hands desperate to mediate the situation.

"Damn it all," Yaya said, letting out a sigh as she swept by us. "Well, we might as well drink our sorrows away. Bartender, I need a double!"

Caroline and I snickered at Yaya as she made herself comfortable at the bar.

"Thank you for being here," Caroline said softly, almost... grateful. Her gaze flickered away, then back, like she didn't want to admit it. "I wanted you here more than I realized. And my algorithm was torturing me today. Some video edits of you dancing and lifting up your shirt in the locker room keeps popping up on my timeline."

"Fucking Bailey," I laughed, spinning her in a circle before I pulled her into me and whispered with a sly grin, "You know, you can't get rid of me that easily." Her hand found its way up my arm, holding on tight as the DJ started playing a slow song.

Her mom's eyes met mine as she walked by, and surprisingly, I found approval in her nod. Maybe after tonight I was no longer the enemy.

Two women joined us on the dance floor. One paused, calculating as she looked me up and down, taking in every detail. Her lips twisted into a smirk, the kind that knew more than it should. "Damn, Caroline," she purred. "Are you going to introduce us?"

"Of course," Caroline replied, although I could tell she didn't really want to, "This is Reese. Reese, these are my cousins."

One of them leaned in slightly, assessing me. "Love that for you, Caroline."

Their laughter faded as they made their way to the DJ booth to request a song. I drew Caroline in closer, my hands resting just above the dip of her waist, feeling the soft fabric of her dress beneath my fingers.

"I need to talk to you about something," I whispered in her ear, inhaling that intoxicating shampoo of hers. "I never knew."

"Never knew what?" she asked, absentmindedly.

I felt the subtle sway of Caroline's body against mine, living for the way she began to relax against me.

"I never knew about the dance," I confessed. "First off, if I was going to ask you to a dance, I would've done it myself."

There was a pause, and her blue eyes searched my face.

"You didn't know?" she asked, disbelief lining the edges of her words. "But you were there. Your girlfriend was there, she—"

Her gaze held me, intense and questioning, as if she was trying to understand but was now reading the truth written in my eyes.

"She wasn't my girlfriend... I just asked her because we sat next to each other in math. I don't think I talked to her much after that dance. I knew something happened at the punch table, but I had no idea about any of what you told me."

She stayed quiet, letting my words sink in. In the soft glow of candlelight, I caught the flicker of something in Caroline's eyes—hurt, maybe disbelief.

"All this time... you really thought I'd do that to you?" My chest tightened as I continued. "I'm sorry it happened, but I need you to know—I'd never do something like that."

She leaned into me gently, her head coming to rest against my shoulder. "I'm sorry for everything. We spent all these years hating each other because I thought—"

I couldn't hold back a grin—she was so ridiculous and sweet that it made my chest ache. Before she could say another word, I leaned down and pressed a soft kiss to the top of her head, cutting her off gently. "It's okay, baby."

Her gaze flickered away for a second before snapping back to mine, a storm of emotions swirling behind those eyes.

"What happens now?" she whispered. "When things go back to how they were? When we have to face reality and we're actually done... when you have to release me?"

For the first time in what felt like forever, she was letting me in. And damn, if it didn't make me want to hold on even tighter. This fucking reputation of mine, which I'd never intended to own, but somehow couldn't escape. We continued to move together, our audience fading, leaving only us. Her hand was so small and relaxed in mine, her other arm draped over my shoulder.

"Caroline, you've been here in this town my whole life, and now that I see you, *really* see you, I can't go back to how things were. Things stopped being fake for me almost as soon as we started."

"But this was never supposed to be real," she said, her voice catching on doubt. "I'm so wrong for you, and you're... you're—"

"I don't give a fuck what I am as long as I'm with you."

Before she could respond, we shifted on the dance floor, and two figures made their approach—her Nana and Papa. Her Nana's eyes locked onto mine, sharp and discerning.

"And who is this strapping young man?"

Caroline stiffened beside me, her grip on my hand tightening. I knew this was her father's parents, two people she said had been the hardest in the entire family to impress.

I extended my other hand toward her Nana. "Reese," I said, my voice steady. "Nice to meet you."

"It's a pleasure," she said with a tight smile, her eyes flicking upward to meet mine. "You know, I have seen Caroline many times over the years, and never have I seen her glowing this way. You two make a beautiful couple."

"Thank you," I grinned, glancing at Caroline. "I think so too."

Caroline's papa stepped forward, not looking pleased. "And what exactly do you do for a living?"

Caroline spoke before I could. "He's only going to be the best pitcher in the MLB soon."

Her Papa's expression shifted, like she instantly lightened the mood. "Baseball?" he asked, curiously, as he turned to Caroline once more. "Don't you forget to bring us to a game then, dear. I'll bring that jersey of mine I won back in 1981."

Caroline laughed a real laugh for the first time all night. "Will do, Papa."

The wedding had drained me, and Caroline stayed behind to help her parents and sister—they all had suites at the event center for the night. By the time I pulled into my driveway, all I wanted was sleep. But as I rolled to a stop, I noticed the downstairs lights were still on. At this hour, that could only mean one thing—someone was up. And from the looks of it, something was going on.

I killed the engine and dragged myself up the steps to the front door.

"Hello?" I pushed the front door open, but no one was in sight. My dad's office door was open, though, a sliver of light was peaking through. I stepped closer, peering through the gap. The chair was empty, pushed away from the desk like he'd just gotten up and walked out.

Something drew me in. The closet door was open and usually never was. A box lay on the floor inside the door, half-buried beneath a pile of discarded papers and old ledgers. Its lid hung off, corners bent. I crouched down to get a closer look.

A flood of emotions hit me all at once. My fingers traced the cardboard, revealing envelopes, photographs, and cards discolored with age. I lifted a photo to the light, glimpsing *her* smile—so much like mine—and felt the sharp sting of betrayal. Anger consumed me as I recognized the names across the envelopes. All addressed to me from my mom.

I went through the memories, pictures of her and Boston. A

wristwatch buried inside had long stopped working, frozen at a point in time I'd never known about. She had been reaching out all this time. She was right about everything. Betrayal coiled in my chest like a snap about to strike. I had lost years with my Mother and with Boston because of him. My dad. He'd kept this all from me.

My fingers clenched around the edges of the cardboard box as I lifted it out of the room. The clinking noises floating down the hall told me exactly where to go. Ice against glass, and probably whiskey being opened, was all too familiar to me. I stepped into the dark bar area where my father stood, his back to me. He poured himself a drink with his sleeves rolled up. I could feel the tension in the room.

With a thud that echoed my frustration, I tossed the box onto the bartop. The contents jumped around slightly. "What the fuck is this?"

Dad turned slowly, barely flinching at my abrupt entrance. His eyes met mine for a quick moment, then he took a slow sip of his whiskey.

"It's nothing," he said calmly. The word "nothing" rolled off his tongue so easily, like another one of his courtroom lies. But the proof was right in front of him—proof that it was definitely fucking some-thing—everything—hidden and kept from me.

"That's all you have to say?"

All these years, she had been trying, reaching out. Everything had been intercepted. In the corners of my mind, I'd always fought the vicious thoughts of her not wanting me. I felt empty, and I'd tried to fill that void with anything else—baseball, women, friends. Nothing ever filled it. He was the reason for that void.

He was silent at first, then tilted his head slightly before finally speaking. "Reese, you don't understand. Everything I did was for you. To protect you."

I let out a slow breath, my fingers tightening around the keys in my pocket, the sharp edges digging into my palm. "Was it?... because from where I'm standing, you took something from me—years I can never get back. Were you really thinking about me? Or were you just doing what was best for you and your ego?"

I turned, heading straight for the front door. I didn't even want to look at him anymore.

"Where are you going?" His question stopped me mid-step. "You have the draft in a few days—you need your head in the right place."

I turned to face him again. The man who had stolen so much from me, hurt me more than he helped me, stood steady and unflinching. My gaze met his. "Does it matter?"

Then, when I thought I'd finally get out of there, his voice cut through the silence again. I paused, hand hovering over the doorknob.

"Where have you been all day?"

"Caroline's sister's wedding," I snapped. The audacity of that question made my blood boil. My jaw clenched, my breath came sharp, and if I wasn't already fuming, I sure as hell was then.

He paused mid-sip. "Her again?" he asked, his voice a low drawl. "What are you doing with that girl?"

"Come on, Dad," I said, frustrated. I ran my hands through my hair. "You try to control so much of my life already. You made sure I didn't have a relationship with my mom or Boston. You put so much pressure on me with baseball all my life. Do you have to have this too? You wanna arrange a marriage for me?"

His gaze studied the whiskey as it swirled in the glass. He chuckled. "There's a difference between controlling you and protecting you."

"There's a thin line, Dad."

"I'm just saying, you're going places—she's not," he snapped. "You're going to have more money than you know what to do with, and people—they see that. Not just her, but Cindee too. They're going to use you, take advantage of you, and you're too damn blind to see it."

I let out a bitter laugh, pulling my tie loose and over my head with one sharp tug. "Then so be it." I tossed it onto the floor, my chest heaving. "I'd rather learn the hard way. I'd rather know for myself than have you decide who I can trust."

His nostrils flared, his free hand clenching into fists at his sides. When he spoke again, his voice was raw and strained like he was finally showing real emotion. "You are the only thing in this world I have ever truly cared about." His eyes burned with something fierce, something desperate. "And the only way I knew to keep you safe was to keep you close. To *protect* you. That is my job and it has always been my job."

"No. Your job was to be my father," I bit out, trembling with frustration.

If keeping me close was about protecting me, then why did it feel like I've spent my whole life trying to escape him? My jaw locked, the years of buried resentment pressing down on me. Then, without another glance, I grabbed the doorknob, and yanked it open. The door slammed shut behind me, rattling in its frame, but it still wasn't loud enough to drown out the pounding in my chest.

thirty-three

CAROLINE

Just as I laid my head down after what felt like a never ending day, there was a knock at my door. My parents had got the bridal suite for Charlotte, themselves a room, and Cooper and I separate rooms. Which meant it was probably a devastated Charlotte at the door.

With a reluctant sigh, I pushed myself up and swung my legs over the edge of the bed. After shuffling forward, I unlocked the door and pulled it open. My arm was sore from being on auto-pilot all day as Charlotte's lip gloss assistant. My hair was twisted into a messy bun, a loose shirt was hanging off one shoulder, and the absence of a bra was unmistakable. "Let me guess," I exhaled, "more lip gloss?"

"Not unless it's coming straight from your lips," Reese said back to me. I took him in. His button-up shirt had the top buttons undone. His tie was gone, and his hair was tousled like he'd been raking his fingers through it all night.

"I thought you went home?"

Something happened. I could see it in the way he was standing. In the tension in his jaw. Whatever it was, he seemed upset. And he'd come to me. Not just anywhere—to me. That thought alone made my chest full and my throat tight with an emotion I had never quite felt before.

"I did," he said. His gaze avoided mine, but I noticed how the muscles along his jaw clenched. "And I shouldn't have. Can't be around my dad tonight. Can I come in?"

The sight of him like this surprised me. It was raw and unguarded in a way that made my stomach flip, like some part of him had unraveled, and I was the place he'd sought to put himself back together. I was worried, but no matter how shaken he was or what happened with his dad, he'd still come to *me*. And all I wanted was to make him feel as safe as he always made me feel.

"Are you okay?" I asked, my hand pushing the door open wider, inviting him in.

He stepped into the room, and the door fell shut behind him. My fingers brushed his arm as he walked past me, and it felt like a jolt of electricity, a way to show him that I was there, that whatever this was—whatever we were—I cared about him.

"I am now," Reese murmured, making his way through the room as he claimed the chair beside my bed, settling into it. He relaxed back, muscles easing beneath the fabric of his crumpled shirt.

I dropped onto the edge of the bed, the mattress dipping slightly as I studied Reese. "What happened?"

"I'm just ready to figure out where I'm going," he said, with a bone-deep tiredness in his voice. "Which team I'm on." His hands—those large pitcher's hands—clenched into fists, then relaxed again. "It's long overdue that I get some space from my dad."

My fingers traced the pattern of the comforter beneath me, my hands always needing to fidget with something.

"Was he upset that you were with me?" The question slipped out, but I wasn't quite sure if I wanted to hear his answer.

The chair creaked as Reese leaned forward, elbows planting themselves on his knees. "I think he's just unhappy with me," he said, shaking his head. "Upset that I'm challenging him on his opinions about my mom."

"I'm sorry he's putting you through that," I whispered. "I wish parents always put us first, put what was best for us first."

"Me too," he said, rising from his seat. I watched, captivated, as his fingers danced over the buttons of his dress shirt, each one coming undone with deliberate slowness. The fabric parted, revealing a glimpse of tanned skin and those abs I would recognize anywhere.

"Oh," I teased, "do I get a show?"

"Anytime you want," he said with a half-smile. Reese threw his shirt over the chair before his pants made their way down his legs. He folded them, then threw them on the chair next to his shirt.

"I'll have to remember that," I said, grinning.

"Scoot over, Chaos," he said. His words were soft, but still held that effortless authority that clung to him like it was built in.

He slid onto the bed, claiming more space. My heart picked up speed as I shifted closer, leaving him no choice but to put his arm around me. The sheets tangled around our legs as I brushed my lips against his shoulder and whispered, "I'm usually the one running to you when I'm upset, but I like it when the roles are reversed."

His exhale was almost a chuckle, warm and teasing. "Oh, do you now?" he drawled, his words gradually turning darker. My stomach tightened at the sound. "What else do you like?"

My fingers trailed up his arm, feeling the heat of his skin beneath them. His muscles tensed as I moved to his chest, my palm flat against the hard ripples, feeling the goosebumps rise.

His hand caught mine, pinning it to his chest for a moment. "Roll over," he growled, and my thighs clenched involuntarily.

I did as he said, turning, the sheets sliding against my skin as I pressed my ass against him. He was gripping my hips in an instant, his hard length already pressing into the curve of my back.

"You're everything I never knew I needed," he said, his lips at my ear, voice rough with emotion. "You're mine."

I felt him shift, his hips grinding against me, his length rocking against my ass. I gasped, arching into him, and he let out a low, satisfied groan. He pulled me back against him, his cock sliding between my thighs, so close but not yet where I wanted him.

One of his large hands stayed gripping my waist, and he used the other to spread my legs, reaching into my center until his fingers found my clit. He started rubbing tight circles that sent sparks shooting through me. His fingers trailed to my dripping slit, the slickness of my arousal coating his fingertips as he inserted one finger, and then another. I gasped, biting down on my lip to stifle the moan threatening to escape.

"Fuck, you're so wet," he whispered, his breath hot against the back of my neck. His fingers inched deeper, plunging inside me with a precision that made me arch into his touch. I wanted more, I wanted him, so I reached behind me, trailing my fingertips over his shaft. "You want it," he murmured, as if he was reading my mind. "Then say it."

I did, the word slipping from my lips in a breathless moan. "Please."

He took my hand in his, intertwining our fingers, holding me in place as he positioned himself at my entrance. "I'm so fucking addicted to this tight pussy," he said, his voice raw as he pushed inside, stretching me, and making me clench around his cock. "Jesus Christ, I can't get enough," he hissed, his hips moving in a slow, torturous rhythm, filling me completely.

"You feel so good," I cried out, my nails digging into the sheets. I was trembling, every nerve in my body buzzing with the sensation of him—thick, hard, and unrelenting—rolling his hips into me with a deep, delicious rhythm.

My heart was pounding so hard I swear he could feel it. My entire body was tingling from the pure intensity of it all. This felt different. He was claiming me, holding me in a way I'd never felt before— tender, sensual, all-consuming. There was an overwhelming shift between us. A rush of emotions were crashing over me, drowning me in sensations I wasn't sure if I could ever recover from. For the first time, I felt cherished, desired. Seen.

"God, yes," I moaned into my pillow, as his hand on my hip tightened. His fingers dug into my skin as he pulled me back against him, our bodies moving in sync. His other hand released mine, reaching around to rub my clit, the dual sensations of him inside me and his fingers moving bringing me to the edge.

His lips were on my neck, teeth grazing the sensitive skin. "You're so perfect, baby. You take me so fucking well."

He pulled out almost completely before he slammed back into me, picking up speed. His muscles tensed and released with every thrust. I was losing myself in the pleasure that was building with every movement of his hips.

"I'm about to—" I couldn't get the words out, though. I came with a cry, my body shaking as the pleasure tore through me.

"Me, too," he breathed out, following me over the edge, his hips stuttering as he buried himself deep inside me, his low groan muffling against my skin.

We stayed like that for a long moment, both of us trembling and breathless. Then he rolled onto his back, pulling me with him until I was sprawled across his chest. His heartbeat was still racing, his skin still hot and damp with sweat.

He pressed a soft kiss to my temple, and a shiver ran through me. "Mine," he whispered. And I didn't argue—because he was right. I was completely his.

I kept my head on his chest, listening to his heartbeat begin to steady. It was the most calming sound I'd ever heard.

"What's going to happen with us when you move away?" I let the question slip from my mouth, unable to hold back the thought that was consuming my mind.

His fingers traced my scalp with a gentle pressure that massaged away the knots of tension. The motion was hypnotic, lulling me into a state where only his touch and the shared warmth beneath the sheets existed.

"Nothing," he finally breathed, his voice barely more than a vibration against my ear.

I looked back just enough to eye him. "Nothing?" I scoffed. "You said that like it just explained everything."

His eyes—those eyes of his—still entrancing, even in the darkness, held mine. Reese's hands resumed their gentle movement through my hair. "If you think I'm just letting you go, then you're wrong," he said. "I might be busy, but I'll come see you anytime I can, and hopefully, you'll come see me when you can too."

I laughed in disbelief. "You're acting like you could be moving down the street—what if it's somewhere across the country?" How could he be so nonchalant about this? I was just now letting him in —I had started to really like him. More than like, maybe. And even though I knew amazing things were coming for him, I couldn't help but wish for a pause button—a way to freeze time in this moment, before the inevitable drift began.

"Then we'll figure it out," he said, simply. I knew he was trying not to be too harsh about the reality of the situation. Maybe he wasn't ready to accept the truth, but even if we did try to stay in touch, see each other when we could, we'd inevitably drift apart.

"You just have no stress in the world, do you?" I said, the words airy but edged. "I always have stress and worries, and anxiety. But you, nothing."

He chuckled, not needing to say anything else, apparently. I knew he understood why I was worried, even as he laid there, the epitome of calm in the face of our uncertain future. It was one of the things that drew me to him, this fact that he could somehow stand tall in any scary situation and not be moved. Yet here I was, perpetually on the edge, about to lose it, not knowing how he and I could possibly continue on this path together.

The warmth of his arms circled around me, drawing me further into the solid comfort of his chest. "Because that sounds like chaos to me."

<h1 style="text-align:center">thirty-four</h1>

REESE

"I personally hope you get drafted to Los Angeles," my sister said, flashing a grin over her shoulder at me. "Because I need a selfie with the Hollywood sign. Maybe even make a dance video nearby."

"You're starting to sound like a real cheerleader now."

"That's because I am," she squealed, then started placing items on her plate from the gourmet buffet that had been set up at the draft.

"Yeah, you are," I acknowledged, grabbing my elbow. "Heard you kicked ass at try-outs."

"The best part is that Wendy didn't make the team," she said with a slight grin. "But I can't really take all the credit because I had a good coach."

"Yeah, but you did the work," I told her, watching as she added salad to her plate last.

"I guess so. But anyway, are they really going to record us all night?" she asked, her gaze locked onto the camera flickering with a red recording light set up in the front of the room.

"Hopefully they only show a quick clip of our reactions." The couch's cool leather pressed against my palms as I leaned back, looking through the glass window at the draft stage.

I unscrewed the cap of my water bottle and took a long swallow just as the door eased open. My stepmom slipped in, her arms immediately finding me in a tight embrace. "I am so proud of you. No matter what order you go in, first or last, you are the best in my eyes, and any team is so lucky to have you."

"Thank you," I said, still in her embrace. "But let's be real. We all know I'm going top five."

"He's going first," my dad announced, walking in after her. "No doubt about it."

With a small nod, I retreated further into the leather couch. My thumbs tapped across my phone screen, wondering what Caroline was doing right now.

"Heard some jackass was hosting a party in here like he's some big deal."

I looked up at the comment. Boston leaned lazily against the doorframe. Behind him, like a shadow, emerged our mother. My eyes darted to my dad in confusion.

"Son," he began, "I know you've been upset with me, but our relationship means more to me than you know." He paused, giving a nod toward Boston and my mom as he continued. "I can suck up being in a room with her if you want her to be part of your life. Today is about you and all the important people in your life supporting you."

He didn't wait for a response—he turned and retreated to the other side of the room where my sister and stepmom stood.

"Glad you're both here," I said, greeting Boston and his mom —*our* mom. My gaze shifted pointedly toward Boston, who was going to be having his own draft party next year. "Well, sort of glad he's here."

Boston smirked. "Yeah, keep talking, and watch you won't be drafted until tomorrow," he shot back.

"Yeah, you wish," I said, playfully.

Out of the corner of my eye, I caught the tears glossing Cindee's eyes. Her hand, warm and trembling, found its way to my back. "Reese," she began, her voice quivering on the edge of emotion. "I knew today would be emotional, but getting to see you two getting along and being together... might be my favorite thing in the world."

"Just give us time. The 'get along' part might have an expiration of about twenty minutes," I joked as her face began to lighten.

"Yeah, don't go planning any family outings just yet," Boston added.

The room started to fill with strangers as the draft began. My name was called second, and my time on the stage was almost dreamlike, like an out of body experience where every clap and cheer blurred together. I accepted my new team's baseball cap, and shook the MLB Commissioner's hand before they allowed me to exit the stage.

Once I got back into the designated room backstage, my family cheered, their smiles wide and eyes shimmering with pride. I felt the love and their support, but my mind raced toward one person —Caroline.

"Congratulations, son," my dad said, his hand firm on my shoulder.

"Thank you," I said, as I reached for my phone. I was grateful for my family, don't get me wrong, but it was Caroline's fiery spirit that I missed, her spark that I craved lately—it made me feel alive. She was the only person I wanted to talk to about this moment.

The screen lit up under my touch, and I had more alerts than I expected—meaning everyone must have been watching. But I ignored all the other alerts, looking for just one name.

CAROLINE

Minnesota, huh? Does that mean I need a winter coat?

ME

It does indeed

CAROLINE

Well I can probably do that but not so sure if
I can pull off those earmuff things

ME

Trust me, you could pull off anything, Chaos

CAROLINE

I miss hearing you say that...

CAROLINE

Oh, no... what's wrong with me?

ME

Love that you miss me. Send me a picture
and show me how much.

CAROLINE

Nah, would rather make you wait to see me
in person

ME

I'll deal with you later for that

CAROLINE

Tell me more

ME

Patience

ME

Got some interviews to do and we'll be here
late but we're driving back early tomorrow

CAROLINE

Sounds good. Congrats again! So happy
for you.

thirty-five

CAROLINE

Reese and I had been inseparable since the moment he came back into town, stealing every second we could before time ran out. Yesterday, we'd spent the entire day on his boat, the sun warming our skin, the gentle waves rocking us blissfully while I was in his arms. He was starting to feel like home, my safe place—and he was right about how much I needed it. And now, just when we'd finally found our rhythm, when everything felt right and effortless with nothing standing in the way, he was leaving. Today.

I reached out, hesitating for just a moment before pressing the doorbell—it was a sleek, modern black circle with a camera. With a small smile, I pressed the button and lifted my shirt just over the camera lens, hoping to be spontaneous and surprise him.

But the giggle died in my throat when the door creaked open sooner than expected. Reese appeared, and a flush crept up my neck as I quickly shoved my shirt back down.

A silent moment hung between us before he grinned and said, "Uh... did you just flash the camera?"

I forced a slow blink, tucking a strand of hair behind my ear like I wasn't internally combusting at the fact that he'd just caught me.

"Maybe," I drawled, aiming for cool and landing somewhere near delusional.

His brow lifted, those sharp green eyes flickering with pure mischief. "You do know that footage goes straight to my dad's phone, right?"

My stomach hit the floor as cold terror rushed through me like I'd been thrown in ice water. He bit his lip, barely holding back a laugh as I choked on air.

"Shut up," I sputtered, voice cracking. "Please tell me you're kidding."

His smirk deepened. He was *definitely* not kidding. Reese just leaned against the door frame, amused. "Don't worry about it," he laughed, "Can guarantee you that wasn't the first pair he's seen."

My cheeks still burned as I crossed my arms. "I can never show my face around him again."

"You're going to have to... he's here in his office," Reese snickered.

"I have to go," I whispered, covering my eyes in embarrassment.

"Get in here," Reese's hands grabbed mine from my face and pulled me inside, the door closing behind me.

He led me down the familiar hallway, moving toward his bedroom. He pushed open the door to his room, where suitcases were open and filled. Shirts, jeans, everything—folded and packed in tight.

"I hate admitting this," I found myself saying, "but we've only been apart a few hours and I missed you. How am I going to do this whole long distance thing?"

He straightened, and flashed me a dimple. "Sit on the bed," he said, simply. "Spread your legs, and I can show you how much I've missed you too."

"Very funny," I rolled my eyes, "with my luck, your dad will walk in here and get another show." The thought of his father witnessing anything more than he already had made me want to live the rest of my days under a rock.

A laugh rumbled out of Reese as his arms wrapped around my

waist, pulling me in close, and the scent of him—warm and spicy—filled my senses. It was like coming home to a warm, clean house, if that house was a person.

"Are you sure you don't want to come with me?" His lips brushed against mine in a kiss so tender it was in direct contradiction to his reckless spirit.

I clung to him, my arms entwined around his solid form. "I can't. But I'll be there to visit in a few weeks," I whispered, feeling the steady thump of his heart.

"I have my own place, you know. It has a nice view of downtown, there's some vacant dance studio space around me. I'm just saying... you could stay with me, start up your own career."

His words painted images of a life that would be a dream. A new city full of opportunities, a life with him and endless possibilities. But it wasn't the real world, and I couldn't allow myself to be swept away by how good it sounded.

"I appreciate that—I do." My fingers trailed over his shirt. "But it's not that easy. I don't have the money to just pick up and go, to start a business. And I can't follow you around like a lost puppy."

"You're not a lost puppy. I got a pretty nice signing bonus. Maybe I could invest in you." His gaze didn't waver, but there was a softness on his face. "And there's nothing tying you down here. You could start a career anywhere."

I felt the pull of his persuasion, saw the determination in his jawline, his puppy dog eyes—he was pulling out all the stops. But this was not how I envisioned the beginning of my journey after college—dependent on someone else's fortune.

"I can't start my career with your signing bonus, but we'll figure this out, okay? I'll be there in a few weeks, and we take it day by day, remember?"

"Yeah, guess I'll go along with this plan," he said, with a deep sigh. "But doesn't mean I have to like it."

"I don't like it either," I said just before a knock on the door fractured our stillness.

His father's muffled voice filtered through the door. "Reese, we need to leave so we have time before your flight takes off."

"Last chance, Chaos."

"I'll see you in a few weeks," I whispered. The reality that he was really leaving was starting to settle in.

How was I going to find the strength to let him go? I hoped that this goodbye was only temporary, but that didn't make it hurt any less. Anything could happen in a few weeks, and long distance had never been known to be easy. His thumb traced the line of my jaw, and I tilted my face up to his as our lips met again. "Knew you'd say that," Reese murmured against my mouth.

I drew back slightly, my heart pounding in my chest as I met those penetrating green eyes. "You're always so strong and calm," I said, my voice barely above a whisper. "Do you ever freak out? Worry?"

His fingers lingered on my chin, his touch soft yet impossibly steady, like he was trying to memorize me with his hands.

"Nah," Reese murmured. "But I'm not always strong. You wanna know when I'm weak?" His eyes locked onto mine, stealing the breath from my lungs. "When it comes to you."

Without thinking, my arms pulled him closer, until I could feel the steady beat of his heart again. "Okay, never mind," I pouted, burrowing my face into the fabric of his shirt, seeking comfort. "Maybe I'll just go in your suitcase."

Reese's laughter vibrated through his chest. "You, baby, would get a seat next to me in first class," he teased.

I drew back slightly, looking up at him. "You're just making this worse," I whined. "You better get going."

"Alright," he said reluctantly. "Bye, Chaos."

A tear escaped even though I fought it. I whispered a choked, "Not a goodbye... a see you soon," as the tear traced a path down my cheek. His fingers brushed ever so lightly against my skin, capturing the tear.

"See you soon," Reese said, then let me go. And just like that, I watched him turn away, gripping the handles of his luggage.

Just before stepping through the door, he hesitated. One last glance over his shoulder—a look that said all the words he didn't. Then, he was gone—disappearing into the car, then down the street, making reality slap me in the face.

His empty room felt too still, too quiet. My gaze landed on an envelope sitting on his desk, my name written across it. My fingers trembled, tracing the letters before finally tearing it open. Something familiar spilled into my palm—his necklace. The one he never took off. The one he'd worn for as long as I could remember.

A folded note rested inside, his handwriting slightly smudged.

You know how much this means to me. But you mean more. Bring it back to me. -R

My breath caught. My heart tore open.

He was gone, but he wasn't letting me go. He left me the one thing he knew I would have to return to him. This wasn't just a necklace. It was a piece of him. And now, it was in my hands. I'd have to find him. I'd have to return it. To put it back where it belonged—around his neck, right next to his heart. Right where I belonged, too.

I sat on the edge of his bed and I ran my fingers through my hair. His scent lingered there, something I wasn't quite ready to give up. Finally, after I don't know how many minutes—I found the strength to stand. I let out a long sigh and I walked out of his room and into the hallway.

"Caroline?" The voice, soft and sweet, got my attention.

"Hi," I murmured through the tightness in my chest. Reese's sister stood beside his stepmom. "I was just saying goodbye to Reese... and was heading out."

"Come here," Lo beckoned with a gentle tilt of her head.

Making my way to the kitchen, tears blurred my vision as I clutched at Lo's hands. "I'm so sorry about everything."

"It's okay… I know that plan was more Reese's idea than yours." She paused, offering a gentle smile. "But the next time Wendy Clark tries to attack my skills, I might need you again."

"Anytime."

"Reese told us PB&J's were your favorite. Well… that and manicotti, but Mom isn't the best at Italian," Lo said, her words bittersweet. "Want one?"

"He said you like them without the crust," his stepmom added, opening the fridge just behind Lo. "I may not be great at pasta but I can make a mean PB&J."

Tears fell from depths I didn't know existed. "They are my favorite," I sobbed, my voice catching on the laughter and sorrow that raced through my mind. Reese remembered that from high school—I used to toss my leftover crusts and trash into the bed of his truck.

"Used to have them every day for lunch," I whispered, almost to myself. A sudden embrace pulled me in—Lo's arms tightening around me, not just in comfort but in understanding. No words, no questions, just quiet solidarity. The space Reese once occupied so vibrantly was now so empty, and all that remained was this dreadful ache—the kind that settled deep, heavy, and unshakable.

thirty-six

REESE

Whack! A firm pat on my back pulled me from my focus, the warmth of it lingering through my jersey. "Carrington!" Skip's voice broke through my focus, and I turned to see him walking towards me. "Little short-handed tonight, might need you to close. Don't be surprised if I call your name in the ninth. Be ready."

I nodded, my muscles tensed at his words. "I'll be ready," I promised, as the weight of the opportunity settled heavily on my shoulders. It could be my first big shot at proving I was worth drafting.

There was another pitcher that wasn't fully recovered and still on the injury list, a fact that certainly played into Skip's decision. But, regardless, I'd take it. Skip nodded, signaling the end of our brief exchange. I settled onto the wooden bench in front of my locker, and reached for my phone.

The screen glowed alive at my touch. A long list of unread messages were displayed, but there were no new alerts from Caroline. Nothing after I'd sent her a good morning text. There was an uneasy feeling in my stomach. She typically called or messaged me throughout the day, but today, of all days, her silence stood out. I knew she couldn't make it to my first game. The distance was something we hadn't figured out. She hadn't been able to visit me yet, which I understood. But this silence? It was unlike her.

"Focus," I whispered to myself. "Don't let it get to you." This was my moment—my chance to make a name for myself here. With or without hearing from her, I had a promise to keep, a game to close.

I flicked across the screen, searching for something—a distraction, anything to fill the void of her ghosting me all day. Bailey popped up on my timeline. He was live, talking to the camera at the gym in all his glory. I was cringing at him flexing under the harsh gym lights.

"Alright, I will do three more reps," Bailey grunted, sweat trailing down his face. "But you better keep sending those unicorns," he warned with a wink, the chat cheering him on.

And then he squinted at the screen. "Oh shoot, my man Reese is in here," he announced, with a big grin. "Which means he wants me to take off my shirt, hang on."

I couldn't help but snicker despite the tension knotting in my stomach. Bailey was still Bailey, just as outrageous as always. He pulled his tank top over his head, muscles glistening like he'd put some kinda baby oil on himself, tattooed skin flexing. I shook my head. I tapped across the screen as I typed, "God please put it back on."

The screen erupted in a digital mayhem of unicorns and fireworks, the chat moving too fast to keep up. Bailey's grin widened, appreciative of his adoring audience. "Alright, chat, thank you for the gifts. Everyone tell my boy Reese good luck on his first game."

The response was immediate and overwhelming. The kind wishes of support and each "good luck" flooded the screen. Shaking off the amusement, I swiped away from Bailey's live stream and turned on a playlist as I pulled out my headphones. Others had started to fill the locker room around me as the music filled my ears. It was time to get my head right, to warm up. Time to step into the limelight and show them all what Reese Carrington was made of.

Tonight, under the stadium lights, it would be just me and the mound—a place I knew better than the back of my hand.

Before I knew it, it was time to take the field. I glanced at my phone one last time, but there was still no message from Caroline. This wasn't the time for distractions, though, so with a decisive click, the phone went dark and I tossed it in my bag.

The game started slow. Innings passed by with no runs on the board from either team. It wasn't until the bottom of the fourth that we broke through—a sharp line drive double. A sac fly to right field sent him home. The score was one to nothing. But, then in the top of the fifth, they answered with a two-run home run.

By the bottom of the seventh inning, we were locked in a tie. Then, the call came. "Carrington," the pitching coach called from the bullpen phone, "Time to get loose."

I nodded. The world shrank as I began with easy throws to warm up.

"Your girl here to watch you play for the first time?" the backup catcher asked as I gripped the ball, winding up for another pitch.

I let out a slow breath, forcing my expression to stay neutral. "Nah, she couldn't make it," I said, trying to sound unfazed. But I was far from unfazed. Would she ever make it to one of my games? Would she ever be in the stands, watching, cheering? I wanted to believe she would be, but hope was starting to feel like a losing bet. She should have visited already. But so far, there was always some reason she couldn't make it. Maybe I'd fallen too deep and this was all on me.

"Ramp it up, Carrington," said one of the pitching coaches. "Game speed."

I nodded, locking in. The ball ripped toward the catcher's mitt, each pitch sharper, faster. It was my best stuff. As I fired another fastball, a steady certainty settled in—win or lose, *this* was exactly where I was meant to be.

The ninth inning crept up before I knew it. I walked to the mound, forcing out slow breaths. As I stood there, the air seemed charged with electricity, an anticipation hanging thick from the crowd. It was surreal. I'd worked all my life for this moment, dreamed about it since I was a kid. All I wanted to do was take it all in and believe that I was here for a reason, and I wouldn't fail.

And then, for the first time in my life, I went completely still. Blindsided. The roar of the crowd, the pounding of my heart, the rush of adrenaline surging through my veins—Gone. Like someone had just hit pause.

My gaze snagged on her, just beyond home plate—impossible to miss, like a firework in the night sky. Caroline. My chest tightened. I narrowed my eyes, not trusting what I was seeing. The double take confirmed it. She was there.

She had come.

A grin spread across my face, my fingers adjusted the brim of my hat—a silent salute to the woman who was the challenge I would never be able to resist. Confidence ran through my veins, drowning out the crowd's roar and putting my head in the game. Nothing could hold me back now. Not with her here, watching.

The catcher's voice came through my earpiece. "Fastball."

I coiled, muscles tensing, and with a quick burst, I unleashed the pitch. The batter swung and the crack of the ball meeting the bat fractured the silence. The ball went foul. I felt the weight of stares, Caroline's among them. The second pitch hurtled across the plate, and the batter lashed out once more. This time, the ball sailed forcefully toward first base, where the baseman snagged it easily.

"Out!" The umpire signaled. The crowd erupted into cheers. One down.

With the second batter staring me down, my fingers brushed the seams of the ball. Another fastball. I'd let this one be my fastest yet. His bat sliced through the afterglow of my pitch, swinging too late. Once, twice, thrice—he flailed, each swing mistimed. Three strikes. He retreated, and I could breathe again for a moment.

I glanced up where the stadium lights made my vision blur, and I allowed myself a moment to bask in it. Just one more out, then it would be up to our batting skills to win it. The moment the batter connected with my fastball, a shot of panic rushed through my veins like lightning. The ball soared, but as it hurtled towards the outfield, I could see our center fielder was right there, and caught it in a dive. Out three. I'd done it.

As I stepped off the mound and into the dugout, the world around me faded into a hazy blur. It was no longer about me; it was about us; the team. Our first batter stepped up, he swung straight into the shortstop's glove.

Our second batter took his stand. He attacked the first pitch with ferocity, sending it deep to the warning track. For a second, we all thought it might clear the fence—but he was held at second with a double. The next batter made it on base, and then after him, a hit to deep center field sent our guys sprinting home. The game was over. We'd won.

The stadium's buzz echoed in my ears as I bypassed the route to the locker room. I had to get to her.

Caroline stood waiting with a cheeky grin in the front row near the dugouts.

"You've got a lot of nerve not texting me today, Chaos," I teased, but there was an edge to my voice—I'd missed her more than I even realized.

She just smiled, that secret little smirk that drove me insane. "I couldn't ruin the surprise."

I narrowed my eyes. "Always keeping me on my toes," I murmured, my gaze locking onto hers. "Thought you couldn't visit."

"That was true," she said softly, stepping closer. "But, I'm not visiting."

My heart stopped. "What do you mean?"

She took a slow breath, her fingers brushing against mine. "Accepted a cheer coach position here in town," she said, her voice barely above a whisper. "It's not the same as having my own studio, but one day, I want to open my own. And when I do... I want to do it with my own money, on my own terms." Her eyes searched mine, a mix of nervousness and excitement. "But until then... I want to be here. With you."

My chest tightened, my world tilted. She was *staying*.

"If you don't kiss me right now," I threatened, voice rough with everything I felt for her, "I swear to God—"

She didn't let me finish. Her lips crashed into mine, and suddenly it wasn't just a kiss—it was every late-night conversation, every moment of missing her, every second I'd spent wishing she was mine and that nothing stood between us.

When we finally broke apart, I pressed my forehead to hers, grinning like an idiot. "I love you, Chaos." The words tumbled out, reckless and real.

Her fingers curled into my shirt, tugging me closer. "I love you, too."

She removed the pendant necklace I had left with her from around her neck and gently fastened it around mine. Right where it belonged. And just like that, my whole world shifted. She was here, and she was staying. We both understood that the road ahead wouldn't always be easy, but it was ours. We'd get through it together, hand in hand, through the good days and bad. I wanted all of it—late night arguments until we made up, shared dreams, and a love that could survive anything. Finally, we weren't just wishing for the right time or being forced to be apart. We had it all—every sunrise, every breathtaking, ordinary, beautiful second together. Caroline was the chaos to my order, the question to every answer, and the destiny I never knew I needed until I found her. And after everything we'd been through, loving each other wasn't just a choice. It was our greatest victory.

epilogue

REESE

"How's my hair?" Bailey asked, nudging my elbow with his. The light caught the subtle highlights in the strands he'd carefully styled with gel.

I let out a chuckle, the sound lost in the ocean breeze. "Bro, I'm the one getting married," I said, shaking my head, "and you're asking me about *your* hair?"

The salty air wrapped around us, carrying with it the faint scent of floral sweetness from the truckloads of arrangements Sam and her team had brought in. The setting sun cast an amber glow over the beach, painting our footprints in the sand with a warm, golden hue.

"You're right, you're right," he conceded, with a goofy grin. "But there's one thing for sure—you look damn good today. I swear, if she doesn't cry when she sees you, I will make a scene."

"Reese is supposed to cry when he sees Caroline, not the other way around," Boston piped up from the other side, his voice carrying over the waves softly lapping against the shore.

"I don't know about that," Bailey lifted up his sunglasses. "I've cried six times staring at him already." His eyes were bloodshot before he lowered his glasses back into place.

In the fading light, I stood there, on the edge of forever, thinking about the man I was about to become—a husband. I hoped I would always be good enough for her.

The first chords of a song signaled that the ceremony was starting. I extended my arms, one to each side, as the two women who meant the world to me each claimed a side. To my right, my stepmother's hand rested lightly on mine. She had stepped into the void in my life without hesitation, always making me feel like her own.

To my left, my mother's grip was tentative and eager, as if she couldn't be more proud. We had spent the past five years navigating our estranged relationship, getting to know each other, and now we were closer than I ever thought possible. With a mom on each arm, it finally felt like everything had fallen into place—like I was whole.

As we reached the end of the aisle, I guided my mothers to their seats, the fabric of their gowns pooling against the pale sand. Turning away, I made my way to the gazebo. As the music continued, Boston appeared at the top of the aisle, my sister on his arm.

They stepped forward at a slow pace down the aisle. Lo shot me a smile that reminded me of her childhood giggles and all the mischief she'd put me through over the years. She was a college cheerleader now, and I couldn't be more proud of her.

Beside her, Boston was giving me a look of pride and respect—an acknowledgment of the rivalry that had changed both of our lives. Boston and I both played for New York teams now, so on the field we were still rivals, but off the field, we were closer than we ever had been—we were brothers.

Bailey and Sam took their first synchronized steps down the aisle. Bailey's grin was as wide as the ocean behind us. Our closest friends and family came slowly after. Then, in a moment that seemed to change the air around me, everyone on the beach rose from their chairs. And there she was. Walking down the aisle with her father's arm for guidance.

My heart throbbed in rhythm with the waves lapping at the shore. All the air in my lungs was stolen as Caroline floated down the aisle. Her blonde hair was intricately pinned up with elegant swirls framing her face. She'd told me her dress was simple, but on her, it was anything but. My throat tightened, the swell of emotions overwhelming me. A single tear betrayed my composure, carving a path down my cheek. With a subtle motion, I tried my best to wipe away the evidence of all my vulnerability exposed.

Her father's hand met mine with an unexpected gentleness, his grip firm yet infused with silent trust.

"Take care of her," he nodded. I could only nod back, the words lodged around the lump in my throat.

"You look beautiful, Chaos," I whispered, knowing this beautiful tornado of a woman would be mine forever, and I'd be her calmness in any storm.

"You look handsome, Baby," she countered, her blue eyes glowing with happiness.

The ocean whispered its approval as we said our vows. With Caroline's hand in mine, we leaped together into marriage, right there on the beach in the most beautiful place on earth. But nothing was as stunning as her.

As the ceremony dissolved into the evening, our guests made their way to the party area. Out of the corner of my eye, a flash of golden curls appeared. Jasper launched himself toward me as he yelled, "Uncle Reese! When do we get to do that dance we've been working on?"

A laugh escaped me as I ruffled his curly mane. "Right now, J. Let's go!"

A smile tugged at my lips as I scooped Jasper and his little sister into my arms, their giggles mingling with the salty breeze and the music. The sand gave way beneath my feet as we approached the designated area where the DJ had set up his deck.

"Reese, be careful!" Chandler yelled, always overly cautious about her little ones. Boston stood beside her laughing, an arm draped around her shoulders.

"Always," I replied with a glance back. I set the kids down in the dance area. Their small hands grasped mine, and together we spun into a dance that was ours alone—carefree and wild. Parker and Willow joined us. Bailey and the crew vaulted onto the floor. We lifted the kids, spinning them round and round.

As I caught my niece's giggle, Caroline found me. Her arms, delicate yet strong, grasped me, drawing me into an orbit that was exclusively ours.

"Tonight, you're mine," she whispered, her breath warm on my neck. The sea breeze carried her words away, but they etched themselves into my heart. I held her, my hands memorizing her all over again. The world around us dimmed—the laughter, the music, the crashing of the waves all faded into a hazy backdrop for the life we were creating.

"Forever and always, Chaos," I whispered into her ear, a vow that transcended time. I knew then, as her eyes locked with mine, that every tomorrow would be better with her by my side. My wife, my heart, my anchor in a sea of always shifting sands—I would hold onto her tight tonight and every night, for the rest of my life.

acknowledgments

<u>To my family</u> - Thank you for supporting me—I love you all so much! I am so grateful to have you in my life.

<u>To my friends</u> - Thank you for supporting and encouraging me. I love you!

<u>Alpha Extraordinaire</u> - Thank you, *Ruth Gough*. For your friendship, kindness, and encouragement through every chapter.

<u>Beta Babes</u> - *Mimi Monson, Roxxanne Vernon, Kaitlyn Garrett, McKinsey Jones, and Brandi Augustine.* Thank you for supporting me! Your feedback, kind words, and time are more than I could ever ask for. I can't thank you enough.

<u>ARC/Street Team</u> - Thank you for your support throughout my series, I appreciate you all more than you know!